Anne Severn and the Fieldings

May Sinclair

Contents

ANNE SEVERN AND THE FIELDINGS

BY

May Sinclair

I
CHILDREN

Anne Severn had come again to the Fieldings. This time it was because her mother was dead.

She hadn't been in the house five minutes before she asked "Where's Jerrold?"

"Fancy," they said, "her remembering."

And Jerrold had put his head in at the door and gone out again when he saw her there in her black frock; and somehow she had known he was afraid to come in because her mother was dead.

Her father had brought her to Wyck-on-the-Hill that morning, the day after the funeral. He would leave her there when he went back to India.

She was walking now down the lawn between the two tall men. They were taking her to the pond at the bottom where the goldfish were. It was Jerrold's father who held her hand and talked to her. He had a nice brown face marked with a lot of little fine, smiling strokes, and his eyes were quick and kind.

"You remember the goldfish, Anne?"

"I remember everything."

She had been such a little girl before, and they said she had forgotten.

But she remembered so well that she always thought of Mr. Fielding as Jerrold's father. She remembered the pond and the goldfish. Jerrold held her tight so that she shouldn't tumble in. She remembered the big grey and yellow house with its nine ball-topped gables; and the lawn, shut in by clipped yew hedges, then spreading downwards, like a fan, from the last green terrace where the two enormous peacocks stood, carved out of the yew.

Where it lay flat and still under the green wall she saw the tennis court. Jerrold was there, knocking balls over the net to please little Colin. She could see him fling back his head and laugh as Colin ran stumbling, waving his racquet before him like a stiff flag. She heard Colin squeal with excitement as the balls flew out of his reach.

Her father was talking about her. His voice was sharp and anxious.

"I don't know how she'll get on with your boys." (He always talked about Anne as if she wasn't there.) "Ten's an awkward age. She's too old for Colin and too young for Eliot and Jerrold."

She knew their ages. Colin was only seven. Eliot, the clever one, was very big; he was fifteen. Jerrold was thirteen.

She heard Jerrold's father answering in his quiet voice.

"You needn't worry. Jerry'll look after Anne all right."

"And Adeline."

"Oh yes, of course, Adeline." (Only somehow he made it sound as if she wouldn't.)

Adeline was Mrs. Fielding. Jerrold's mother.

Anne wanted to get away from the quiet, serious men and play with Jerrold; but their idea seemed to be that it was too soon. Too soon after the funeral. It would be all right to go quietly and look at the goldfish; but no, not to play. When she thought of her dead mother she was afraid to tell them that she didn't want to go and look at the goldfish. It was as if she knew that something sad waited for her by the pond at the bottom. She would be safer over there where Jerrold was laughing and shouting. She would play with him and he wouldn't be afraid.

The day felt like a Sunday, quiet, quiet, except for the noise of Jerrold's laughter. Strange and exciting, his boy's voice rang through her sadness; it made her turn her head again and again to look after him; it called to her to forget and play.

Little slim brown minnows darted backwards and forwards under the olive green water of the pond. And every now and then the fat goldfish came nosing along, orange, with silver patches, shining, making the water light round them, stiff mouths wide open. When they bobbed up, small bubbles broke from them and sparkled and went out.

Anne remembered the goldfish; but somehow they were not so fascinating as they used to be.

A queer plant grew on the rock border of the pond. Green fleshy stems, with blunt spikes all over them. Each carried a tiny gold star at its tip. Thick, cold juice would come out of it if you squeezed it. She thought it would smell like lavender.

It had a name. She tried to think of it.

Stonecrop. Stonecrop. Suddenly she remembered.

Her mother stood with her by the pond, dark and white and slender. Anne held out her hands smeared with the crushed flesh of the stonecrop; her mother stooped and wiped them with her pockethandkerchief, and there was a smell of lavender. The goldfish went swimming by in the olive-green water.

Anne's sadness came over her again; sadness so heavy that it kept her from crying; sadness that crushed her breast and made her throat ache.

They went back up the lawn, quietly, and the day felt more and more like Sunday, or like--like a funeral day.

"She's very silent, this small daughter of yours," Mr. Fielding said.

"Yes," said Mr. Severn.

His voice came with a stiff jerk, as if it choked him. He remembered, too.

The grey and yellow flagstones of the terrace were hot under your feet.

Jerrold's mother lay out there on a pile of cushions, in the sun. She was very large and very beautiful. She lay on her side, heaved up on one elbow. Under her thin white gown you could see the big lines of her shoulder and hip, and of her long full thigh, tapering to the knee.

Anne crouched beside her, uncomfortably, holding her little body away from the great warm mass among the cushions.

Mrs. Fielding was aware of this shrinking. She put out her arm and drew Anne to her side again.

"Lean back," she said. "Close. Closer."

And Anne would lean close, politely, for a minute, and then stiffen and shrink away again when the soft arm slackened.

Eliot Fielding (the clever one) lay on his stomach, stretched out across the terrace. He leaned over a book: *Animal Biology*. He was absorbed in a diagram of a rabbit's heart and took no notice of his mother or of Anne.

Anne had been at the Manor five days, and she had got used to Jerrold's mother's caresses. All but one. Every now and then Mrs. Fielding's hand would stray to the back of Anne's neck, where the short curls, black as her frock, sprang out in a thick bunch. The fingers stirred among the roots of Anne's hair, stroking, stroking, lifting the bunch and letting it fall again. And whenever they did this Anne jerked her head away and held it stiffly out of their reach.

She remembered how her mother's fingers, slender and silk-skinned and loving, had done just that, and how their touch went thrilling through the back of her neck, how it made her heart beat. Mrs. Fielding's fingers didn't thrill you, they were blunt and fumbling. Anne thought: "She's no business to touch me like that. No business to think she can do what mother did."

She was always doing it, always trying to be a mother to her. Her father had told her she was going to try. And Anne wouldn't let her. She would not let her.

"Why do you move your head away, darling?"

Anne didn't answer.

"You used to love it. You used to come bending your funny little neck and turning first one ear and than the other. Like a little cat. And now you won't let me touch you."

"No. No. Not--like that."

"Yes. Yes. Like this. You don't remember."

"I *do* remember."

She felt the blunt fingers on her neck again and started up. The beautiful, wilful woman lay back on her cushions, smiling to herself.

"You're a funny little thing, aren't you?" she said.

Anne's eyes were glassed. She shook her head fiercely and spilled tears.

Jerrold had come up on to the terrace. Colin trotted after him. They were looking at her. Eliot had raised his head from his book and was looking at her.

"It *is* rotten of you, mater," he said, "to tease that kid."

"I'm not teasing her. Really, Eliot, you do say things--as if nobody but yourself had any sense. You can run away now, Anne darling."

Anne stood staring, with wild animal eyes that saw no place to run to.

It was Jerrold who saved her.

"I say, would you like to see my new buck rabbit?"

"Rather!"

He held out his hand and she ran on with him, along the terrace, down the steps at the corner and up the drive to the stable yard where the rabbits were. Colin followed headlong.

And as she went Anne heard Eliot saying, "I've sense enough to remember that her mother's dead."

In his worst tempers there was always some fierce pity.

Mrs. Fielding gathered herself together and rose, with dignity, still smiling. It was a smile of great sweetness, infinitely remote from all discussion.

"It's much too hot here," she said. "You might move the cushions down there under the beech-tree."

That, Eliot put it to himself, was just her way of getting out of it. To Eliot the irritating thing about his mother was her dexterity in getting out. She never lost her temper, and never replied to any serious criticism; she simply changed the subject, leaving you with your disapproval on your hands.

In this Eliot's young subtlety misled him. Adeline Fielding's mind was not the clever, calculating thing that, at fifteen, he thought it. Her one simple idea was to be happy and, as a means to that end, to have people happy about her. His father, or Anne's father, could have told him that all her ideas were simple as feelings and impromptu. Impulse moved her, one moment, to seize on the faithful, defiant little heart of Anne, the next, to get up out of the sun. Anne's tears spoiled her bright world; but not for long. Coolness was now the important thing, not Anne and not Anne's mother. As for Eliot's disapproval, she was no longer aware of it.

"Oh, to be cool, to be cool again! Thank you, my son."

Eliot had moved all the cushions down under the tree, scowling as he did it, for he knew that when his mother was really cool he would have to get up and move them back again.

With the perfect curve of a great supple animal, she turned and settled in her lair, under her tree.

Presently, down the steps and across the lawn, Anne's father came towards her, grave, handsome, and alone.

Handsome even after fifteen years of India. Handsomer than when he was young. More distinguished. Eyes lighter in the sallowish bronze. She liked his lean, eager, deerhound's face, ready to start off, sniffing the trail. A little strained, leashed now, John's eagerness. But that was how he used to come to her, with that look of being ready, as if they could do things together.

She had tried to find his youth in Anne's face; but Anne's blackness and whiteness were her mother's; her little nose was still soft and vague; you couldn't tell what she would be like in five years' time. Still, there was something; the same strange quality; the same forward-springing grace.

Before he reached her, Adeline was smiling again. A smile of the delicate, instinctive mouth, of the blue eyes shining between curled lids, under dark eyebrows; of the innocent white nose; of the whole soft, milk-white face. Even her sleek, dark hair smiled, shining. She was conscious of her power to make him come to her, to make herself felt through everything, even through his bereavement.

The subtle Eliot, looking over the terrace wall, observed her and thought, "The mater's jolly pleased with herself. I wonder why."

It struck Eliot also that a Commissioner of Ambala and a Member of the Legislative Council and a widower ought not to look like Mr. Severn. He was too lively, too adventurous.

He turned again to the enthralling page. "The student should lay open the theoracic cavity of the rabbit and dissect away the thymous gland and other tissues which hide the origin of the great vessels; so as to display the heart..."

Yearp, the vet, would show him how to do that.

"His name's Benjy. He's a butterfly smut," said Jerrold.

The rabbit was quiet now. He sat in Anne's arms, couching, his forepaws laid on her breast. She stooped and kissed his soft nose that went in and out, pushing against her mouth, in a delicate palpitation. He was white, with black ears and a black oval at the root of his tail. Two wing-shaped patches went up from his nose like a moustache. That was his butterfly smut.

"He *is* sweet," she said.

Colin said it after her in his shrill child's voice: "He is sweet." Colin had a habit of repeating what you said. It was his way of joining in the conversation.

He stretched up his hand and stroked Benjy, and Anne felt the rabbit's heart beat sharp and quick against her breast. A shiver went through Benjy's body.

Anne kissed him again. Her heart swelled and shook with maternal tenderness.

"Why does he tremble so?"

"He's frightened. Don't touch him, Col-Col."

Colin couldn't see an animal without wanting to stroke it. He put his hands in his pockets to keep them out of temptation. By the way Jerrold looked at him you saw how he loved him.

About Colin there was something beautiful and breakable. Dusk-white face; little tidy nose and mouth; dark hair and eyes like the minnows swimming under the green water. But Jerrold's face was strong; and he had funny eyes that made you keep looking at him. They were blue. Not tiresomely blue, blue all the time, like his mother's, but secretly and surprisingly blue, a blue that flashed at you and hid again, moving queerly in the set squareness of his face, presenting at every turn a different Jerrold. He had a pleasing straight up and down nose, his one constant feature. The nostrils slanted slightly upward, making shadows there. You got to know these things after watching him attentively. Anne loved his mouth best of all, cross one minute (only never with Colin), sweet the next, tilted at the corners, ready for his laughter.

He stood close beside her in his white flannels, straight and slender. He was looking at her, just as he looked at Colin.

"Do you like him?" he said.

"Who? Colin?"

"No. Benjy."

"I *love* him."

"I'll give him to you if you'd like to have him."

"For my own? To keep?"

"Rather."

"Don't you want him?"

"Yes. But I'd like you to have him."

"Oh, Jerrold."

She knew he was giving her Benjy because her mother was dead.

"I've got the grey doe, and the fawn, and the lop-ear," he said.

"Oh--I *shall* love him."

"You mustn't hold him too tight. And you must be careful not to touch his stomach. If you squeeze him there he'll die."

"Yes. If you squeeze his stomach he'll die," Colin cried excitedly.

"I'll be ever so careful."

They put him down, and he ran violently round and round, drumming with his hind legs on the floor of the shed, startling the does that couched, like cats, among the lettuce leaves and carrots.

"When the little rabbits come half of them will be yours, because he'll be their father."

"Oh--"

For the first time since Friday week Anne was happy. She loved the rabbit, she loved little Colin. And more than anybody or anything she loved Jerrold.

Yet afterwards, in her bed in the night nursery, when she thought of her dead mother, she lay awake crying; quietly, so that nobody could hear.

It was Robert Fielding's birthday. Anne was to dine late that evening, sitting beside him. He said that was his birthday treat.

Anne had made him a penwiper of green cloth with a large blue bead in the middle for a knob. He was going to keep it for ever. He had no candles on his birthday cake at tea, because there would have been too many.

The big hall of the Manor was furnished like a room.

The wide oak staircase came down into it from a gallery that went all around. They were waiting there for Mrs. Fielding who was always a little late. That made you keep on thinking about her. They were thinking about her now.

Up there a door opened and shut. Something moved along the gallery like a large light, and Mrs. Fielding came down the stairs, slowly, prolonging her effect. She was dressed in her old pearl-white gown. A rope of pearls went round her neck and hung between her breasts. Roll above roll of hair jutted out at the back of her head; across it, the foremost curl rose like a comb, shining. Her eyes, intensely blue in her milk-white face, sparkled between two dark wings of hair. Her mouth smiled its enchanting and enchanted smile. She was aware that her husband and John watched her from stair to stair; she was aware of their men's eyes, darkening. Then suddenly she was aware of John's daughter.

Anne was coming towards her across the hall, drawn by the magic, by the eyes, by the sweet flower smell that drifted (not lavender, not lavender). She stood at the foot of the staircase looking up. The heavenly thing swept down to her and she broke into a cry.

"Oh, you're beautiful. You're beautiful."

Mrs. Fielding stopped her progress.

"So are you, you little darling."

She stooped quickly and kissed her, holding her tight to her breast, crushed down into the bed of the flower scent. Anne gave herself up, caught by the sweetness and the beauty.

"You rogue," said Adeline. "At last I've got you."

She couldn't bear to be repulsed, to have anything about her, even a cat or a dog, that had not surrendered.

Every evening, soon after Colin's Nanna had tucked Anne up in her bed and left her, the door of the night nursery would open, letting a light in. When Anne saw the light coming she shut her eyes and burrowed under the blankets, she knew it was Auntie Adeline trying to be a mother to her. (You called them Auntie Adeline and Uncle Robert to please them, though they weren't relations.)

Every night she would hear Aunt Adeline's feet on the floor and her candle clattering on the chest of drawers, she would feel her hands drawing back the blankets and her face bending down over her. The mouth would brush her forehead. And she would lie stiff and still, keeping her eyes tight shut.

To-night she heard voices at the door and somebody else's feet going tip-toe behind Aunt Adeline's. Somebody else whispered "She's asleep." That was Jerrold. Jerrold. She felt him standing beside his mother, looking at her, and her eyelids fluttered; but she lay still.

"She isn't asleep at all," said Aunt Adeline. "She's shamming, the little monkey."

Jerrold thought he knew why. He turned into the old nursery that was the schoolroom now, and found Eliot there, examining a fly's leg under his microscope. It was Eliot that he wanted..

"I say, you know, Mum's making a jolly mistake about that kid. Trying to go on as if she was Anne's mother. You can see it makes her sick. It would me, if my mother was dead."

Eliot looked as if he wasn't listening, absorbed in his fly's leg.

"Somebody's got to tell her."

"Are you going to," said Eliot, "or shall I?"

"Neither. I shall get Dad to. He'll do it best."

Robert Fielding didn't do it all at once. He put it off till Adeline gave him his chance. He found her alone in the library and she had begun it.

"Robert, I don't know what to do about that child."

"Which child?"

"Anne. She's been here five weeks, and I've done everything I know, and she hasn't shown me a scrap of affection. It's pretty hard if I'm to house and feed the little thing and look after her like a mother and get nothing. Nothing but half a cold little face to kiss night and morning. It isn't good enough."

"For Anne?"

"For me, my dear. Trying to be a mother to somebody else's child who doesn't love you, and isn't going to love you."

"Don't try then."

"Don't try?"

"Don't try and be a mother to her. That's what Anne doesn't like."

They had got as far as that when John Severn stood in the doorway. He was retreating before their appearance of communion when she called him back.

"Don't go, John. We want you. Here's Robert telling me not to be a mother to Anne."

"And here's Adeline worrying because she thinks Anne isn't going to love her."

Severn sat down, considering it.

"It takes time," he said.

She looked at him, smiling under lowered brows.

"Time to love me?"

"Time for Anne to love you. She--she's so desperately faithful."

The dressing-bell clanged from the belfry. Robert left them to finish a discussion that he found embarrassing.

"I said I'd try to be a mother to her. I *have* tried, John; but the little thing won't let me."

"Don't try too hard. Robert's right. Don't--don't be a mother to her."

"What am I to be?"

"Oh, anything you like. A presence. A heavenly apparition. An impossible ideal. Anything but that."

"Do you think she's going to hold out for ever?"

"Only against that. As long as she remembers. It puts her off."

"She doesn't object to Robert being a father to her."

"No. Because he's a better father than I am; and she knows it."

Adeline flushed. She understood the implication and was hurt, unreasonably. He saw her unreasonableness and her pain.

"My dear Adeline, Anne's mother will always be Anne's mother. I was never anywhere beside Alice. I've had to choose between the Government of India and my daughter. You'll observe that I don't try to be a father to Anne; and that, in consequence, Anne likes me. But she'll *love* Robert."

"And 'like' me? If I don't try."

"Give her time. Give her time."

He rose, smiling down at her.

"You think I'm unreasonable?"

"The least bit in the world. For the moment."

"My dear John, if I didn't love your little girl I wouldn't care."

"Love her. Love her. She'll love you too, in her rum way. She's fighting you now. She wouldn't fight if she didn't feel she was beaten. Nobody could hold out against you long."

She looked at the clock.

"Heavens! I must go and dress."

She thought: "He didn't hold out against me, poor dear, five minutes. I suppose he'll always remember that I jilted him for Robert."

And now he wanted her to see that if Anne's mother would be always Anne's mother, his wife would be always his wife. Was he desperately faithful, too? Always?

How could he have been? It was characteristic of Alice Severn that when she had to choose between her husband and her daughter she had chosen Anne. It was characteristic of John that when he had to choose between his wife and his Government, he had not chosen Alice. He must have had adventures out in India, conducted with the discretion becoming in a Commissioner and a Member of the Legislative Council, but adventures. Perhaps he was going back to one of them.

Severn dressed hastily and went into the schoolroom where Anne sat reading in her solitary hour between supper time and bed-time. He took her on his knee, and she snuggled there, rubbing her head against his shoulder. He thought of Adeline, teasing, teasing for the child's caresses, and every time repulsed.

"Anne," he said, "don't you think you can love Auntie Adeline?"

Anne straightened herself. She looked at him with candid eyes. "I don't know, Daddy, really, if I can."

"Can't you love her a little?"

"I--I would, if she wouldn't try--"

"Try?"

"To do like Mummy did."

Robert was right. He knew it, but he wanted to be sure.

Anne went on. "It's no use, you see, her trying. It only makes me think of Mummy more."

"Don't you *want* to think of her?"

"Yes. But I want to think by myself, and Auntie Adeline keeps on getting in the way."

"Still, she's awfully kind to you, isn't she?"

"Awfully."

"And you mustn't hurt her feelings."

"Have I? I didn't mean to."

"You wouldn't if you loved her."

"You haven't ever hurt her feelings, have you, Daddy?"

"No."

"Well, you see, it's because I keep on thinking about Mummy. I want her back--I want her so awfully."

"I know, Anne, I know."

Anne's mind burrowed under, turning on its tracks, coming out suddenly.
"Do you love Auntie Adeline, Daddy?"
It was terrible, but he owned that he had brought it on himself.
"I can't say. I've known her such a long time; before you were born."
"Before you married Mummy!"
"Yes."
"Well, won't it do if I love Uncle Robert and Eliot and Colin? And Jerrold?"
That night he said to Adeline, "I know who'll take my place when I'm gone."
"Who? Robert?"
"No, Jerrold."
In another week he had sailed for India and Ambala.

*   *   *   *   *

Jerrold was brave.
When Colin upset the schoolroom lamp Jerrold wrapped it in the tablecloth and threw it out of the window just in time. He put the chain on Billy, the sheepdog, when he went mad and snapped at everybody. It seemed odd that Jerrold should be frightened.
A minute ago he had been happy, rolling over and over on the grass, shouting with laughter while Sandy, the Aberdeen, jumped on him, growling his merry puppy's growl and biting the balled fists that pushed him off.
They were all out on the lawn. Anne waited for Jerry to get up and take her into Wyck, to buy chocolates.
Every time Jerrold laughed his mother laughed too, a throaty, girlish giggle.
"I love Jerry's laugh," she said. "It's the nicest noise he makes."
Then, suddenly, she stopped it. She stopped it with a word.
"If you're going into Wyck, Jerry, you might tell Yearp----"
Yearp.
He got up. His face was very red. He looked mournful and frightened too. Yes, frightened.
"I--can't, Mother."
"You can perfectly well. Tell Yearp to come and look at Pussy's ears, I think

she's got canker."

"She hasn't," said Jerry defiantly.

"She jolly well has," said Eliot.

"Rot."

"You only say that because you don't like to think she's got it."

"Eliot can go himself. *He's* fond of Yearp."

"You'll do as you're told, Jerry. It's downright cowardice."

"It isn't cowardice, is it, Daddy?"

"Well," said his father, "it isn't exactly courage."

"Whatever it is," his mother said, "you'll have to get over it. You go on as if nobody cared about poor Binky but yourself."

Binky was Jerry's dog. He had run into a motor-bicycle in the Easter holidays and hurt his back, so that Yearp, the vet, had had to come and give him chloroform. That was why Jerrold was afraid of Yearp. When he saw him he saw Binky with his nose in the cup of chloroform; he heard him snorting out his last breath. And he couldn't bear it.

"I could send one of the men," his father was saying.

"Don't encourage him, Robert. He's got to face it."

"Yes, Jerrold, you'd better go and get it over. You can't go on funking it for ever."

Jerrold went. But he went alone, he wouldn't let Anne go with him. He said he didn't want her to be mixed up with it.

"He means," said Eliot, "that he doesn't want to think of Yearp every time he sees Anne."

It was true that Eliot was fond of Yearp's society. He would spend hours with him, learning how to dissect frogs and rabbits and pigeons. He drove about the country with Yearp seeing the sick animals, the ewes at lambing time and the cows at their calving. And he spent half the midsummer holidays reading *Animal Biology* and drawing diagrams of frogs' hearts and pigeons' brains. He said he wasn't going to Oxford or Cambridge when he left Cheltenham; he was going to Barts. He wanted to be a doctor. But his mother said he didn't know what he'd want to be in three years' time. She thought him awful, with his frogs' hearts and horrors.

Next to Jerrold and little Colin Anne loved Eliot. He seemed to know when she was thinking about her mother and to understand. He took her into the woods to look for squirrels; he showed her the wildflowers and told her all their names: bugloss, and lady's smock and speedwell, king-cup, willow herb and meadow sweet, crane's bill and celandine.

One day they found in the garden a tiny egg-shaped shell made of gold-coloured lattice work. When they put it under the microscope they saw inside it a thing like a green egg. Every day they watched it; it put out two green horns, and a ridge grew down the middle of it, and one morning they found the golden shell broken. A long, elegant fly with slender wings crawled beside it.

When Benjy died of eating too much lettuce Eliot was sorry. Aunt Adeline said it was all put on and that he really wanted to cut him up and see what he was made of. But Eliot didn't. He said Benjy was sacred. That was because he knew they loved him. And he dug the grave and lined it with moss and told Aunt Adeline to shut up when she said it ought to have been lettuce leaves.

Aunt Adeline complained that it was hard that Eliot couldn't be nice to her when he was her favorite.

"Little Anne, little Anne, what have you done to my Eliot?" She was always saying things like that. Anne couldn't think what she meant till Jerrold told her she was the only kid that Eliot had ever looked at. The big Hawtrey girl from Medlicote would have given her head to be in Anne's shoes.

But Anne didn't care. Her love for Jerrold was sharp and exciting. She brought tears to it and temper. It was mixed up with God and music and the deaths of animals, and sunsets and all sorrowful and beautiful and mysterious things. Thinking about her mother made her think about Jerrold; but she never thought about Eliot at all when he wasn't there.

She would run away from Eliot any minute if she heard Jerrold calling. It was Jerrold, Jerrold, all the time, said Aunt Adeline.

And when Eliot was busy with his microscope and Jerrold had turned from her to Colin, there was Uncle Robert. He seemed to know the moments when she wanted him. Then he would take her out riding with him over the estate that stretched from Wyck across the valley of the Speed and beyond it for miles over the hills. And he would show her the reaping machines at work, and the great carthorses, and the prize bullocks in their stalls at the Manor Farm. And Anne told him her secret, the secret she had told to nobody but Jerrold.

"Some day," she said, "I shall have a farm, with horses and cows and pigs and little calves."

"Shall you like that?"

"Yes," said Anne. "I would. Only it can't happen till Grandpapa's dead. And I don't want him to die."

They were saying now that Colin was wonderful. He was only seven, yet he could play the piano like a grown-up person, very fast and with loud noises in the bass. And he could sing like an angel. When you heard him you could hardly believe that he was a little boy who cried sometimes and was afraid of ghosts. Two masters came out from Cheltenham twice a week to teach him. Eliot said Colin would be a professional when he grew up, but his mother said he should be nothing of the sort and Eliot wasn't to go putting nonsense like that into his head. Still, she was proud of Colin when his hands went pounding and flashing over the keys. Anne had to give up practising because she did it so badly that it hurt Colin to hear her.

He wasn't in the least conceited about his playing, not even when Jerrold stood beside him and looked on and said, "Clever Col-Col. Isn't he a wonderful kid? Look at him. Look at his little hands, all over the place."

He didn't think playing was wonderful. He thought the things that Jerrold did were wonderful. With his child's legs and arms he tried to do the things that Jerrold did. They told him he would have to wait nine years before he could do them. He was always talking about what he would do in nine years' time.

And there was the day of the walk to High Slaughter, through the valley of the Speed to the valley of the Windlode, five miles there and back. Eliot and Jerrold and Anne had tried to sneak out when Colin wasn't looking; but he had seen them and came running after them down the field, calling to them to let him come. Eliot shouted "We can't, Col-Col, it's too far," but Colin looked so pathetic, standing there in the big field, that Jerrold couldn't bear it.

"I think," he said, "we might let him come."

"Yes. Let him," Anne said.

"Rot. He can't walk it."

"I can," said Colin. "I can."

"I tell you he can't. If he's tired he'll be sick in the night and then he'll say it's ghosts."

Colin's mouth trembled.

"It's all right, Col-Col, you're coming." Jerrold held out his hand.

"Well," said Eliot, "if he crumples up *you* can carry him."

"I can," said Jerrold.

"So can I," said Anne.

"Nobody," said Colin "shall carry me. I can walk."

Eliot went on grumbling while Colin trotted happily beside them. "You're a fearful ass, Jerrold. You're simple ruining that kid. He thinks he can come butting into everything. Here's the whole afternoon spoiled for all three of us. He can't walk. You'll see he'll drop out in the first mile."

"I shan't, Jerrold."

And he didn't. He struggled on down the fields to Upper Speed and along the river-meadows to Lower Speed and Hayes Mill, and from Hayes Mill to High Slaughter. It was when they started to walk back that his legs betrayed him, slackening first, then running, because running was easier than walking, for a change. Then dragging. Then being dragged between Anne and Jerrold (for he refused to be carried). Then staggering, stumbling, stopping dead; his child's mouth drooping.

Then Jerrold carried him on his back with his hands clasped under Colin's soft hips. Colin's body slipped every minute and had to be jerked up again; and when it slipped his arms tightened round Jerrold's neck, strangling him.

At last Jerrold, too, staggered and stumbled and stopped dead.

"I'll take him," said Eliot. He forbore, nobly, to say "I told you so."

And by turns they carried him, from the valley of the Windlode to the valley of the Speed, past Hayes Mill, through Lower Speed, Upper Speed, and up the fields to Wyck Manor. Then up the stairs to the schoolroom, pursued by their mother's cries.

"Oh Col-Col, my little Col-Col! What have you done to him, Eliot?"

Eliot bore it like a lamb.

Only after they had left Colin in the schoolroom, he turned on Jerrold.

"Some day," he said, "Col-Col will be a perfect nuisance. Then you and Anne'll have to pay for it."

"Why me and Anne?"

"Because you'll both be fools enough to keep on giving in to him."

"I suppose," said Jerrold bitterly, "you think you're clever."

Adeline came out and overheard him and made a scene in the gallery before Pinkney, the footman, who was bringing in the schoolroom tea. She said Eliot was clever enough and old enough to know better. They were all old enough. And Jerrold said it was his fault, not Eliot's, and Anne said it was hers, too. And Adeline declared that it was all their faults and she would have to speak to their father. She kept it up long after Eliot and Jerrold had retreated to the bathroom. If it had been anybody but her little Col-Col. She wouldn't *have* him dragged about the country till he dropped.

She added that Col-Col was her favourite.

It was the last week of the holidays. Rain had come with the west wind. The hills were drawn back behind thick sheets of glassy rain. Shining spears of rain dashed themselves against the west windows. Jets of rain rose up, whirling and spraying, from the terrace. Rain ran before the wind in a silver scud along the flagged path under the south front.

The wind made hard, thudding noises as if it pounded invisible bodies in the air. It screamed high above the drumming and hissing of the rain.

It excited the children.

From three o'clock till tea-time the sponge fight stormed up and down the passages. The house was filled with the sound of thudding feet and shrill laughter.

Adeline lay on the sofa in the library. Eliot was with her there.

She was amused, but a little plaintive when they rushed in to her.

"It's perfectly awful the noise you children are making. I'm tired out with it."

Jerrold flung himself on her. "Tired? What must *we* be?"

But he wasn't tired. His madness still worked in him. It sought some supreme expression.

"What can we play at next?" said Anne.

"What can we play at next?" said Colin.

"Something quiet, for goodness sake," said his mother.

They were very quiet, Jerrold and Anne and Colin, as they set the booby-trap for Pinkney. Very quiet as they watched Pinkney's innocent approach. The sponge caught him--with a delightful, squelching flump--full and fair on the top of his sleek head.

Anne shrieked with delight. "Oh Jerry, did you *hear* him say 'Damn'?"

They rushed back to the library to tell Eliot. But Eliot couldn't see that it was funny. He said it was a rotten thing to do.

"When he's a servant and can't do anything to *us*."

"I never thought of that," said Jerrold. (It *was* pretty rotten.) ... "I could ask him to bowl to me and let him get me out."

"He'd do that in any case."

"Still--I'll have *asked* him."

But it seemed that Pinkney was in no mood to think of cricket, and they had to be content with begging his pardon, which he gave, as he said, "freely." Yet it struck them that he looked sadder than a booby-trap should have made him.

It was just before bed-time that Eliot told them the awful thing.

"I suppose you know," he said, "that Pinkney's mother's dying?"

"I didn't," said Jerrold. "But I might have known. I notice that when you're excited, *really* excited, something awful's bound to happen.... Don't cry, Anne. It was beastly of us, but we didn't know."

"No. It's no use crying," said Eliot. "You can't do anything."

"That's it," Anne sobbed. "If we only could. If we could go to him and tell him we wouldn't have done it if we'd known."

"You jolly well can't. It would only bother the poor chap. Besides, it was Jerry did it. Not you."

"It *was* me. I filled the sponge. We did it together."

What they had done was beastly--setting booby-traps for Pinkney, and laughing at him when his mother was dying--but they had done it together. The pain of her sin had sweetness in it since she shared it with Jerry. Jerry's arm was round her as she went upstairs to bed, crying. They sat together on her bed, holding each other's hands; they faced it together.

"You'd never have done it, Anne, if I hadn't made you."

"I wouldn't mind so much if we hadn't laughed at him."

"Well, we couldn't help *that*. And it wasn't as if we'd known."

"If only we could tell him--"

"We can't. He'd hate us to go talking to him about his mother."

"He'd hate us."

Then Anne had an idea. They couldn't talk to Pinkney but they could write. That wouldn't hurt him. Jerry fetched a pencil and paper from the schoolroom; and Anne wrote.

Dear Pinkney: We didn't know. We wouldn't have done it if we'd   known. We are awfully sorry.

Yours truly,

ANNE SEVERN.

P.S. You aren't to answer this.

JERROLD FIELDING.

Half an hour later Jerrold knocked at her door.

"Anne--are you in bed?"

She got up and stood with him at the door in her innocent nightgown.

"It's all right," he said. "I've seen Pinkney. He says we aren't to worry. He knew we wouldn't have done it if we'd known."

"Was he crying?"

"No. Laughing.... All the same, it'll be a lesson to us," he said.

"Where's Jerrold?"

Robert Fielding called from the dogcart that waited by the porch. Eliot sat beside him, very stiff and straight, painfully aware of his mother who stood on the flagged path below, and made yearning faces at him, doing her best, at this last moment, to destroy his morale. Colin sat behind him by Jerrold's place, tearful but excited. He was to go with them to the station. Eliot tried hard to look as if he didn't care; and, as his mother said, he succeeded beautifully.

It was the end of the holidays.

"Adeline, you might see where Jerrold is."

She went into the house and saw Anne and Jerrold coming slowly down the stairs together from the gallery. At the turn they stopped and looked at each other, and suddenly he had her in his arms. They kissed, with close, quick kisses and then stood apart, listening.

Adeline went back. "The monkey," she thought; "and I who told her she didn't know how to do it."

Jerrold ran out, very red in the face and defiant. He gave himself to his mother's large embrace, broke from it, and climbed into the dogcart. The mare bounded forward, Jerrold and Eliot raised their hats, shouted and were gone.

Adeline watched while the long lines of the beech-trees narrowed on them, till the dogcart swung out between the ball-topped pillars of the Park gates.

Last time their going had been nothing to her. Today she could hardly bear it. She wondered why.

She turned and found little Anne standing beside her. They moved suddenly apart. Each had seen the other's tears.

Outside Colin's window the tree rocked in the wind. A branch brushed backwards and forwards, it tapped on the pane. Its black shadow shook on the grey, moonlit wall.

Jerrold's empty bed showed white and dreadful in the moonlight, covered with a sheet. Colin was frightened.

A narrow passage divided his room from Anne's. The doors stood open. He called "Anne! Anne!"

A light thud on the floor of Anne's room, then the soft padding of naked feet, and Anne stood beside him in her white nightgown. Her hair rose in a black ruff round her head, her eyes were very black in the sharp whiteness of her face.

"Are you frightened, Colin?"

"No. I'm not exactly frightened, but I think there's something there."

"It's nothing. Only the tree."

"I mean--in Jerry's bed."

"Oh no, Colin."

"Dare you," he said, "sit on it?"

"Of course I dare. *Now* you see. *Now* you won't be frightened."

"You know," Colin said, "I don't mind a bit when Jerrold's there. The ghosts never come then, because he frightens them away."

The clock struck ten. They counted the strokes. Anne still sat on Jerrold's bed with her knees drawn up to her chin and her arms clasped round them.

"I'll tell you a secret," Colin said. "Only you mustn't tell."

"I won't."

"Really and truly?"

"Really and truly."

"I think Jerrold's the wonderfullest person in the whole world. When I grow up I'm going to be like him."

"You couldn't be."

"Not now. But when I'm grown-up, I say."

"You couldn't be. Not even then. Jerrold can't sing and he can't play."

"I don't care."

"But you mustn't do what he can't if you want to be like him."

"When I'm singing and playing I shall pretend I'm not."

"You needn't. You won't ever be him."

"I--shall."

"Col-Col, I don't want you to be like him. I don't want anybody else to be like Jerrold in the whole world."

"But," said Colin, "I shall be like him."

Every night Adeline still came to see Anne in bed. The little thing had left off pretending to be asleep. She lay with eyes wide open, yielding sweetly to the embrace.

To-night her eyelids lay shut, slack on her eyes, and Adeline thought "She's really asleep, the little lamb. Better not touch her."

She was going away when a sound stopped her. A sound of sobbing.

"Anne--Anne--are you crying?"

A tremulous drawing-in of breath, a shaking under the bed-clothes. On Anne's white cheek the black eyelashes were parted and pointed with her tears. She had been crying a long time.

Adeline knelt down, her face against Anne's face.

"What is it darling? Tell me."

Anne shivered.

"Oh Anne, I wish you loved me. You don't, ducky, a little bit."

"I do. I do. Really and truly."

"Then give me a kiss. The proper kind."

Anne gave her the tight, deep kiss that was the proper kind.

"Now--tell me what it is." She knew by Anne's surrender that, this time, it was not her mother.

"I don't know."

"You *do* know. Is it Jerry? Do you want Jerry?"

At the name Anne's crying broke out again, savage, violent.

Adeline held her close and let the storm beat itself out against her heart.

"You can't want him more than I do, little Anne."

"You'll have him when he comes back. And I shan't. I shall be gone."

"You'll come again, darling. You'll come again."

II
ADOLESCENTS

For the next two years Anne came again and again, staying four months at Wyck and four months in London with Grandmamma Severn and Aunt Emily, and four months with Grandpapa Everitt at the Essex Farm.

When she was twelve they sent her to school in Switzerland for three years. Then back to Wyck, after eight months of London and Essex in between.

Only the times at Wyck counted for Anne. Her calendar showed them clear with all their incidents recorded; thick black lines blotted out the other days, as she told them off, one by one. Three years and eight months were scored through in this manner.

Anne at fifteen was a tall girl with long hair tied in a big black bow at the cape of her neck. Her vague nose had settled into the forward-raking line that made her the dark likeness of her father. Her body was slender but solid; the strong white neck carried her head high with the poise of a runner. She looked at least seventeen in her clean-cut coat and skirt. Probably she wouldn't look much older for another fifteen years.

Robert Fielding stared with incredulity at this figure which had pursued him down the platform at Wyck and now seized him by the arm.

"Is it--is it Anne?"

"Of course it is. Why, didn't you expect me?"

"I think I expected something smaller and rather less grown-up."

"I'm not grown-up. I'm the same as ever."

"Well, you're not little Anne any more."

She squeezed his arm, hanging on it in her old loving way. "No. But I'm still me. And I'd have known *you* anywhere."

"What? With my grey hair?"

"I love your grey hair."

It made him handsome, more lovable than ever. Anne loved it as she loved his face, tanned and tightened by sun and wind, the long hard-drawn lines, the thin, kind mouth, the clear, greenish brown eyes, quick and kind.

Colin stood by the dogcart in the station yard. Colin was changed. He was no longer the excited child who came rushing to you. He stood for you to come to him, serious and shy. His child's face was passing from prettiness to a fine, sombre beauty.

"What's happened to Col-Col? He's all different?"

"Is he? Wait," Uncle Robert said, "till you've seen Jerrold."

"Oh, is Jerrold going to be different, too?"

"I'm afraid he'll *look* a little different."

"I don't care," she said. "He'll *be* him."

She wanted to come back and find everybody and everything the same, looking exactly as she had left them. What they had once been for her they must always be.

They drove slowly up Wyck Hill. The tree-tops meeting overhead made a green tunnel. You came out suddenly into the sunlight at the top. The road was the same. They passed by the Unicorn Inn and the Post Office, through the narrow crooked street with the church and churchyard at the turn; and so into the grey and yellow Market Square with the two tall elms standing up on the little green in the corner. They passed the Queen's Head; the powder-blue sign hung out from the yellow front the same as ever. Next came the fountain and the four forked roads by the signpost, then the dip of the hill to the left and the grey ball-topped stone pillars of the Park gates on the right.

At the end of the beech avenue she saw the house; the three big, sharp-pointed gables of the front: the little gable underneath in the middle, jutting out over the porch. That was the bay of Aunt Adeline's bed-room. She used to lean out of the lattice windows and call to the children in the garden. The house was the same.

So were the green terraces and the wide, flat-topped yew walls, and the great peacocks carved out of the yew; and beyond them the lawn, flowing out under banks of clipped yew down to the goldfish pond. They were things that she had seen again and again in sleep and memory; things that had made her heart ache thinking of them; that took her back and back, and wouldn't let her be. She had only to leave off what she was doing and she saw them; they swam before her eyes, covering the Swiss mountains, the flat Essex fields, the high white London houses. They waited for her at the waking end of dreams.

She had found them again.

A gap in the green walls led into the flower garden, and there, down the path between tall rows of phlox and larkspurs and anchusa, of blue heaped on blue, Aunt Adeline came holding up a tall bunch of flowers, blue on her white gown, blue on her own milk-white and blue. She came, looking like a beautiful girl; the same, the same; Anne had seen her in dreams, walking like that, tall among the tall flowers.

She never hurried to meet you; hurrying would have spoiled the beauty of her movement; she came slowly, absent-mindedly, stopping now and then to pluck yet another of the blue spires. Robert stood still in the path to watch her. She was smiling a long way off, intensely aware of him.

"Is *that* Anne?" she said.

"Yes, Auntie, *really* Anne."

"Well, you *are* a big girl, aren't you?"

She kissed her three times and smiled, looking away again over her flowerbeds. That was the difference between Aunt Adeline and Uncle Robert. His eyes made you important; they held you all the time he talked to you; when he smiled, it was for you altogether and not for himself at all. Her eyes never looked at you long; her smile wandered, it was half for you and half for herself, for something she was thinking of that wasn't you.

"What have you done with your father?" she said.

"I was to tell you. Daddy's ever so sorry; but he can't come till to-morrow. A horrid man kept him on business."

"Oh?" A little crisping wave went over Aunt Adeline's face, a wave of vexation. Anne saw it.

"He is *really* sorry. You should have heard him damning and cursing."

They laughed. Adeline was appeased. She took her husband's arm and drew him to herself. Something warm and secret seemed to pass between them.

Anne said to herself: "That's how people look--" without finishing her thought.

Lest she should feel shut out he turned to her.

"Well, are you glad to be back again, Anne?" he said.

"Glad? I'm never glad to be anywhere else. I've been counting the weeks and the days and the minutes."

"The minutes?"

"Yes. In the train."

They had come up on to the flagged terrace. Anne looked round her.

"Where's Jerrold?" she said.

And they laughed again. "There's no doubt," said Uncle Robert, "about it being the same Anne."

A day passed. John Severn had come. He was to stay with the Fieldings for the last weeks of his leave. He had followed Adeline from the hot terrace to the cool library. When she wanted the sun again he would follow her out.

Robert and Colin were down at the Manor Farm. Eliot was in the schoolroom, reading.

Jerrold and Anne sat together on the grass under the beech trees, alone.

They had got over the shock of the first encounter, when they met at arms' length, not kissing, but each remembering, shyly, that they used to kiss. If they had not got over the "difference," the change of Anne from a child to a big girl, of Jerrold from a big boy to a man's height and a man's voice, it was because, in some obscure way, that difference fascinated them. The great thing was that underneath it they were both, as Anne said, "the same."

"I don't know what I'd have done, Jerrold, if you hadn't been."

"You might have known I would be."

"I did know."

"I say, what a thundering lot of hair you've got. I like it."

"Do you like what Auntie Adeline calls my new nose?"

"Awfully."

She meditated. "Jerrold, do you remember Benjy?"

"Rather."

"Dear Benjy... Do you know, I can hardly believe I'm here. I never thought I should come again."

"But why shouldn't you?"

"I don't know. Only I think every time something'll happen to prevent me. I'm afraid of being ill or dying before I can get away. And they might send me anywhere any day. It's awful to be so uncertain."

"Don't think about it. You're here now."

"Oh Jerrold, supposing it was the last time--"

"It isn't the last time. Don't spoil it by thinking."

"You'd think if you were me."

"I say--you don't mean they're not decent to you?"

"Who, Grandmamma and Grandpapa? They're perfect darlings. So's Aunt Emily. But they're awfully old and they can't play at anything, except bridge. And it isn't the same thing at all. Besides, I don't--"

She paused. It wasn't kind to the poor things to say "I don't love them the same."

"Do you like us so awfully, then?"

"Yes."

"I'm glad you like us."

They were silent.

Up and down the flagged terrace above them Aunt Adeline and Uncle Robert walked together. The sound of his voice came to them, low and troubled.

Anne listened, "Is anything wrong?" she said. "They've been like that for ages."

"Daddy's bothered about Eliot."

"Eliot?"

"About his wanting to be a doctor."

"Is Auntie Adeline bothered?"

"No. She would be if she knew. But she doesn't think it'll happen. She never thinks anything will happen that she doesn't like. But it will. They can't keep him off it. He's been doing medicine at Cambridge because they won't let him go and do it at Bart's. It's just come out that he's been at it all the time. Working like blazes."

"Why shouldn't he be a doctor if he likes?"

"Because he's the eldest son. It wouldn't matter so much if it was only Colin or me. But Eliot ought to have the estate. And he says he won't have it. He doesn't want it. He says Daddy's got to leave it to me. That's what's worrying the dear old thing. He thinks it wouldn't be fair."

"Who to?"

Jerrold laughed. "Why, to **Eliot**. He's got it into his dear old head that he **ought** to have it. He can't see that Eliot knows his own business best. It **would** be most awfully in his way... It's pretty beastly for me, too. I don't like taking it when I know Daddy wants Eliot to have it. That's to say, he **doesn't** want; he'd like me to have it, because I'd take care of it. But that makes him all the more stuck on Eliot, because he thinks it's the right thing. I don't like having it in any case."

"Why ever not?"

"Well, I **can** only have it if Daddy dies, and I'd rather die myself first."

"That's how I feel about my farm."

"Beastly, isn't it? Still, I'm not worrying. Daddy's frightfully healthy, thank Heaven. He'll live to be eighty at the very least. Why--I should be fifty."

"You're all right," said Anne. "But it's awful for me. Grandpapa might die any day. He's seventy-five **now**. It'll be ages before you're fifty."

"And I may never be it. India may polish me off long before that." He laughed his happy laugh. The idea of his own death seemed to Jerrold irresistibly funny.

"India?"

He laughed again at her dismay.

"Rather. I'm going in for the Indian Civil."

"Oh Jerrold--you'll be away years and years, nearly all the time, like Daddy, and I shan't ever see you."

"I shan't start for ages. Not for five years. Lots of time to see each other in."

"Lots of time for **not** seeing each other ever again."

She sat staring mournfully, seeing before her the agony of separation.

"Nonsense," said Jerrold. "Why on earth shouldn't you come out to India too? I say, that would be a lark, wouldn't it? You would come, wouldn't you?"

"Like a shot," said Anne.

"Would you give up your farm to come?"

"I'd give up anything."

"That's all right. Let's go and play tennis."

They played for two hours straight on end, laughing and shouting. Adeline, intensely bored by Eliot and his absurd affairs, came down the lawn to look at them. She loved their laughter. It was good to have Anne there. Anne was so happy.

John Severn came to her.

"Did you ever see anything happier than that absurd boy?" she said. "Why can't Eliot be jolly and contented, too, like Jerrold?"

"Don't you think the chief reason may be that he *isn't* Jerrold?"

"Jerrold's adorable. He's never given me a day's trouble since he was born."

"No. It's other women he'll give trouble to," said John, "before he's done."

Colin was playing. All afternoon he had been practising with fury; first scales, then exercises. Then a pause; and now, his fingers slipped into the first movement of the Waldstein Sonata.

Secretly, mysteriously he began; then broke, sharply, impatiently, crescendo, as the passion of the music mounted up and up. And now as it settled into its rhythm his hands ran smoothly and joyously along.

The west window of the drawing-room was open to the terrace. Eliot and Anne sat out there and listened.

"He's wonderful, isn't he?" she said.

Eliot shook his head. "Not so wonderful as he was. Not half so wonderful as he ought to be. He'll never be good enough for a professional. He knows he won't."

"What's happened?"

"Nothing. That's just it. Nothing ever will happen. He's stuck. It's the same with his singing. He'll never be any good if he can't go away and study somewhere. If it isn't Berlin or Leipzig it ought to be London. But father can't live there and the mater won't go anywhere without him. So poor Col-Col's got to stick here doing nothing, with the same rotten old masters telling him things he knew years ago.... It'll be worse next term when he goes to Cheltenham. He won't be able to practice, and nobody'll care a damn.... Not that that would matter if he cared himself."

Colin was playing the slow movement now, the grave, pure passion, pressed out from the solemn bass, throbbed, tense with restraint.

"Oh Eliot, he *does* care."

"In a way. Not enough to keep on at it. You've got to slog like blazes, if you want to get on."

"Jerrold won't, ever, then."

"Oh yes he will. *He'll* get on all right, because he *doesn't* care; because work comes so jolly easy to him. He hasn't got to break his heart over it.... The trouble with Colin is that he cares, awfully, for such a lot of other things. Us, for instance. He'll leave off in the middle of a movement if he hears Jerrold yelling for him. He ought to be able to chuck us all; we're all of us in his way. He ought to hate us. He ought to hate Jerrold worst of all."

Adeline and John Severn came round the corner of the terrace.

"What's all this about hating?" he said.

"What do you mean, Eliot?" said she.

Eliot raised himself wearily. "I mean," he said, "you'll never be any good at anything if you're not prepared to commit a crime for it."

"I know what I'd commit a crime for," said Anne. "But I shan't tell."

"You needn't. *You'd* do it for anybody you were gone on."

"Well, I would. I'd tell any old lie to make them happy. I'd steal for them if they were hungry. I'd kill anybody who hurt them."

"I believe you would," said Eliot.

"We know who Anne would commit her crimes for."

"We don't. We don't know anything she doesn't want us to," said Eliot, shielding her from his mother's mischief.

"That's right, Eliot, stick up for her," said John. He knew what she was thinking of. "Would Jerrold commit a crime?" he said.

"Sooner than any of us. But not for the Indian Civil. He'd rob, butcher, lie himself black in the face for anything he really cared for."

"He would for Colin," said Anne.

"Rob? Butcher and lie?" Her father meditated.

"It sounds like Jerrold, doesn't it?" said Adeline. "Absurd children. Thank goodness they don't any of them know what they're talking about.... And here's tea."

Indoors the music stopped suddenly and Colin came out, ready.

"What's Jerrold doing?" he said.

It was, as Eliot remarked, a positive obsession.

Tea was over. Adeline and Anne sat out together on the terrace. The others had gone. Adeline looked at her watch.

"What time is it?" said Anne.

"Twenty past five."

Anne started up. "And I'm going to ride with Jerrold at half-past."

"Are you? I thought you were going to stay with me."

Anne turned. "Do you want me to, Auntie?"

"What do you think?"

"If you really want me to, of *course* I'll stay. Jerry won't mind."

"You darling... And I used to think you were never going to like me. Do you remember?"

"I remember I was a perfect little beast to you."

"You were. But you do love me a bit now, don't you?"

"What do you *think*?"

Anne leaned over her, covering her, supporting herself by the arms of the garden chair. She brought her face close down, not kissing her, but looking into her eyes and smiling, teasing in her turn.

"You love me," said Adeline; "but you'd cut me into little bits if it would please Jerrold."

Anne drew back suddenly, straightened herself and turned away.

"Run off, you monkey, or you'll keep him waiting. I don't want you ... Wait ... Where's Uncle Robert?"

"Down at the farm."

"Bother his old farm. Well--you might ask that father of yours to come and amuse me."

"I'll go and get him now. Are you sure you don't want me?"

"Quite sure, you funny thing."

Anne ran, to make up for lost time.

The sun had come round on to the terrace. Adeline rose from her chair. John Severn rose, stiffly.

She had made him go with her to the goldfish pond, made him walk round the garden, listening to him and not listening, detaching herself wilfully at every turn, to gather more and more of her blue flowers; made him come into the drawing-room and look on while she arranged them exquisitely in the tall Chinese jars. She had brought him out again to sit on the terrace in the sun; and now, in her restlessness, she was up again and calling to him to follow.

"It's baking here. Shall we go into the library?"

"If you like." He sighed as he said it.

As long as they stayed out of doors he felt safe and peaceful; but he was afraid of the library. Once there, shut in with her in that room which she was consecrating to their communion, heaven only knew what sort of fool he might make of himself. Last time it was only the sudden entrance of Robert that had prevented some such manifestation. And to-day, her smile and her attentive attitude told him that she expected him to be a fool, that she looked to his folly for her entertainment.

He had followed her like a dog; and as if he had been a dog her hand patted a place on the couch beside her. And because he was a fool and foredoomed he took it.

There was a silence. Then suddenly he made up his mind.

"Adeline, I'm very sorry, but I find I've got to go to-morrow."

"Go? Up to town?"

"Yes."

"But--you're coming back again."

"I'm--afraid--not."

"My dear John, you haven't been here a week. I thought you were going to stay with us till your leave was up."

"So did I. But I find I can't."

"Whyever not?"

"Oh--there are all sorts of things to be seen to."

"Nonsense, what do you suppose Robert will say to you, running off like this?"

"Robert will understand."

"It's more than I do."

"You can see, can't you, that I'm going because I must, not because I want to."

"Well, I think it's horrid of you. I shall miss you frightfully."

"Yes, you were good enough to say I amused you."

"You're not amusing me now, my dear ... Are you going to take Anne away from me too?"

"Not if you'd like to keep her."

"Of course I'd like to keep her."

He paused, brooding, wrenching one of his lean hands with the other.

"There's one thing I must ask you--"

"Ask, ask, then."

"I told you Anne would care for you if you gave her time. She does care for you."

"Yes. Odd as it may seem, I really believe she does."

"Well--don't let her be hurt by it."

"Hurt? Who's going to hurt her?"

"You, if you let her throw herself away on you when you don't want her."

"Have I behaved as if I didn't want her?"

"You've behaved like an angel. All the same, you frighten me a little. You've a terrible fascination for the child. Don't use it too much. Let her feelings alone. Don't work on them for the fun of seeing what she'll do next. If she tries to break away don't bring her back. Don't jerk her on the chain. Don't--amuse yourself with Anne."

"So that's how you think of me?"

"Oh, you know how I think."

"Do I? Have I ever known? You say the cruellest things. Is there anything else I'm not to do to her?"

"Yes. For God's sake don't tease her about Jerrold."

"My dear John, you talk as if it was serious. I assure you Jerrold isn't thinking about Anne."

"And Anne isn't 'thinking' about Jerrold. They don't think, poor dears. They don't know what's happening to them. None of us know what's happening to us till it happens. Then it's too late."

"Well, I'll promise not to do any of these awful things if you'll tell me, honestly, why you're going."

He stared at her.

"Tell you? You know why. I am going for *the same reason* that I came. How can you possibly ask me to stay?"

"Of course, if you feel like that about it--"

"You'll say I'd no business to come if I feel like that. But I knew I wasn't hurting anybody but myself. I knew *you* were safe. There's never been anybody but Robert."

"Never. Never for a minute."

"I tell you I know that. I always have known it. And I understand it. What I can't understand is why, when that's that, you make it so hard for me."

"Do I make it hard for you?"

"Damnably."

"You poor thing. But you'll get over it."

"I'm not young enough to get over it. Does it look like getting over it? It's been going on for twenty-two years."

"Oh come, not all the time, John."

"Pretty nearly. On and off."

"More off than on, I think."

"What does that matter when it's 'on' now? Anyhow I've got to go."

"Go, if you must. Do the best for yourself, my dear. Only don't say I made you."

"I'm not saying anything."

"Well--I'm sorry."

All the same her smile declared her profound and triumphant satisfaction with herself. It remained with her after he had gone. She would rather he had stayed, following her about, waiting for her, ready to her call, amusing her; but his going was the finer tribute to her power: the finest, perhaps, that he could have well paid. She hadn't been prepared for such a complete surrender.

Something had happened to Eliot. He sulked. Indoors and out, working and playing, at meal-times and bed-time he sulked. Jerrold said of him that he sulked in his sleep.

Two things made his behaviour inexplicable. To begin with, it was uncalled for. Robert Fielding, urged by John Severn in a last interview, had given in all along the line. Not only had Eliot leave to stick to his medicine (which he would have done in any case), but he was to go to Bart's to work for his doctor's degree when his three years at Cambridge were ended. His father had made a new will, leaving the estate to Jerrold and securing to the eldest son an income almost large enough to make up for the loss. Eliot, whose ultimate aim was research work, now saw all the ways before him cleared. He had no longer anything to sulk for.

Still more mysteriously, his sulking appeared to be related to Anne. He had left off going for walks alone with her in the fields and woods; he didn't show her things under his microscope any more. If she leaned over his shoulder he writhed himself away; if his hand blundered against hers he drew it back as if her touch burnt him. More often than not he would go out of the room if she came into it. Yet as long as she was there he couldn't keep his eyes off her. She would be sitting still, reading, when she would be aware, again and again, of Eliot's eyes, lifted from his book to fasten on her. She could feel them following her when she walked away.

One wet day in August they were alone together in the schoolroom, reading. Suddenly Anne felt his eyes on her. Their look was intent, penetrating, disturbing; it burned at her under his jutting, sombre eyebrows.

"Is there anything funny about me?" she said.

"Funny? No. Why?"

"Because you keep on looking at me."

"I didn't know I was looking at you."

"Well, you were. You're always doing it. And I can't think why."

"It isn't because I want to."

He held his book up so that it hid his face.

"Then don't do it," she said. "You needn't."

"I shan't," he snarled, savagely, behind his screen.

But he did it again and again, as if for the life of him he couldn't help it. There was something about it mysterious and exciting. It made Anne want to look at Eliot when he wasn't looking at her.

She liked his blunt, clever face, the half-ugly likeness of his father's with its jutting eyebrows and jutting chin, its fine grave mouth and greenish-brown eyes; mouth and eyes that had once been so kind and were now so queer. Eliot's face made her keep on wondering what it was doing. She *had* to look at it.

One day, when she was looking, their eyes met. She had just time to see that his mouth had softened as if he were pleased to find her looking at him. And his eyes were different; not cross, but dark now and unhappy; they made her feel as if she had hurt him.

They were in the library. Uncle Robert was there, sitting in his chair behind them, at the other end of the long room. She had forgotten Uncle Robert.

"Oh, Eliot," she said, "have I done anything?"

"Not that I know of." His face stiffened.

"You look as if I had. Have I?"

"Don't talk such putrid rot. As if I cared what you did. Can't you leave me alone?"

And he jumped up and left the room.

And there was Uncle Robert in his chair, watching her, looking kind and sorry.

"What's the matter with him?" she said. "Why is he so cross?"

"You mustn't mind. He doesn't mean it."

"No, but it's so funny of him. He's only cross with me; and I haven't done anything."

"It isn't that."

"What is it, then? I believe he hates me."

"No. He doesn't hate you, Anne. He's going through a bad time, that's all. He can't help being cross."

"Why can't he? He's got everything he wants."

"Has he?"

Uncle Robert was smiling. And this time his smile was for himself. She didn't understand it.

Anne was going away. She said she supposed now that Eliot would be happy.

Grandmamma Severn thought she had been long enough running loose with those Fielding boys. Grandpapa Everitt agreed with her and they decided that in September Anne should go to the big girls' college in Cheltenham. Grandmamma and Aunt Emily had left London and taken a house in Cheltenham and Anne was to live with them there.

Colin and she were going in the same week, Colin to his college and Anne to hers.

They were discussing this prospect. Colin and Jerrold and Anne in Colin's room. It was a chilly day in September and Colin was in bed surrounded by hot water bottles. He had tried to follow Jerrold in his big jump across the river and had fallen in. He was not ill, but he hoped he would be, for then he couldn't go back to Cheltenham next week.

"If it wasn't for the hot water bottles," he said, "I *might* get a chill."

"I wish I could get one," said Anne. "But I can't get anything. I'm so beastly strong."

"It isn't so bad for you. You haven't got to live with the girls. It'll be perfectly putrid in my house now that Jerrold isn't there."

"Haven't you *any* friends, Col-Col?"

"Yes. There's little Rogers. But even he's pretty rotten after Jerry."

"He would be."

"And that old ass Rawly says I'll be better this term without Jerrold. He kept on gassing about fighting your own battles and standing on your own feet. You never heard such stinking rot."

"You're lucky it's Cheltenham," Jerrold said, "and not some other rotten hole. Dad and I'll go over on half-holidays and take you out. You and Anne."

"You'll be at Cambridge."

"Not till next year. And it isn't as if Anne wasn't there."

"Grannie and Aunt Emily'll ask you every week. I've made them. It'll be a bit slow, but they're rather darlings."

"Have they a piano?" Colin asked.

"Yes. And they'll let you play on it all the time."

Colin looked happier. But he didn't get his chill, and when the day came he had to go.

Jerrold saw Anne off at Wyck station.

"You'll look after Col-Col, won't you?" he said. "Write and tell me how he gets on."

"I'll write every week."

Jerrold was thoughtful.

"After all, there's something in that idea of old Rawlings', that I'm bad for him.

He's got to do without me."

"So have I."

"You're different. You'll stand it, if you've got to. Colin won't. And he doesn't chum up with the other chaps."

"No. But think of me and all those awful girls--after you and Eliot" (she had forgotten Eliot's sulkiness) "and Uncle Robert. And Grannie and Aunt Emily after Auntie Adeline."

"Well, I'm glad Col-Col'll have you sometimes."

"So'm I... Oh, Jerrold, here's the beastly train."

It drew up along the platform.

Anne stood in her carriage, leaning out of the window to him.

His hand was on the ledge. They looked at each other without speaking.

The guard whistled. Carriage doors slammed one after another. The train moved forward.

Jerrold ran alongside. "I say, you'll let Col-Col play on that piano?"

Anne was gone.

III
ANNE AND JERROLD

"'Where have you been all the day, Rendal, my son?
Where have you been all the day, my pretty one?...'"

Five years had passed. It was August, nineteen ten.

Anne had come again. She sat out on the terrace with Adeline, while Colin's song drifted out to them through the open window.

It was her first day, the first time for three years. Anne's calendar was blank from nineteen seven to nineteen ten. When she was seventeen she had left Cheltenham and gone to live with Grandpapa Everitt at the Essex farm. Grandpapa Everitt wanted her more than Grandmamma Severn, who had Aunt Emily; so Anne had stayed with him all that time. She had spent it learning to farm and looking after Grandpapa on his bad days. For the last year of his life all his days had been bad. Now he was dead, dead three months ago, and Anne had the farm. She was going to train for five years under the man who had worked it for Grandpapa; after that she meant to manage it herself.

She had been trying to tell Aunt Adeline all about it, but you could see she wasn't interested. She kept on saying "Yes" and "Oh" and "Really"? in the wrong places. She never could listen to you for long together, and this afternoon she was evidently thinking of something else, perhaps of John Severn, who had been home on leave and gone again without coming to the Fieldings.

"'I've been to my sweetheart, mother, make my bed soon, For I'm sick to my heart and I fain would lie down...'"

Mournful, and beautiful, Colin's song came through the windows, and Anne thought of Jerrold who was not there. He was staying in Yorkshire with some friends of his, the Durhams. He would be back to-morrow. He would have got away from the Durhams.

...'"make my bed soon..."'

To-morrow. To-morrow.

"Who are the Durhams, Auntie?"

"He's Sir Charles Durham. Something important in the Punjaub. Some high government official. He'll be useful to Jerrold if he gets a job out there. They're going back in October. I suppose I shall have to ask. Maisie Durham before they sail."

Maisie Durham. Maisie Durham. But to-morrow he would have got away.

"'What will you leave your lover, Rendal, my son? What will you leave your lover, my pretty one? A rope to hang her, mother, A rope to hang her, mother, make my bed soon,   For I'm sick to my heart and I fain would lie down.'"

"Sing something cheerful, Colin, for Goodness sake," said his mother. But Colin sang it again.

"'A rope to hang her'"

"Bless him, you'd think he'd known all the wicked women that ever were. My little Col-Col."

"You like him the best, don't you?"

"No. Indeed I do not. I like my laughing boy best. You wouldn't catch Jerry singing a dismal song like that."

"Darling, you used to say Colin was your favourite."

"No, my dear. Never. Never. It was always Jerrold. Ever since he was born. He never cried when he was a baby. Colin was always crying."

"Poor Col-Col."

"There you are. Nobody'll ever say, 'Poor Jerrold'. I like happy people, Anne. In this tiresome world it's people's duty to be happy."

"If it was, would they be? Don't look at me as if I wasn't."

"I wasn't thinking of you, ducky... You might tell Pinkney to take *all* those tea-things off the terrace and put them *back* into the lounge."

The beech-trees stood in a half ring at the top of the highest field. Jerrold had come back. He and Anne sat in the bay of the beeches, looking out over the hills.

Curve after curve of many-coloured hills, rolling together, flung off from each other, an endless undulation. Rounded heads carrying a clump of trees like a comb; long steep groins packed with tree-tops; raking necks hog-maned with stiff plantations. Slopes that spread out fan-wise, opened wide wings. An immense stretching and flattening of arcs up to the straight blue wall on the horizon. A band of trees stood up there like a hedge.

Calm, clean spaces emerging, the bright, sharp-cut pattern of the fields; squares and fans and pointed triangles, close fitted; emerald green of the turnips; yellow of the charlock lifted high and clear; red brown and pink and purple of ploughed land and fallows; red gold of the wheat and white green of the barley; shimmering in a wash of thin air.

Where Anne and Jerrold sat, green pastures, bitten smooth by the sheep, flowed down below them in long ridges like waves. On the right the bright canary coloured charlock brimmed the field. Its flat, vanilla and almond scent came to them.

"What's Yorkshire like?"

"Not a patch on this place. I can't think what there is about it that makes you feel so jolly happy."

"But you'd always be happy, Jerrold, anywhere."

"Not like that. I mean a queer, uncanny feeling that you sort of can't make out."

"I know. I know... There's nothing on earth that gets you like the smell of charlock."

Anne tilted up her nose and sniffed delicately.

"Fancy seeing this country suddenly for the first time," he said.

"There's such a lot of it. You wouldn't see it properly. It takes ages just to tell one hill from another."

He looked at her. She could feel him meditating, considering.

"I say, I wonder what it would feel like seeing each other for the first time."

"Not half so nice as seeing each other now. Why, we shouldn't remember any of the jolly things we've done: together."

He had seen Maisie Durham for the first time. She wondered whether that had made him think of it.

"No, but the effect might be rather stunning--I mean of seeing *you*."

"It wouldn't. And you'd be nothing but a big man with a face I rather liked. I suppose I should like your face. We shouldn't *know* each other, Jerrold."

"No more we should. It would be like not knowing Dad or Mummy or Colin. A thing you can't conceive."

"It would be like not knowing anything at all ... Of course, the best thing would be both."

"Both?"

"Knowing each other and not knowing."

"You can't have it both ways," he said.

"Oh, can't you! You don't half know me as it is, and I don't half know you. We might both do anything any day. Things that would make each other jump."

"What sort of things?"

"That's the exciting part of it--we wouldn't know."

"I believe you *could*, Anne--make me jump."

"Wait till I get out to India."

"You're really going?"

"Really going. Daddy may send for me any day."

"I may be sent there. Then we'll go out together."

"Will Maisie Durham be going too?"

"O Lord no. Not with us. At least I hope not ... Poor little Maisie, I was a beast to say that."

"Is she little?"

"No, rather big. But you think of her as little. Only I don't think of her."

They stood up; they stood close; looking at each other, laughing. As he laughed his eyes took her in, from head to feet, wondering, admiring.

Anne's face and body had the same forward springing look. In their very stillness they somehow suggested movement. Her young breasts sprang forwards, sharp pointed. Her eyes had no sliding corner glances. He was for ever aware of Anne's face turning on its white neck to look at him straight and full, her black-brown eyes shining and darkening and shining under the long black brushes of her eyebrows. Even her nose expressed movement, a sort of rhythm. It rose in a slender arch, raked straight forward, dipped delicately and rose again in a delicately questing tilt. This tilt had the delightful air of catching up and shortening the curl of her upper lip. The exquisite lower one sprang forward, sharp and salient from the little dent above her innocent, rounded chin. Its edge curled slightly forward in a line firm as ivory and fine as the edge of a flower. As long as he lived he would remember the way of it.

And she, she was aware of his body, slender and tense under his white flannels. It seemed to throb with the power it held in, prisoned in the smooth, tight muscles. His eyes showed the colour of dark hyacinths, set in his clear, sun-browned skin. He smiled down at her, and his mouth and little fawn brown moustache followed the tilted shadow of his nostrils.

Suddenly her whole body quivered as if his had touched it. And when she looked at him she had the queer feeling that she saw him for the first time. Never before like that. Never before.

But to him she was the same Anne. He knew her face as he knew his mother's face or Colin's. He knew, he remembered all her ways.

And this was not what he wanted. He wanted some strange wonder and excitement; he wanted to find it in Anne and in nobody but Anne, and he couldn't find it. He wanted to be in love with Anne and he wasn't. She was too near him, too much a part of him, too well-known, too well-remembered. She made him restless and impatient, looking, looking for the strangeness, the mystery he wanted and couldn't find.

If only he could have seen her suddenly for the first time.

It was extraordinary how happy it made her to be with Aunt Adeline, walking slowly, slowly, with her round the garden, stretched out beside her on the terrace, following her abrupt moves from the sun into the shade and back again; or sitting for hours with her in the big darkened bedroom when Adeline had one of the bad headaches that attacked her now, brushing her hair, and putting handkerchiefs soaked in eau-de-cologne on her hot forehead.

Extraordinary, because this inactivity did violence to Anne's nature; besides, Auntie Adeline behaved as if you were uninteresting and unimportant, not attending to a word you said. Yet her strength lay in her inconsistency. One minute her arrogance ignored you and the next she came humbly and begged for your caresses; she was dependent, like a child, on your affection. Anne thought that pathetic. And there was always her fascination. That was absolute; above logic and morality, irrefutable as the sweetness of a flower. Everybody felt it, even the servants whom she tormented with her incalculable wants. Jerrold and Colin, even Eliot, now that he was grown-up, felt it. As for Uncle Robert he was like a young man in the beginning of first love.

Adeline judged people by their attitude to her. Anne, whether she listened to her or not, was her own darling. Her husband and John Severn were adorable, Major Markham of Wyck Wold and Mr. Hawtrey of Medlicote, who admired her, were perfect dears, Sir John Corbett of Underwoods, who didn't, was that silly old thing. Resist her and she felt no mean resentment; you simply dropped out of her scene. Thus her world was peopled with her adorers.

Anne couldn't have told you whether she felt the charm on its own account, or whether the pleasure of being with her was simply part of the blessed state of being at Wyck-on-the-Hill. Enough that Auntie Adeline was there where Uncle Robert and Eliot and Colin and Jerrold were; she belonged to them; she belonged to the house and garden; she stood with the flowers.

Anne was walking with her now, gathering roses for the house. The garden was like a room shut in by the clipped yew walls, and open to the sky. The sunshine poured into it; the flagged walks were pale with heat.

Anne's cat, Nicky, was there, the black Persian that Jerrold had given her last birthday. He sat in the middle of the path, on his haunches, his forelegs straight and stiff, planted together. His face had a look of sweet and solemn meditation.

"Oh Nicky, oh you darling!" she said.

When she stroked him he got up, arching his back and carrying his tail in a flourishing curve, like one side of a lyre; he rubbed against her ankles. A white butterfly flickered among the blue larkspurs; when Nicky saw it he danced on his hind legs, clapping his forepaws as he tried to catch it. But the butterfly was too quick for him. Anne picked him up and he flattened himself against her breast, butting under her chin with his smooth round head in his loving way.

And as Adeline wouldn't listen to her Anne talked to the cat.

"Clever little thing, he sees everything, all the butterflies and the dicky-birds and the daddy-long-legs. Don't you, my pretty one?"

"What's the good of talking to the cat?" said Adeline. "He doesn't understand a word you say."

"He doesn't understand the words, he says, but he feels the feeling ... He was the most beautiful of all the pussies, he was, he was."

"Nonsense. You're throwing yourself away on that absurd animal, for all the affection you'll get out of him."

"I shall get out just what I put in. He expects to be talked to."

"So do I."

"I've been trying to talk to you all afternoon and you won't listen. And you don't know how you can hurt Nicky's feelings. He's miserable if I don't tell him he's a beautiful pussy the minute he comes into my room. He creeps away under the washstand and broods. We take these darling things and give them little souls and hearts, and we've no business to hurt them. And they've such a tiny time to live, too... Look at him, sitting up to be carried, like a child."

"Oh wait, my dear, till you *have* a child. You ridiculous baby."

"Oh come, Jerrold's every bit as gone on him."

"You're a ridiculous pair," said Adeline.

"If Nicky purred round *your* legs, you'd love him, too," said Anne.

Uncle Robert was not well. He couldn't eat the things he used to eat; he had to have fish or chicken and milk and beef-tea and Benger's food. Jerrold said it was only indigestion and he'd be all right in a day or two. But you could see by the way he walked now that there was something quite dreadfully wrong. He went slowly, slowly, as if every step tired him out.

"Sorry, Jerrold, to be so slow."

But Jerrold wouldn't see it.

They had gone down to the Manor Farm, he and Jerrold and Anne. He wanted to show Jerrold the prize stock and what heifers they could breed from next year. "I should keep on with the short horns. You can't do better," he said.

Then they had gone up the fields to see if the wheat was ready for cutting yet. And he had kept on telling Jerrold what crops were to be sown after the wheat, swedes to come first, and vetch after the swedes, to crowd out the charlock.

"You'll have to keep the charlock down, Jerrold, or it'll kill the crops. You'll have the devil of a job." He spoke as though Jerrold had the land already and he was telling him the things he wanted him to remember.

They came back up the steep pasture, very slowly, Uncle Robert leaning on Jerrold's arm. They sat down to rest under the beech-trees at the top. They looked at the landscape, the many-coloured hills, rolling together, flung off from each other, an endless undulation.

"Beautiful country. Beautiful country," said Uncle Robert as if he had never seen it before.

"You should see *my* farm," Anne said. "It's as flat as a chess-board and all squeezed up by the horrid town. Grandpapa sold a lot of it for building. I wish I could sell the rest and buy a farm in the Cotswolds. Do you ever have farms to sell, Uncle Robert?"

"Well, not to sell. To let, perhaps, if a tenant goes. You can have the Barrow Farm when old Sutton dies. He can't last long. But," he went on, "you'll find it very different farming here."

"How different?"

"Well, in some of those fields you'll have to fight the charlock all the time. And in some the soil's hard. And in some you've got to plough across the sun because of the slope of the land... Remember, Jerrold, Anne's to have the Barrow Farm, if she wants it, when Sutton dies."

Jerrold laughed. "My dear father, I shall be in India."

"I'll remind you, Uncle Robert."

Uncle Robert smiled. "I'll tell Barker to remember," he said. Barker was his agent.

It was as if he were thinking that when Sutton died he might not be there. And he had said that Sutton wouldn't last long. Anne looked at Jerrold. But Jerrold's face was happy. He didn't see it.

They left Uncle Robert in the library, drinking hot water for tea.

"Jerrold," Anne said, "I'm sure Uncle Robert's ill."

"Oh no. It's only indigestion. He'll be as right as rain in a day or two."

Anne's cat Nicky was dying.

Jerrold struggled with his sleep, pushing it back and back before him, trying to remember.

There was something; something that had hung over him the night before. He had been afraid to wake and find it there. Something--.

Now he remembered.

Nicky was dying and Anne was unhappy. That was what it was; that was what he had hated to wake to, Anne's unhappiness and the little cat.

There was nothing else. Nothing wrong with Daddy--only indigestion. He had had it before.

The room was still dark, but the leaded squares of the window lattices barred a sky pale with dawn. In her room across the passage Anne would be sitting up with Nicky. He remembered now that he had to get up early to make her some tea.

He lit a candle and went to her door to see if she were still awake. Her voice answered his gentle tapping, "Who's there?"

"Me. Jerrold. May I come in?"

"Yes. But don't bring the light in. He's sleeping."

He put out the candle and made his way to her. Against the window panes he could see the outline of her body sitting upright in a chair. She glimmered there in her white wrapper and he made out something black stretched straight and still in her lap. He sat down in the window-seat and watched.

The room was mysterious, full of dusk air that thinned as the dawn stirred in it palpably, waking first Anne's white bed, a strip of white cornice and a sheet of watery looking-glass. Nicky's saucer of milk gleamed white on the dark floor at Anne's feet. The pale ceiling lightened; and with a sliding shimmer of polished curves the furniture rose up from the walls. Presently it stood clear, wine-coloured, shining in the strange, pure light.

And in the strange, pure light he saw Anne, in her white wrapper with the great rope of her black hair, plaited, hanging down her back. The little black cat lay in her white lap, supported by her arm.

She smiled at Jerrold strangely. She spoke and her voice was low and strange.

"He's asleep, Jerry. He kept on looking at me and mewing. Then he tried to climb into my lap and couldn't. And I took him up and he was quiet then. I think he was pleased that I took him ... I've given him the morphia pill and I don't think he's in pain. He'll die in his sleep."

"Yes. He'll die in his sleep."

He hardly knew what he was saying. He was looking at Anne, and it was as if now, at last, he saw her for the first time. This, this was what he wanted, this mysterious, strangely smiling Anne, this white Anne with the great plaited rope of black hair, who belonged to the night and the dawn.

"I'm going to get you some tea," he said.

He went down to the kitchen where everything had been left ready for him over-night. He lit the gas-ring and made the tea and brought it to her with cake and bread and butter on a little tray. He set it down beside her on the window-seat. But Anne could neither eat nor drink. She cried out to him.

"Oh, Jerry, look at him. Do you think he's dying now?"

He knelt down and looked. Nicky's eyes were two slits of glaze between half-shut lids. His fur stood up on his bulging, frowning forehead. His little, flat cat's face was drawn to a point with a look of helpless innocence and anguish. His rose-leaf tongue showed between his teeth as he panted.

"Yes. I'm awfully afraid he's dying."

They waited half an hour, an hour. They never knew how long. Once he said to her, "Would you rather I went or stayed?" And she said, "Stayed, if you don't mind."

Through the open window, from the fields of charlock warm in the risen sun, the faint, smooth scent came to them.

Then Nicky began to cough with a queer quacking sound. Jerrold went to her, upsetting the saucer as he came.

"It's his milk," she said. "He couldn't drink it." And with that she burst into tears.

"Oh, Anne, don't cry. Don't cry, Anne darling."

He put his arm round her. He laid his hand on her hair and stroked it. He stooped suddenly and kissed her face; gently, quietly, because of the dead thing in her lap.

It was as if he had kissed her for the first time.

For one instant she had her arm round his neck and clung to him, hiding her face on his shoulder. Then suddenly she loosed herself and stood up before him, holding out the body of the little cat.

"Take him away, please, Jerry, so that I don't see him."

He took him away.

All day the sense of kissing her remained with him, and all night, with the scent of her hair, the sweet rose-scent of her flesh, the touch of her smooth rose-leaf skin. That was Anne, that strangeness, that beauty of the clear, cold dawn, that scent, that warm sweet smoothness, that clinging of passionate arms. And he had kissed her gently, quietly, as you kiss a child, as you kiss a young, small animal.

He wanted to kiss her close, pressing down on her mouth, deep into her sweet flesh; to hold her body tight, tight, crushed in his arms. If it hadn't been for Nicky that was the way he would have kissed her.

To-morrow, to-morrow, he would kiss Anne that way.

IV
ROBERT

But when to-morrow came he did not kiss her. He was annoyed with Anne because she insisted on taking a gloomy view of his father's illness.

The doctors couldn't agree about it. Dr. Ransome of Wyck said it was gastritis. Dr. Harper of Cheltenham said it was colitis. He had had that before and had got better. Now he was getting worse, fast. For the last three days he couldn't keep down his chicken and fish. Yesterday not even his milk. To-day, not even his ice-water. Then they both said it was acute gastritis.

"He's never been like this before, Jerrold."

"No. But that doesn't mean he isn't going to get better. People with acute gastritis do get better. It's enough to make him die, everybody insisting that he's going to. And it's rot sending for Eliot."

That was what Anne had done.

Eliot had written to her from London: 10 Welbeck St., **Sept. 35th, 1910.**

My dear Anne:

I wish you'd tell me how Father really is. Nobody but you has
any intelligence that matters. Between Mother's wails and
Jerrold's optimism I don't seem to be getting the truth. If it's
serious I'll come down at once.

Always yours,

Eliot.

And Anne had answered:

My dear Eliot,

It *is* serious. Dr. Ransome and Dr. Harper say so. They think now it's acute gastritis. I wish you'd come down. Jerrold is heart-breaking. He won't see it; because he couldn't bear it if he did. I know Auntie wants you.

Always very affectionately yours,

Anne.

She addressed the letter to Dr. Eliot Fielding, for Eliot had taken his degree.

And on that to-morrow of Jerrold's Eliot had come. Jerrold told him he was a perfect idiot, rushing down like that, as if Daddy hadn't an hour to live.

"You'll simply terrify him," he said. "He hasn't got a chance with all you people grousing and croaking round him."

And he went off to play in the lawn tennis tournament at Medlicote as a protest against the general pessimism. His idea seemed to be that if he, Jerrold, could play in a lawn tennis tournament, his father couldn't be seriously ill.

"It's perfectly awful of Jerrold," his mother said. "I can't make him out. He adores his father, yet he behaves as if he hadn't any feeling."

She and Anne were sitting in the lounge after luncheon, waiting for Eliot to come from his father's room.

"Didn't you *tell* him, Anne?"

"I did everything I know.... But darling, he isn't unfeeling. He does it because he can't bear to think Uncle Robert won't get better. He's trying to make himself believe he will. I think he does believe it. But if he stayed away from the tournament that would mean he didn't."

"If only *I* could. But I must. I *must* believe it if I'm not to go mad. I don't know what I shall do if he doesn't get better. I can't live without him. It's been so perfect, Anne. It can't come to an end like this. It can't happen. It would be too cruel."

"It would," Anne said. But she thought: "It just will happen. It's happening now."

"Here's Eliot," she said.

Eliot came down the stairs. Adeline went to him.

"Oh Eliot, what do you think of him?"

Eliot put her off. "I can't tell you yet."

"You think he's very bad?"

"Very."

"But you don't think there isn't any hope?"

"I can't tell yet. There may be. He wants you to go to him. Don't talk much to him. Don't let him talk. And don't, whatever you do, let him move an inch."

Adeline went upstairs. Anne and Eliot were alone. "You **can** tell," she said. "You don't think there's any hope."

"I don't. There's something quite horribly wrong. His temperature's a hundred and three."

"Is that bad?"

"Very."

"I do wish Jerry hadn't gone."

"So do I."

"It'll be worse for him, Eliot, than for any of us when he knows."

"I know. But he's always been like that, as long as I can remember. He simply can't stand trouble. It's the only thing he funks. And his funking it wouldn't matter if he'd stand and face it. But he runs away. He's running away now. Say what you like, it's a sort of cowardice."

"It's his only fault."

"I know it is. But it's a pretty serious one, Anne. And he'll have to pay for it. The world's chock full of suffering and all sorts of horrors, and you can't go turning your back to them as Jerrold does without paying for it. Why, he won't face anything that's even a little unpleasant. He won't listen if you try to tell him. He won't read a book that hasn't a happy ending. He won't go to a play that isn't a comedy... It's an attitude I can't understand. I don't like horrors any more than he does; but when I hear about them I want to go straight where they are and do something to stop them. That's what I chose my profession for."

"I know. Because you're so sorry. So sorry. But Jerry's sorry too. So sorry that he can't bear it."

"But he's got to bear it. There it is and he's got to take it. He's only making things worse for himself by holding out and refusing. Jerrold will never be any good till he *has* taken it. Till he's suffered damnably."

"I don't want him to suffer. I don't want it. I can't bear him to bear it."

"He must. He's got to."

"I'd do anything to save him. But I can't."

"You can't. And you mustn't try to. It would be the best thing that could happen to him."

"Oh no, not to Jerry."

"Yes. To Jerry. If he's ever to be any good. You don't want him to be a moral invalid, do you?"

"No... Oh Eliot, that's Uncle Robert's door."

Upstairs the door opened and shut and Adeline came to the head of the stairs.

"Oh Eliot, come quick----"

Eliot rushed upstairs. And Anne heard Adeline sobbing hysterically and crying out to him.

"I can't--I can't. I can not bear it!"

She saw her trail off along the gallery to her room; she heard her lock herself in. She had every appearance of running away from something. From something she could not bear. Half an hour passed before Eliot came back to Anne.

"What was it?" she said.

"What I thought. Gastric ulcer. He's had a haemorrhage."

That was what Aunt Adeline had run away from.

"Look here, Anne, I've got to send Scarrott in the car for Ransome. Then he'll have to go on to Cheltenham to fetch Colin."

"Colin?" This was the end then.

"Yes. He'd better come. And I want you to do something. I want you to drive over to Medlicote and bring Jerrold back. It's beastly for you. But you'll do it, won't you?"

"I'll do anything."

It was the beastliest thing she had ever had to do, but she did it.

From where she drew up in the drive at Medlicote she could see the tennis courts. She could see Jerrold playing in the men's singles. He stood up to the net, smashing down the ball at the volley; his back was turned to her as he stood.

She heard him shout. She heard him laugh. She saw him turn to come up the court, facing her.

And when he saw her, he knew.

He had waited ten minutes in the gallery outside his father's room. Eliot had asked Anne to go in and help him while Jerrold stood by the door to keep his mother out. She was no good, Eliot said. She lost her head just when he wanted her to do things. You could have heard her all over the house crying out that she couldn't bear it.

She opened her door and looked out. When she saw Jerrold she came to him, slowly, supporting herself by the gallery rail. Her eyes were sore with crying and there was a flushed thickening about the edges of her mouth.

"So you've come back," she said. "You might go in and tell me how he is."

"Haven't you seen him?"

"Of course I've seen him. But I'm afraid, Jerrold. It was awful, awful, the haemorrhage. You can't think how awful. I daren't go in and see it again. I shouldn't be a bit of good if I did. I should only faint, or be ill or something. I simply can not bear it."

"You mustn't go in," he said.

"Who's with him?"

"Eliot and Anne."

"Anne?"

"Yes."

"Jerrold, to think that Anne should be with him and me not."

"Well, she'll be all right. She can stand things."

"It's all very well for Anne. He isn't *her* husband."

"You'd better go away, Mother."

"Not before you tell me how he is. Go in, Jerrold."

He knocked and went in.

His father was sitting up in his white, slender bed, raised on Eliot's arm. He saw his face, strained and smoothed with exhaustion, sallow white against the pillows, the back-drawn-mouth, the sharp, peaked nose, the iron grey hair, pointed with sweat, sticking to the forehead. A face of piteous, tired patience, waiting. He saw Eliot's face, close, close beside it by the edge of the pillow, grave and sombre and intent.

Anne was crossing the room from the bed to the washstand. Her face was very white but she had an air of great competence and composure. She carried a white basin brimming with a reddish froth. He saw little red specks splashed on the sleeve of her white linen gown. He shuddered.

Eliot made a sign to him and he went back to the door where his mother waited.

"Is he better?" she whispered. "Can I come in?"

Jerrold shook his head. "Better not--yet."

"You'll send for me if--if--"

"Yes."

He heard her trailing away along the gallery. He went into the room. He stood at the foot of the bed and stared, stared at his father lying there in Eliot's arms. He would have liked to have been in Eliot's place, close to him, close, holding him. As it was he could do nothing but stand and look at him with that helpless, agonized stare. He *had* to look at him, to look and look, punishing himself with sight for not having seen.

His eyes felt hot and brittle; they kept on filling with tears, burned themselves dry and filled again. His hand clutched the edge of the footrail as if only so he could keep his stand there.

A stream of warm air came through the open windows. Everything in the room stood still in it, unnaturally still, waiting. He was aware of the pattern of the window curtains. Blue parrots perched on brown branches among red flowers on a white ground; it all hung very straight and still, waiting.

Anne looked at him and spoke. She was standing beside the bed now, holding the clean basin and a towel, ready.

"Jerrold, you might go and get some more ice. It's in the bucket in the bathroom. Break it up into little pieces, like that. You split it with a needle."

He went to the bath-room, moving like a sleepwalker, wrapped in his dream-like horror. He found the ice, he broke it into little pieces, like that. He was very careful and conscientious about the size, and grateful to Anne for giving him something to do. Then he went back again and took up his station at the foot of the bed and waited. His father still lay back on his pillow, propped by Eliot's arm. His hands were folded on his chest above the bedclothes.

Anne still stood by the bed holding her basin and her towel ready. From time to time they gave him little pieces of ice to suck.

Once he opened his eyes, looked round the room and spoke. "Is your mother there?"

"Do you want her?" Eliot said.

"No. It'll only upset her. Don't let her come in."

He closed his eyes and opened them again.

"Is that Anne?"

"Yes. Who did you think it was?"

"I don't know...I'm sorry, Anne."

"Darling--" the word broke from a tender inarticulate sound she made.

Then: "Jerrold--," he said.

Jerrold came closer. His father's right arm unfolded itself and stretched out towards him along the bed.

Anne whispered, "Take his hand." Jerrold took it. He could feel it tremble as he touched it.

"It's all right, Jerry," he said. "It's all right." He gave a little choking cough. His eyes darkened with a sudden anxiety, a fear. His hand slackened. His head sank forward. Anne came between them. Jerrold felt the slight thrust of her body pushing him aside. He saw her arms stretched out, and the white gleam of the basin, then, the haemorrhage, jet after jet. Then his father's face tilted up on Eliot's arm, very white, and Anne stooping over him tenderly, and her hand with the towel, wiping the red foam from his lips.

Then eyes glazed between half-shut lids, mouth open, and the noise of death.

Eliot's arm laid down its burden. He got up and put his hand on Jerrold's shoulder and led him out of the room. "Go out into the air," he said. "I'll tell Mother."

Jerrold staggered downstairs, and through the hall and out into the blinding sunshine.

Far down the avenue he could hear the whirring of the car coming back from Cheltenham; the lines of the beech trees opened fan-wise to let it through. He saw Colin sitting up beside Scarrott.

Above his head a lattice ground and clattered. Somebody was going through the front rooms, shutting the windows and pulling down the blinds.

Jerrold turned back into the house to meet Colin there.

Upstairs his father's door opened and shut softly and Anne came out. She moved along the gallery to her room. Between the dark rails he could see her white skirt, and her arm, hanging, and the little specks of red splashed on the white sleeve.

Jerrold was afraid of Anne, and he saw no end to his fear. He had been dashed against the suffering he was trying to put away from him and the shock of it had killed in one hour his young adolescent passion. She would be for ever associated with that suffering. He would never see Anne without thinking of his father's death. He would never think of his father's death without seeing Anne. He would see her for ever through an atmosphere of pain and horror, moving as she had moved in his father's room. He couldn't see her any other way. This intolerable memory of her effaced all other memories, memories of the child Anne with the rabbit, of the young, happy Anne who walked and rode and played with him, of the strange, mysterious Anne he had found yesterday in her room at dawn. That Anne belonged to a time he had done with. There was nothing left for him but the Anne who had come to tell him his father was dying, who had brought him to his father's death-bed, who had bound herself up inseparably with his death, who only moved from the scene of it to appear dressed in black and carrying the flowers for his funeral.

She was wrapped round and round with death and death, nothing but death, and with Jerrold's suffering. When he saw her he suffered again. And as his way had always been to avoid suffering, he avoided Anne. His eyes turned from her if he saw her coming. He spoke to her without looking at her. He tried not to think of her. When he had gone he would try not to remember.

His one idea was to go, to get away from the place his father had died in and from the people who had seen him die. He wanted new unknown faces, new unknown voices that would not remind him------

Ten days after his father's death the letter came from John Severn. He wrote:

"... I'm delighted about Sir Charles Durham. You are a lucky devil. Any chap Sir Charles takes a fancy to is bound to get on. He can't help himself. You're not afraid of hard work, and I can tell you we give our Assistant Commissioners all they want and a lot more.

"It'll be nice if you bring Anne out with you. If you're stationed anywhere near us we ought to give her the jolliest time in her life between us."

"But Jerrold," said Adeline when she had read this letter. "You're not going out *now*. You must wire and tell him so."

"Why not now?"

"Because, my dear boy, you've got the estate and you must stay and look after it."

"Barker'll look after it. That's what he's there for."

"Nonsense, Jerrold. There's no need for you to go out to India."

"There *is* need. I've got to go."

"You haven't. There's every need for you to stop where you are. Eliot will be going abroad if Sir Martin Crozier takes him on. And if Colin goes into the diplomatic service Goodness knows where he'll be sent to."

"Colin won't be sent anywhere for another four years."

"No. But he'll be at Cheltenham or Cambridge half the time. I must have one son at home."

"Sorry, Mother. But I can't stand it here. I've got to go, and I'm going."

To all her arguments and entreaties he had one answer: He had got to go and he was going.

Adeline left him and went to look for Eliot whom she found in his room packing to go back to London. She came sobbing to Eliot.

"It's too dreadfully hard. As if it weren't bad enough to lose my darling husband I must lose all my sons. Not one of you will stay with me. And there's Anne going off with Jerrold. *She* may have him with her and I mayn't. She's taken everything from me. You'd have said if a wife's place was anywhere it was with her dying husband. But no. *She* was allowed to be with him and *I* was turned out of his room."

"My dear Mother, you know you weren't."

"I *was*. You turned me out yourself, Eliot, and had Anne in."

"Only because you couldn't stand it and she could."

"I daresay. She hadn't the same feelings."

"She had her own feelings, anyhow, only she controlled them. She stood it because she never thought of her feelings. She only thought of what she could do to help. She was magnificent."

"Of course you think so, because you're in love with her. She must take you, too. As if Jerrold wasn't enough."

"She hasn't taken me. She probably won't if I ask her. You shouldn't say those things, Mother. You don't know what you're talking about."

"I know I'm the most unhappy woman in the world. How am I going to live? I can't stand it if Jerry goes."

"He's got to go, Mother."

"He hasn't. Jerrold's place is here. He's got a duty and a responsibility. Your dear father didn't leave him the estate for him to let it go to wrack and ruin. It's most cruel and wrong of him."

"He can't do anything else. Don't you see why he wants to go? He can't stand the place without Father."

"I've got to stand it. So he may."

"Well, he won't, that's all. He simply funks it."

"He always was an arrant coward where trouble was concerned. He doesn't think of other people and how bad it is for them. He leaves me when I want him most."

"It's hard on you, Mother; but you can't stop him. And I don't think you ought to try."

"Oh, everybody tells me what *I* ought to do. My children can do as they like. So can Anne. She and Jerrold can go off to India and amuse themselves as if nothing had happened and it's all right."

But Anne didn't go off to India.

When she spoke to Jerrold about going with him his hard, unhappy face showed her that he didn't want her.

"You'd rather I didn't go," she said gently.

"It isn't that, Anne. It isn't that I don't want you. It's--it's simply that I want to get away from here, to get away from everything that reminds me--I shall go off my head if I've got to remember every minute, every time I see somebody who--I want to make a clean break and grow a new memory."

"I understand. You needn't tell me."

"Mother doesn't. I wish you'd make her see it."

"I'll try. But it's all right, Jerrold. I won't go."

"Of course you'll go. Only you won't think me a brute if I don't take you out with me?"

"I'm not going out with you. In fact, I don't think I'm going at all. I only wanted to because of going out together and because of the chance of seeing you when you got leave. I only thought of the heavenly times we might have had."

"Don't--don't, Anne."

"No, I won't. After all, I shouldn't care a rap about Ambala if you weren't there. And you may be stationed miles away. I'd rather go back to Ilford and do farming. Ever so much rather. India would really have wasted a lot of time."

"Oh, Anne, I've spoilt all your pleasure."

"No, you haven't. There isn't any pleasure to spoil--now."

"What a brute--what a cad you must think me."

"I don't, Jerry. It's not your fault. Things have just happened. And you see, I understand. I felt the same about Auntie Adeline after Mother died. I didn't want to see her because she reminded me--and yet, really, I loved her all the time."

"You won't go back on me for it?"

"I wouldn't go back on you whatever you did. And you mustn't keep on thinking I *want* to go to India. I don't care a rap about India itself. I hate Anglo-Indians and I simply loathe hot places. And Daddy doesn't want me out there, really. I shall be much happier on my farm. And it'll save a lot of expense, too. Just think what my outfit and passage would have cost."

"You wouldn't have cared what it cost if--"

"There isn't any if. I'm not lying, really." Not lying. Not lying. She would have given up more than India to save Jerrold that pang of memory. Only, when it was all over and he had sailed without her, she realized in one wounding flash that what she had given up was Jerrold himself.

V

ELIOT AND ANNE

Anne did not go back to her Ilford farm at once. Adeline had made that impossible.

At the prospect of Anne's going her resentment died down as suddenly as it had risen. She forgot that Anne had taken her sons' affection and her place beside her husband's deathbed. And though she couldn't help feeling rather glad that Jerrold had gone to India without Anne, she was sorry for her. She loved her and she meant to keep her. She said she simply could not bear it if Anne left her, and *was* it the time to choose when she wanted her as she had never wanted her before? She had nobody to turn to, as Anne knew. Corbetts and Hawtreys and Markhams and people were all very well; but they were outsiders.

"It's the inside people that I want now, Anne. You're deep inside, dear."

Yes, of course she had relations. But relations were no use. They were all wrapped up in their own tiresome affairs, and there wasn't one of them she cared for as she cared for Anne.

"I couldn't care more if you were my own daughter. Darling Robert felt about you just the same. You *can't* leave me."

And Anne didn't. She never could resist unhappiness. She thought: "I was glad enough to stop with her through all the happy times. I'd be a perfect beast to go and leave her now when she's miserable and hasn't got anybody."

It would have been better for Anne if she could have gone. Robert Fielding's death and Jerrold's absence were two griefs that inflamed each other; they came together to make one immense, intolerable wound. And here at Wyck, she couldn't move without coming upon something that touched it and stung it to fresh pain. But Anne was not like Jerrold, to turn from what she loved because it hurt her. For as long as she could remember all her happiness had come to her at Wyck. If unhappiness came now, she had got, as Eliot said, "to take it."

And so she stayed on through the autumn, then over Christmas to the New Year; this time because of Colin who was suffering from depression. Colin had never got over his father's death and Jerrold's going; and the last thing Jerrold had said to her before he went was; "You'll look after Col-Col, won't you? Don't let him go grousing about by himself."

Jerrold had always expected her to look after Colin. At seventeen there was still something piteous and breakable about him, something that clung to you for help. Eliot said that if Colin didn't look out he'd be a regular neurotic. But he owned that Anne was good for him.

"I don't know what you do to him, but he's better when you're there."

Eliot was the one who appeared to have recovered first. He met the shock of his father's death with a defiant energy and will.

He was working now at bacteriology under Sir Martin Crozier. Covered with a white linen coat, in a white-washed room of inconceivable cleanness, surrounded by test-tubes and mixing jars, Eliot spent the best part of the day handling the germs of the deadliest diseases; making cultures, examining them under the microscope; preparing vaccines. He went home to the brown velvety, leathery study in his Welbeck Street flat to write out his notes, or read some monograph on inoculation; or he dined with a colleague and talked to him about bacteria.

At this period of his youth Eliot had more than ever the appearance of inhuman preoccupation. His dark, serious face detached itself with a sort of sullen apathy from the social scene. He seemed to have no keen interests beyond his slides and mixing jars and test-tubes. Women, for whom his indifference had a perverse fascination, said of him: "Dr. Fielding isn't interested in people, only in their diseases. And not really in diseases, only in their germs."

They never suspected that Eliot was passionate, and that a fierce pity had driven him into his profession. The thought of preventable disease filled him with fury; he had no tolerance for the society that tolerated it. He suffered because he had a clearer vision and a profounder sense of suffering than most persons. Up to the time of his father's death all Eliot's suffering had been other people's. He couldn't rest till he had done something to remove the cause of it.

Add to this an insatiable curiosity as to causes, and you have the main bent of Eliot's mind.

And it seemed to him that there was nobody but Anne who saw that hidden side of him. **She** knew that he was sorry for people, and that being sorry for them had made him what he was, like Jerrold and yet unlike him. Eliot was attracted to suffering by the same sensitiveness that made Jerrold avoid everything once associated with it.

And so the very thing that Jerrold couldn't bear to remember was what drew Eliot closer to Anne. He saw her as Jerrold had seen her, moving, composed and competent, in his father's room; he saw her stooping over him to help him, he saw the specks of blood on her white sleeve; and he thought of her with the more tenderness. From that instant he really loved her. He wanted Anne as he had never conceived himself wanting any woman. He could hardly remember his first adolescent feeling for her, that confused mixture of ignorant desire and fear, so different was it from the intense, clear passion that possessed him now. At night when his work was done, he lay in bed, not sleeping, thinking of Anne with desire that knew itself too well to be afraid. Anne was the one thing necessary to him beside his work, necessary as a living part of himself. She could only not come before his work because Eliot's work came before himself and his own happiness. When he went down every other week-end to Wyck-on-the-Hill he knew that it was to see Anne.

His mother knew it too.

"I wish Eliot would marry," she said.

"Why?" said Anne.

"Because then he wouldn't be so keen on going off to look for germs in disgusting climates."

Anne wondered whether Adeline knew Eliot. For Eliot talked to her about his work as he walked with her at a fine swinging pace over the open country, taking all his exercise now while he could get it. That was another thing he liked about Anne Severn, her splendid physical fitness; she could go stride for stride with him, and mile for mile, and never tire. Her mind, too, was robust and active, and full of curiosity; it listened by the hour and never tired. It could move, undismayed, among horrors. She could see, as he saw, the "beauty" of the long trains of research by which Sir Martin Crozier had tracked down the bacillus of amoebic dysentery and established the difference between typhoid and Malta fever.

Once started on his subject, the grave, sullen Eliot talked excitedly.

"You do see, Anne, how thrilling it is, don't you? For me there's nothing but bacteriology. I always meant to go in for it, and Sir Martin's magnificent. Absolutely top-hole. You see, all these disgusting diseases can be prevented. It's inconceivable that they should be tolerated in a civilized country. People can't care a rap or they couldn't sleep in their beds. They ought to get up and make a public row about it, to insist on compulsory inoculation for everybody whether they like it or not. It really isn't enough to cure people of diseases when they've got them. We ought to see that they never get them, that there aren't any to get... What we don't know yet is the complete behaviour of all these bacteria among themselves. A bad bacillus may be doing good work by holding down a worse one. It's conceivable that if we succeeded in exterminating all known diseases we might release an unknown one, supremely horrible, that would exterminate the race."

"Oh Eliot, how awful. How can *you* sleep in your bed?"

"You needn't worry. It's only a nightmare idea of mine."

And so on and so on, for he was still so young that he wanted Anne to be excited by the things that excited him. And Anne told him all about her Ilford farm and what she meant to do on it. Eliot didn't behave like Aunt Adeline, he listened beautifully, like Uncle Robert and Jerrold, as if it was really most important that you should have a farm and work on it.

"What I want is to sell it and get one here. I don't want to be anywhere else. I can't tell you how frightfully home-sick I am when I'm away. I keep on seeing those gables with the little stone balls, and the peacocks, and the fields down to the Manor Farm. And the hills, Eliot. When I'm away I'm always dreaming that I'm trying to get back to them and something stops me. Or I see them and they turn into something else. I shan't be happy till I can come back for good."

"You don't want to go to India?" Eliot's heart began to beat as he asked his question.

"I want to work. To work hard. To work till I'm so dead tired that I roll off to sleep the minute I get into bed. So tired that I can't dream."

"That isn't right. You're too young to feel like that, Anne."

"I do feel like it. You feel like it yourself--My farm is to me what your old bacteria are to you."

"Oh, if I thought it was the farm--"

"Why, what else did you think it was?"

Eliot couldn't bring himself to tell her. He took refuge in apparent irrelevance.

"You know Father left me the Manor Farm house, don't you?"

"No, I didn't. I suppose he thought you'd want to come back, like me."

"Well, I'm glad I've got it. Mother's got the Dower House in Wyck. But she'll stay on here till--"

"Till Jerrold comes back," said Anne bravely.

"I don't suppose Jerry'll turn her out even then. Unless--"

But neither he nor Anne had the courage to say "unless he marries."

Not Anne, because she couldn't trust herself with the theme of Jerrold's marrying. Not Eliot, because he had Jerrold's word for it that if he married anybody, ever, it would not be Anne.

*   *   *   *   *

It was this assurance that made it possible for him to say what he had been thinking of saying all the time that he talked to Anne about his bacteriology. Bacteriology was a screen behind which Eliot, uncertain of Anne's feelings, sheltered himself against irrevocable disaster. He meant to ask Anne to marry him, but he kept putting it off because, so long as he didn't know for certain that she wouldn't have him, he was at liberty to think she would. He would not be taking her from Jerrold. Jerrold, inconceivable ass, didn't want her. Eliot had made sure of that months ago, the night before Jerrold sailed. He had simply put it to him: what did he mean to do about Anne Severn? And Jerrold had made it very plain that his chief object in going to India was to get away from Anne Severn and Everything. Eliot knew Jerrold too well to suspect his sincerity, so he considered that the way was now honorably open to him.

His only uncertainty was Anne herself. He had meant to give her a year to forget Jerrold in, if she was ever going to forget him; though in moments of deeper insight he realized that Anne was not likely to forget, nor to marry anybody else as long as she remembered.

Yet, Eliot reasoned, women did marry, even remembering. They married and were happy. You saw it every day. He was content to take Anne on her own terms, at any cost, at any risk. He had never been afraid of risks, and once he had faced the chance of her refusal all other dangers were insignificant.

A year was a long time, and Eliot had to consider the probability of his going out to Central Africa with Sir Martin Crozier to investigate sleeping sickness. He wanted the thing settled one way or another before he went.

He put it off again till the next week-end. And in the meanwhile Sir Martin Crozier had seen him. He was starting in the spring and Eliot was to go with him.

It was on Sunday evening that he spoke to Anne, sitting with her under the beeches at the top of the field where she and Jerrold had sat together. Eliot had chosen his place badly.

"I wouldn't bother you so soon if I wasn't going away, but I simply must--must know--"

"Must know what?"

"Whether you care for me at all. Not much, of course, but just enough not to hate marrying me."

Anne turned her face full on him and looked at him with her innocent, candid eyes. And all she said was, "You *do* know about Jerrold, don't you?"

"Oh God, yes. I know all about him."

"He's why I can't."

"I tell you, I know all about Jerrold. He isn't a good enough reason."

"Good enough for me."

"Not unless--" But he couldn't say it.

"Not unless he cares for me. That's why you're asking me, then, because you know he doesn't."

"Well, it wouldn't be much good if I knew he did."

"Eliot, it's awful of me to talk about it, as if he'd said he did. He never said a word. He never will."

"I'm afraid he won't, Anne."

"Don't imagine I ever thought he would. He never did anything to make me think it for a minute, really."

"Are you quite sure he didn't?"

"Quite sure. I made it all up out of my head. My silly head. I don't care what you think of me so long as you don't think it was Jerry's fault. I should go on caring for him whatever he did or didn't do."

"I know you would. But it's possible--"

"To care for two people and marry one of them, no matter which? It isn't possible for me. If I can't have the person I want I won't have anybody."

"It isn't wise, Anne. I tell you I could make you care for me. I know all about you. I know how you think and how you feel. I understand you better than Jerrold does. You'd be happy with me and you'd be safe."

"It's no use. I'd rather be unhappy and in danger if it was with Jerrold."

"You'll be unhappy and in danger without him."

"I don't care. Besides, I shan't be. I shall work. You'll work, too. It'll be so exciting that you'll soon forget all about me."

"You know I shan't. And I'll never give you up, unless Jerrold gets you."

"Eliot--I only told you about Jerrold, because I thought you ought to know. So that you mightn't think it was anything in you."

"It isn't something in me, then? Tell me--if it hadn't been for Jerry, do you think you might have cared for me?"

"Yes. I do. I quite easily might. And I think it would be a jolly good thing if I could, now. Only I can't. I can't."

"Poor little Anne."

"Does it comfort you to think I'd have cared if it hadn't been for Jerry?"

"It does, very much."

"Eliot--you're the only person I can talk to about him. Do you mind telling me whether he said that to you, or whether you just guessed it."

"What?"

"Why, that he wouldn't--ever--"

"I asked him, Anne, because I had to know. And he told me."

"I thought he told you."

"Yes, he told me. But I'm a cad for letting you think he didn't care for you. I believe he did, or that he would have cared--awfully--if my father hadn't died just then. Your being in the room that day upset him. If it hadn't been for that--"

"Yes, but there *was* that. It was like he was when Binky died and he couldn't stand Yearp. Don't you remember how he wouldn't let me go with him to see Yearp because he said he didn't want me mixed up with it. Well--I've been mixed up, that's all."

"Still, Anne, I'm certain he'd have cared--if that's any comfort to you. You didn't make it up out of your dear little head. We all thought it. Father thought it. I believe he wanted it. If he'd only known!"

She thought: If he'd only known how he had hurt her, he who had never hurt anybody in all his beautiful life.

"Dear Uncle Robert. There's no good talking about it. I knew, the minute Jerry said he didn't want me to go to India with him."

"Is that why you didn't go?"

"Yes."

"That was a mistake, Anne. You should have gone."

"How could I, after that? And if I had, he'd only have kept away."

"You should have let him go first and then gone after him. You should have turned up suddenly, in wonderful clothes, looking cheerful and beautiful. So that you wiped out the memory he funked. As it is you've left him nothing else to think of."

"I daresay that's what I should have done. But it's too late. I can't do it now."

"I'm not so sure."

"What, go *after* Jerrold? Hunt him down? Dress up and scheme to make him marry me?"

"Yes. Yes. Yes."

"Eliot, you know I couldn't."

"You said once you'd commit a crime for anybody you cared about."

"A crime, yes. But not that. I'd rather die."

"You're too fastidious. It's only the unscrupulous people who get what they want in this world. They know what they want and go for it. They stamp on everything and everybody that gets in their way."

"Oh, Eliot dear, I know what I want, and I'd go for it. If only Jerrold knew, too."

"He would know if you showed him."

"And that's just what I can't do."

"Well, don't say I didn't give you the best possible advice, against my own interests, too."

"It was sweet of you. But you see how impossible it is."

"I see how adorable you are. You always were."

For the first time in her life Adeline was furious.

She had asked Eliot whether he was or was not going to marry Anne Severn, and was told that he had asked her to marry him that afternoon and that she wouldn't have him.

"Wouldn't have you? What's she thinking of?"

"You'd better ask her," said Eliot, never dreaming that she would.

But that was what Adeline did. She came that night to Anne's room just as Anne was getting into bed. Unappeased by her defenseless attitude, she attacked with violence.

"What's all this about Eliot asking you to marry him?"

Anne uncurled herself and sat up on the edge of her bed.

"Did he tell you?"

"Yes. Of course he told me. He says you refused him. Did you?"

"I'm afraid I did."

"Then Anne, you're a perfect little fool."

"But Auntie, I don't love him."

"Nonsense; you love him as much as most people love the men they marry. He's quite sensible. He doesn't want you to go mad about him."

"He wants more than I can give him."

"Well, all I can say is if you can't give him what he wants you'd no business to go about with him as you've been doing."

"I've been going about with him all my life and I never dreamed he'd want to marry me."

"What did you suppose he'd want?"

"Why, nothing but just to go about. As we always did."

"You idiot."

"I don't see why you should be so cross about it."

Adeline sat down in the armchair at the head of the bed, prepared to "have it out" with Anne.

"I suppose you think my son's happiness is nothing to me? Didn't it occur to you that if you refuse him he'll stick for years in that awful place he's going to? Whereas if he had a wife in England there'd be a chance of his coming home now and then. Perhaps he'd never go out again."

"I'm sorry, Auntie. I can't marry Eliot even to keep him in England. Even to please you."

"Even to save his life, you mean. You don't care if he dies of some hideous tropical disease."

"I care awfully. But I can't marry him. He knows why."

"It's more than I do. If you're thinking of Jerrold, you needn't. I thought you'd done with that schoolgirlish nonsense."

"I'm not 'thinking' of him. I'm not 'thinking' of anybody and I wish you'd leave me alone."

"My dear child, how can I leave you alone when I see you making the mistake of your life? Eliot is absolutely the right person for you, if you'd only the sense to see it. He's got more character than anybody I know. Much more than dear Jerry. He'll be ten times more interesting to live with."

"I thought Jerrold was your favourite."

"No, Eliot, my dear. Always Eliot. He was my first baby."

"Well, I'm awfully sorry you mind so much. And I'd marry Eliot if I could. I simply hate him to be unhappy. But he won't be. He'll live to be frightfully glad I didn't...What, aren't you going to kiss me good-night?"

Adeline had risen and turned away with the great dignity of her righteous anger.

"I don't feel like it," she said. "I think you've been thoroughly selfish and un-kind. I hate girls who go on like that--making a man mad about you by pretending to be his comrade, and then throwing him over. I've had more men in love with me, Anne, than you've seen in your life, but I never did *that*."

"Oh Auntie, what about Father? And you were engaged to him."

"Well, anyhow," said Adeline, softened by the recollection, "I *was* engaged."

She smiled her enchanting smile; and Anne, observing the breakdown of dignity, got up off the bed and kissed her.

"I don't suppose," she said, "that Father was the only one."

"He wasn't. But then, with *me*, my dear, it was their own risk. They knew where they were."

In March, nineteen eleven, Eliot went out to Central Africa. He stayed there two years, investigating malaria and sleeping sickness. Then he went on to the Straits Settlements and finally took a partnership in a practice at Penang.

Anne left Wyck at Easter and returned in August because of Colin. Then she went back to her Ilford farm.

The two years passed, and in the spring of the third year, nineteen fourteen, she came again.

VI
QUEENIE

Something awful had happened. Adeline had told Anne about it.

It seemed that Colin in his second year at Cambridge, when he should have given his whole mind to reading for the Diplomatic Service, had had the imprudence to get engaged. And to a girl that Adeline had never heard of, about whom nothing was known but that she was remarkably handsome and that her family (Courthopes of Leicestershire) were, in Adeline's brief phrase, "all right."

From the terrace they could see, coming up the lawn from the goldfish pond, Colin and his girl.

Queenie Courthope. She came slowly, her short Russian skirt swinging out from her ankles. The brilliance of her face showed clear at a distance, vermilion on white, flaming; hard, crystal eyes, sweeping and flashing; bobbed hair, brown-red, shining in the sun. Then a dominant, squarish jaw, and a mouth exquisitely formed, but thin, a vermilion thread drawn between her staring, insolent nostrils and the rise of her round chin.

This face in its approach expressed a profound, arrogant indifference to Adeline and Anne. Only as it turned towards Colin its grey-black eyes lowered and were soft dark under the black feathers of their brows.

Colin looked back at it with a shy, adoring tenderness.

Queenie could be even more superbly uninterested than Adeline. In Adeline's self-absorption there was a passive innocence, a candor that disarmed you, but Queenie's was insolent and hostile; it took possession of the scene and challenged every comer.

"Hallo, Anne!" Colin shouted. "How did you get here?"

"Motored down."

"I say, have you got a car?"

"Only just."

"Drove yourself?"

"Rather."

Queenie scowled as if there were something disagreeable to her in the idea that Anne should have a car of her own and drive it. She endured the introduction in silence and addressed herself with an air of exclusiveness to Colin.

"What are we going to do?"

"Anything you like," he said.

"I'll play you singles, then."

"Anne might like to play," said Colin. But he still looked at Queenie, as she flamed in her beauty.

"Oh, three's a rotten game. You can't play the two of us unless Miss Severn handicaps me."

"She won't do that. Anne could take us both on and play a decent game."

Queenie picked up her racquet and stood between them, beating her skirts with little strokes of irritated impatience. Her eyes were fixed on Colin, trying, you could see, to dominate him.

"We'd better take it in turns," he said.

"Thanks, Col-Col. I'd rather not play. I've driven ninety-seven miles."

"Really rather?"

Queenie backed towards the court.

"Oh, come on, Colin, if you're coming."

He went.

"What do you think of Queenie?" Adeline said.

"She's very handsome."

"Yes, Anne. But it isn't a nice face. Now, is it?"

Anne couldn't say it was a nice face.

"It's awful to think of Colin being married to it. He's only twenty-one now, and she's seven years older. If it had been anybody but Colin. If it had been Eliot or Jerrold I shouldn't have minded so much. They can look after themselves. He'll never stand up against that horrible girl."

"She does look terribly strong."

"And cruel, Anne, as if she might hurt him. I don't want him to be hurt. I can't bear her taking him away from me. My little Col-Col....I did hope, Anne, that if you wouldn't have Eliot--"

"I'd have Colin? But Auntie, I'm years older than he is. He's a baby."

"If he's a baby he'll want somebody older to look after him."

"Queenie's even better fitted than I am, then."

"Do you think, Anne, she proposed to Colin?"

"No. I shouldn't think it was necessary."

"I should say she was capable of anything. My only hope is they'll tire each other out before they're married and break it off."

All afternoon on the tennis court below Queenie played against Colin. She played vigorously, excitedly, savagely, to win. She couldn't hide her annoyance when he beat her.

"What was I to do?" he said. "You don't like it when I beat you. But if I was beaten you wouldn't like *me*."

Adeline's only hope was not realized. They hadn't had time to tire of each other before the War broke out. And Colin insisted on marrying before he joined up. Their engagement had left him nervous and unfit, and his idea was that, once married, he would present a better appearance before the medical examiners.

But after a month of Queenie, Colin was more nervous and unfit than ever.

"I can't think," said Adeline, "what that woman does to him. She'll wear him out."

So Colin waited, trying to get fitter, and afraid to volunteer lest he should be rejected.

Everybody around him was moving rapidly. Queenie had taken up motoring, so that she could drive an ambulance car at the front. Anne had gone up to London for her Red Cross training. Eliot had left his practice to his partner at Penang and had come home and joined the Army Medical Corps.

Eliot, home on leave for three days before he went out, tried hard to keep Colin back from the War. In Eliot's opinion Colin was not fit and never would be fit to fight. He was just behaving as he always had behaved, rushing forward, trying insanely to do the thing he never could do.

"Do you mean to say they won't pass me?" he asked.

"Oh, they'll pass you all right," Eliot said. "They'll give you an expensive train-ing, and send you into the trenches, and in any time from a day to a month you'll be in hospital with shell-shock. Then you'll be discharged as unfit, having wasted everybody's time and made a damned nuisance of yourself....I suppose I ought to say it's splendid of you to want to go out. But it isn't splendid. It's idiotic. You'll be simply butting in where you're not wanted, taking a better man's place, taking a better man's commission, taking a better man's bed in a hospital. I tell you we don't want men who are going to crumple up in their first action."

"Do you think I'm going to funk then?" said poor Colin.

"Funk? Oh, Lord no. You'll stick it till you drop, till you're paralyzed, till you've lost your voice and memory, till you're an utter wreck. There'll be enough of 'em, poor devils, without you, Col-Col."

"But why should I go like that more than anybody else?"

"Because you're made that way, because you haven't got a nervous system that can stand the racket. The noises alone will do for you. You'll be as right as rain if you keep out of it."

"But Jerrold's coming back. *He*'ll go out at once. How can I stick at home when he's gone?"

"Heaps of good work to be done at home."

"Not by men of my age."

"By men of your nervous organization. Your going out would be sheer waste."

"Why not?" Does it matter what becomes of me?"

"No. It doesn't. It matters, though, that you'll be taking a better man's place."

Now Colin really did want to go out and fight, as he had always wanted to follow Jerrold's lead; he wanted it so badly that it seemed to him a form of self-indulgence; and this idea of taking a better man's place so worked on him that he had almost decided to give it up, since that was the sacrifice required of him, when he told Queenie what Eliot had said.

"All I can say is," said Queenie, "that if you don't go out I shall give *you* up. I've no use for men with cold feet."

"Can't you see," said Colin (he almost hated Queenie in that moment), "what

I'm afraid of? Being a damned nuisance. That's what Eliot says I'll be. I don't know how he knows."

"He doesn't know everything. If *my* brother tried to stop my going to the front I'd jolly soon tell him to go to hell. I swear, Colin, if you back out of it I won't speak to you again. I'm not asking you to do anything I funk myself."

"Oh, shut up. I'm going all right. Not because you've asked me, but because I want to."

"If you didn't I should think you'd feel pretty rotten when I'm out with my Field Ambulance," said Queenie.

"Damn your Field Ambulance!... No, I didn't mean that, old thing; it's splendid of you to go. But you'd no business to suppose I funked. I *may* funk. Nobody knows till they've tried. But I was going all right till Eliot put me off."

"Oh, if you're put off as easily as all that----"

She was intolerable. She seemed to think he was only going because she'd shamed him into it.

That evening he sang:

"'What are you doing all the day, Rendal, my son? What are you doing all the day, my pretty one?'"

He understood that song now.

"'What will you leave to your lover, Rendal, my son?
What will you leave to your lover, my pretty one?
A rope to hang her, mother,
A rope to hang her, mother....'"

"Go it, Col-Col!" Out on the terrace Queenie laughed her harsh, cruel laugh.

"'For I'm sick to my heart and I fain would lie down.'"

"'I'm sick to my heart and I fain would lie down,'" Queenie echoed, with clipped words, mocking him.

He hated Queenie.

And he loved her. At night, at night, she would unbend, she would be tender and passionate, she would touch him with quick, hurrying caresses, she would put her arms round him and draw him to her, kissing and kissing. And with her young, beautiful body pressed tight to him, with her mouth on his and her eyes shining close and big in the darkness, Colin would forget.

Dr. Cutler's Field Ambulance, British Hospital, Antwerp.

September 20th, 1914.

Dearest Auntie Adeline,--I haven't been able to write before. There's been a lot of fighting all round here and we're frightfully busy getting in wounded. And when you've done you're too tired to sit up and write letters. You simply roll into bed and drop off to sleep. Sometimes we're out with the ambulances half the night.

You needn't worry about me. I'm keeping awfully fit. I *am* glad now I've always lived in the open air and played games and ploughed my own land. My muscles are as hard as any Tommie's. So are Queenie's. You see, we have to act as stretcher bearers as well as chauffeurs. You're not much good if you can't carry your own wounded.

Queenie is simply splendid. She really *doesn't* know what fear is, and she's at her very best under fire. It sort of excites her and bucks her up. I can't help seeing how fine she is, though she was so beastly to poor old Col-Col before he joined up. But talk of the War bringing out the best in people, you should simply see her out here with the wounded. Dr. Cutler (the Commandant) thinks no end of her. She drives for him and I drive for a little doctor man called Dicky Cartwright. He's awfully good at his job and decent. Queenie doesn't like him. I can't think why.

Good-bye, darling. Take care of yourself.

Your loving

Anne.

Antwerp. **October 3rd.**

... You ask me what I really think of Queenie at close quarters. Well, the quarters are very close and I know she simply hates me. She was fearfully sick when she found we were both in the same Corps. She's always trying to get up a row about something. She'd like to have me fired out of Belgium if she could, but I mean to stay as long as I can, so I won't quarrel with her. She can't do it all by herself. And when I feel like going back on her I tell myself how magnificent she is, so plucky and so clever at her job. I don't wonder that half the men in our Corps are gone on her. And there's a Belgian Colonel, the one Cutler gets his orders from, who'd make a frantic fool of himself if she'd let him. But good old Queenie sticks to her job and behaves as if they weren't there. That makes them madder. You'd have thought they'd never have had the time to be such asses in, but it's wonderful what a state you can get into in your few odd moments. Dicky says it's the War whips you up and makes it all the easier. I don't know....

FURNES.

November.

That's where we are now. I simply can't describe the retreat. It was too awful, and I don't want to think about it. We've "settled" down in a house we've commandeered and I suppose we shall stick here till we're shelled out of it.

Talking of shelling, Queenie is funny. She's quite annoyed if
anybody besides herself gets anywhere near a shell. We picked up
two more stretcher-bearers in Ostend and a queer little
middle-aged lady out for a job at the front. Cutler took her on
as a sort of secretary. At first Queenie was so frantic that she
wouldn't speak to her, and swore she'd make the Corps too hot to
hold her. But when she found that the little lady wasn't for the
danger zone and only proposed to cook and keep our accounts for
us, she calmed down and was quite decent. Then the other day
Miss Mullins came and told us that a bit of shell had chipped
off the corner of her kitchen. The poor old thing was ever so
proud and pleased about it, and Queenie snubbed her frightfully,
and said she wasn't in any danger at all, and asked her how
she'd enjoy it if she was out all day under fire, like us.

And she was furious with me because I had the luck to get into
the bombardment at Dixmude and she hadn't. She talked as if I'd
done her out of her shelling on purpose, whereas it only meant
that I happened to be on the spot when the ambulances were sent
out and she was away somewhere with her own car. She really is
rather vulgar about shells. Dicky says it's a form of war
snobbishness (he hasn't got a scrap of it), but I think it
really is because all the time she's afraid of one of us being
killed. It must be that. Even Dicky owns that she's splendid,
though he doesn't like her....

Five months later.

The Manor, Wyck-on-the-Hill, Gloucestershire.

May 30th, 1915.

My darling Anne,--Queenie will have told you about Colin. He was through all that frightful shelling at Ypres in April. He's been three weeks in the hospital at Boulogne with shell-shock--had it twice--and now he's back and in that Officers' Hospital in Kensington, not a bit better. I really think Queenie ought to get leave and come over and see him.

Eliot was perfectly right. He ought never to have gone out. Of course he was as plucky as they make them--went back into the trenches after his first shell-shock--but his nerves couldn't stand it. Whether they're treating him right or not, they don't seem to be able to do anything for him.

I'm writing to Queenie. But tell her she must come and see him.

Your loving

Adeline Fielding.
Three months later.

The Manor, Wyck-on-the-Hill, Gloucestershire.

August 30th.

Darling Anne,--Colin has been discharged at last as incurable. He is with me here. I'm so glad to have him, the darling. But oh, his nerves are in an awful state--all to bits. He's an utter wreck, my beautiful Colin; it would make your heart bleed to see him. He can't sleep at night; he keeps on hearing shells; and if he does sleep he dreams about them and wakes up screaming. It's awful to hear a man scream. Anne, Queenie must come home and look after him. My nerves are going. I can't sleep any more than Colin. I lie awake waiting for the scream. I can't take the responsibility of him alone, I can't really. After all, she's his wife, and she made him go out and fight, though she knew what Eliot said it would do to him. It's too cruel that it should have happened to Col-Col of all people. *Make* that woman come.

Your loving

Adeline Fielding.

Nieuport. *September 5th, 1915.*

Darling Auntie,--I'm so sorry about dear Col-Col. And I quite agree that Queenie ought to go back and look after him. But she won't. She says her work here is much more important and that she can't give up hundreds of wounded soldiers for just one man. Of course she is doing splendidly, and Cutler says he can't spare her and she'd be simply thrown away on one case. They think Colin's people ought to look after him. It doesn't seem to matter to either of them that he's her husband. They've got into the way of looking at everybody as a case. They say it's not even as if Colin could be got better so as to be sent out to fight again. It would be sheer waste of Queenie.
But Cutler has given me leave to go over and see him. I shall get to Wyck as soon as this letter.

Dear Col-Col, I wish I could do something for him. I feel as if we could never, never do too much after all he's been through. Fancy Eliot knowing exactly what would happen.

Your loving
Anne.

Nieuport. *September 7th.*

Dear Anne,--Now that you *have* gone I think I ought to tell you
that it would be just as well if you didn't come back. I've got
a man to take your place; Queenie picked him up at Dunkirk the
day you sailed, and he's doing very well.

The fact is we're getting on much better since you left. There's
perfect peace now. You and Queenie didn't hit it off, you know,
and for a job like ours it's absolutely essential that everybody
should pull together like one. It doesn't do to have two in a
Corps always at loggerheads.

I don't like to lose you, and I know you've done splendidly. But
I've got to choose between Queenie and you, and I must keep her,
if it's only because she's worked with me all the time. So now
that you've made the break I take the opportunity of asking you
to resign. Personally I'm sorry, but the good of the Corps must
come before everything.

Sincerely yours,

Robert Cutler.

The Manor, Wyck-on-the-Hill, Gloucestershire.

September 11th, 1915.

Dear Dicky,--This is only to say good-bye, as I shan't see you
again. Cutler's fired me out of the Corps. He *says* it's
because Queenie and I don't hit it off. I shouldn't have thought
that was my fault, but he seems to think it is. He says there's

been perfect peace since I left.

Well, we've had some tremendous times together, and I wish we could have gone on.

Good-bye and Good Luck,

Yours ever,

Anne Severn.

P. S.--Poor Colin Fielding's in an awful state. But he's been a bit better since I came. Even if Cutler'd let me come back I couldn't leave him. This is my job. The queer thing is he's afraid of Queenie, so it's just as well she didn't come home.

Nieuport.

September 15th, 1915.

Dear Old Thing,--We're all furious here at the way you've been treated. I've resigned as a protest, and I'm going into the R. A. M. So has Miss Mullins--: resigned I mean--so Queenie's the only woman left in the Corps. That'll suit her down to the ground.

I gave myself the treat of telling Cutler what I jolly well think of him. But of course you know she made him hoof you out. She's been trying for it ever since you joined. It's all rot his saying you didn't hit it off with her, when everybody knows you were a perfect angel to her. Why, you backed her every time when we were all going for her. It's quite true that the peace of God has settled on the Corps since you left it; but that's only because Queenie doesn't rage round any more.

You'll observe that she never went for Miss Mullins. That's because Miss Mullins kept well out of the line of fire. And if you hadn't jolly well distinguished yourself there she'd have let you alone, too. The real trouble began that day you were at Dixmude. It wasn't a bit because she was afraid you'd be killed. Queenie doesn't want you about when the War medals are handed round. Everybody sees that but old Cutler. He's too much gone on her to see anything. She can twist him round and round and tie him up in knots.

But Cutler isn't in it now. Queenie's turned him down for that young Noel Fenwick who's got your job. Cutler's nose was a sight, I can tell you.

Well, I'm not surprised that Queenie's husband funks her. She's a terror. Worse than war.

Good-bye and Good Luck, Old Thing, till we meet again.

Yours ever,

Dicky Cartwright.

VII
ADELINE

They would never know what it cost her to come back and look after Colin. That knowledge was beyond Adeline Fielding. She congratulated Anne and expected Anne to congratulate herself on being "well out of it." Her safety was revolting and humiliating to Anne when she thought of Queenie and Cutler and Dicky, and Eliot and Jerrold and all the allied armies in the thick of it. She had left a world where life was lived at its highest pitch of intensity for a world where people were only half-alive. To be safe from the chance of sudden violent death was to be only half-alive.

Her one consolation had been that now she would see Jerrold. But she did not see him. Jerrold had given up his appointment in the Punjaub three weeks before the outbreak of the war. His return coincided with the retreat from Mons. He had not been in England a week before he was in training on Salisbury Plain. Anne had left Wyck when he arrived; and before he got leave she was in Belgium with her Field Ambulance. And now, in October of nineteen fifteen, when she came back to Wyck, Jerrold was fighting in France.

At least they knew what had happened to Colin; but about Eliot and Jerrold they knew nothing. Anything might have happened to them since they had written the letters that let them off from week to week, telling them that they were safe. Anything might happen and they might never know.

Anne's fear was dumb and secret. She couldn't talk about Jerrold. She lived every minute in terror of Adeline's talking, of the cries that came from her at queer unexpected moments: between two cups of tea, two glances at the mirror, two careful gestures of her hands pinning up her hair.

"I cannot bear it if anything happens to Jerrold, Anne."

"Oh Anne, I wonder what's happening to Jerrold."

"If only I knew what was happening to Jerrold."

"If only I knew where Jerrold **was**. Nothing's so awful as not knowing."

And at breakfast, over toast and marmalade: "Anne, I've got such an awful feeling that something's happened to Jerrold. I'm sure these feelings aren't given you for nothing... You aren't eating anything, darling. You **must** eat."

Every morning at breakfast Anne had to look through the lists of killed, missing and wounded, to save Adeline the shock of coming upon Jerrold's or Eliot's name. Every morning Adeline gazed at Anne across the table with the same look of strained and agonised enquiry. Every morning Anne's heart tightened and dragged, then loosened and lifted, as they were let off for one more day.

One more day? Not one more hour, one minute. Any second the wire from the War Office might come.

Anne never knew the moment when she was first aware that Colin's mother was afraid of him. Aunt Adeline was very busy, making swabs and bandages. Every day she went off to her War Hospital Supply work at the Town Hall, and Anne was left to take care of Colin. She began to wonder whether the swabs and bandages were not a pretext for getting away from Colin.

"It's no use," Adeline said. "I cannot stand the strain of it. Anne, he's worse with me than he is with you. Everything I say and do is wrong. You don't know what it was like before you came."

Anne did know. The awful thing was that Colin couldn't bear to be left alone, day or night. He would lie awake shivering with terror. If he dropped off to sleep he woke screaming. At first Pinkney slept with him. But Pinkney had joined up, and old Wilkins, the butler, was impossible because he snored.

Anne had her old room across the passage where she had slept when they were children. And now, as then, their doors were left open, so that at a sound from Colin she could get up and go to him.

She was used to the lacerating, unearthly scream that woke her, the scream that terrified Adeline, that made her cover her head tight with the bed-clothes, to shut it out, that made her lock her door to shut out Colin. Once he had come into his mother's room and she had found him standing by her bed and looking at her with the queer frightened face that frightened her. She was always afraid of this happening again.

Anne couldn't bear to think of that locked door. She was used to the sight of Colin standing in her doorway, to the watches beside his bed where he lay shivering, holding her hand tight as he used to hold it when he was a child. To Anne he was "poor Col-Col" again, the little boy who was afraid of ghosts, only more abandoned to terror, more unresisting.

He would start and tremble at any quick, unexpected movement. He would burst into tears at any sudden sound. Small noises, whisperings, murmurings, creakings, soft shufflings, irritated him. Loud noises, the slamming of doors, the barking of dogs, the crowing of cocks, made him writhe in agony. For Colin the deep silence of the Manor was the ambush for some stupendous, crashing, annihilating sound; sound that was always coming and never came. The droop of the mouth that used to appear suddenly in his moments of childish anguish was fixed now, and fixed the little tortured twist of his eyebrows and his look of anxiety and fear. His head drooped, his shoulders were hunched slightly, as if he cowered before some perpetually falling blow.

On fine warm days he lay out on the terrace on Adeline's long chair; on wet days he lay on the couch in the library, or sat crouching over the fire. Anne brought him milk or beef tea or Benger's Food every two hours. He was content to be waited on; he had no will to move, no desire to get up and do things for himself. He lay or sat still, shivering every now and then as he remembered or imagined some horror. And as he was afraid to be left alone Anne sat with him.

"How can you say this is a quiet place?" he said.

"It's quiet enough now."

"It isn't. It's full of noises. Loud, thundering noises going on and on. Awful noises.... You know what it is? It's the guns in France. I can hear them all the time."

"No, Colin. That isn't what you hear. We're much too far off. Nobody could hear them."

"I can."

"I don't think so."

"Do you mean it's noises in my head?"

"Yes. They'll go away when you're stronger."

"I shall never be strong again."

"Oh yes, you will be. You're better already."

"If I get better they'll send me out again."

"Never. Never again."

"I ought to be out. I oughtn't to be sticking here doing nothing.... Anne, you don't think Queenie'll come over, do you?"

"No, I don't. She's got much too much to do out there."

"You know, that's what I'm afraid of, more than anything, Queenie's coming. She'll tell me I funked. She thinks I funked. She thinks that's what's the matter with me."

"She doesn't. She knows it's your body, not you. Your nerves are shaken to bits, that's all."

"I didn't funk, Anne." (He said it for the hundredth time.) "I mean I stuck it all right. I went back after I had shell-shock the first time--straight back into the trenches. It was at the very end of the fighting that I got it again. Then I couldn't go back. I couldn't move."

"I know, Colin, I know."

"Does Queenie know?"

"Of course she does. She understands perfectly. Why, she sees men with shell-shock every day. She knows you were splendid."

"I wasn't. But I wasn't as bad as she thinks me. ... Don't let her see me if she comes back."

"She won't come."

"She will. She will. She'll get leave some day. Tell her not to come. Tell her she can't see me. Say I'm off my head. Any old lie that'll stop her."

"Don't think about her."

"I can't help thinking. She said such beastly things. You can't think what disgusting things she said."

"She says them to everybody. She doesn't mean them."

"Oh, doesn't she!... Is that mother? You might tell her I'm sleeping."

For Colin was afraid of his mother, too. He was afraid that she would talk, that she would talk about the War and about Jerrold. Colin had been home six weeks and he had not once spoken Jerrold's name. He read his letters and handed them to Anne and Adeline without a word. It was as if between him and the thought of Jerrold there was darkness and a supreme, nameless terror.

One morning at dawn Anne was wakened by Colin's voice in her room.

"Anne, are you awake?"

The room was full of the white dawn. She saw him standing in it by her bedside.

"My head's awfully queer," he said. "I can feel my brain shaking and wobbling inside it, as if the convolutions had come undone. Could they?"

"Of course they couldn't."

"The noise might have loosened them."

"It isn't your brain you feel, Colin. It's your nerves. It's just the shock still going on in them."

"Is it never going to stop?"

"Yes, when you're stronger. Go back to bed and I'll come to you."

He went back. She slipped on her dressing-gown and came to him. She sat by his bed and put her hand on his forehead.

"There--it stops when you put your hand on."

"Yes. And you'll sleep."

Presently, to her joy, he slept.

She stood up and looked at him as he lay there in the white dawn. He was utterly innocent, utterly pathetic in his sleep, and beautiful. Sleep smoothed out his vexed face and brought back the likeness of the boy Colin, Jerrold's brother.

That morning a letter came to her from Jerrold. He wrote: "Don't worry too much about Col-Col. He'll be all right as long as you'll look after him."

She thought: "I wonder whether he remembers that he asked me to."

But she was glad he was not there to hear Colin scream.

"Anne, can *you* sleep?" said Adeline. Colin had gone to bed and they were sitting together in the drawing-room for the last hour of the evening.

"Not very well, when Colin has such bad nights."

"Do you think he's ever going to get right again?"

"Yes. But it'll take time."

"A long time?"

"Very long, probably."

"My dear, if it does, I don't know how I'm going to stand it. And if I only knew what was happening to Jerrold and Eliot. Sometimes I wonder how I've lived through these five years. First, Robert's death; then the War. And before that there was nothing but perfect happiness. I think trouble's worse to bear when you've known nothing but happiness before.... If I could only die instead of all these boys, Anne. Why can't I? What is there to live for?"

"There's Jerrold and Eliot and Colin."

"Oh, my dear, Jerrold and Eliot may never come back. And look at poor Colin. *That* isn't the Colin I know. He'll never be the same again. I'd almost rather he'd been killed than that he should be like this. If he'd lost a leg or an arm.... It's all very well for you, Anne. He isn't your son."

"You don't know what he is," said Anne. She thought: "He's Jerrold's brother. He's what Jerrold loves more than anything."

"No," said Adeline. "Everything ended for me when Robert died. I shall never marry again. I couldn't bear to put anybody in Robert's place."

"Of course you couldn't. I know it's been awful for you, Auntie."

"I couldn't bear it, Anne, if I didn't believe that there is Something Somewhere. I can't think how you get on without any religion."

"How do you know I haven't any?"

"Well, you've no faith in Anything. Have you, ducky?"

"I don't know what I've faith in. It's too difficult. If you love people, that's enough, I think. It keeps you going through everything."

"No, it doesn't. It's all the other way about. It's loving people that makes it all so hard. If you didn't love them you wouldn't care what happened to them. If I didn't love Colin I could bear his shell-shock better."

"If *I* didn't love him, I couldn't bear it at all."

"I expect," said Adeline, "we both mean the same thing."

Anne thought of Adeline's locked door; and, in spite of her love for her, she had a doubt. She wondered whether in this matter of loving they had ever meant the same thing. With Adeline love was a passive state that began and ended in emotion. With Anne love was power in action. More than anything it meant doing things for the people that you loved. Adeline loved her husband and her sons, but she had run away from the sight of Robert's haemorrhage, she had tried to keep back Eliot and Jerrold from the life they wanted, she locked her door at night and shut Colin out. To Anne that was the worst thing Adeline had done yet. She tried not to think of that locked door.

"I suppose," said Adeline, "you'll leave me now your father's coming home?"

John Severn's letter lay between them on the table. He was retiring after twenty-five years of India. He would be home as soon as his letter.

"I shall do nothing of the sort," said Anne. "I shall stay as long as you want me. If father wants me he must come down here."

In another three days he had come.

He had grey hair now and his face was a little lined, a little faded, but he was slender and handsome still--handsomer, more distinguished, Adeline thought, than ever.

Again he sat out with her on the terrace when the October days were warm; he walked with her up and down the lawn and on the flagged paths of the flower garden. Again he followed her from the drawing-room to the library where Colin was, and back again. He waited, ready for her.

Again Adeline smiled her self-satisfied, self-conscious smile. She had the look of a young girl, moving in perfect happiness. She was perpetually aware of him.

One night Colin called out to Anne that he couldn't sleep. People were walking about outside under his window. Anne looked out. In the full moonlight she saw Adeline and her father walking together on the terrace. Adeline was wrapped in a long cloak; she held his arm and they leaned toward each other as they walked. His man's voice sounded tender and low.

Anne called to them. "I say, darlings, would you mind awfully going somewhere else? Colin can't sleep with you prowling about there."

Adeline's voice came up to them with a little laughing quiver.

"All right, ducky; we're going in."

It was the end of October; John Severn had gone back to London. He had taken a house in Montpelier Square and was furnishing it.

One morning Adeline came down smiling, more self-conscious than ever.

"Anne," she said, "do you think you could look after Colin if I went up to Evelyn's for a week or two?"

Evelyn was Adeline's sister. She lived in London.

"Of course I can."

"You aren't afraid of being alone with him?"

"Afraid? Of Col-Col? What do you take me for?"

"Well--" Adeline meditated. "It isn't as if Mrs. Benning wasn't here."

Mrs. Benning was the housekeeper.

"That'll make it all right and proper. The fact is, I must have a rest and change before the winter. I hardly ever get away, as you know. And Evelyn would like to have me. I think I must go."

"Of course you must go," Anne said.

And Adeline went.

At the end of the first week she wrote:

12 Eaton Square. November 3d, 1915.

Darling Anne,--Will you be very much surprised to hear that your father and I are going to be married? You mayn't know it, but he has loved me all his life. We *were* to have married once (you knew *that*), and I jilted him. But he has never changed. He has been so faithful and forgiving, and has waited for me so patiently--twenty-seven years, Anne--that I hadn't the heart to refuse him. I feel that I must make up to him for all the pain I've given him.

We want you to come up for the wedding on the 10th. It will be very quiet. No bridesmaids. No party. We think it best not to have it at Wyck, on Colin's account. So I shall just be married from Evelyn's house.

Give us your blessing, there's a dear.

Your loving

Adeline Fielding.

Anne's eyes filled with tears. At last she saw Adeline Fielding completely, as she was, without any fascination. She thought: "She's marrying to get away from Colin. She's left him to me to look after. How could she leave him? How could she?"

Anne didn't go up for the wedding. She told Adeline it wasn't much use asking her when she knew that Colin couldn't be left.

"Or, if you like, that *I* can't leave him."

Her father wrote back:

Your Aunt Adeline thinks you reproach her for leaving Colin. I told her you were too intelligent to do anything of the sort. You'll agree it's the best thing she could do for him. She's no more capable of looking after Colin than a kitten. She wants to be looked after herself, and you ought to be grateful to me for relieving you of the job.

But I don't like your being alone down there with Colin. If he isn't better we must send him to a nursing home.

Are you wondering whether we're going to be happy?

We shall be so long as I let her have her own way; which is what I mean to do.

Your very affectionate father,

JOHN SEVERN.

And Anne answered:

DEAREST DADDY,--I shouldn't dream of reproaching Aunt Adeline any more
than I should reproach a pussycat for catching birds.

Look after her as much as you please--I shall look after Colin.
Whether you like it or not, darling, you can't stop me. And I won't let
Colin go to a nursing home. It would be the worst possible place for
him. Ask Eliot. Besides, he *is* better.

I'm ever so glad you're going to be happy.

Your loving

ANNE.

VIII
ANNE AND COLIN

Autumn had passed. Colin's couch was drawn up before the fire in the drawing-room. Anne sat with him there.

He was better. He could listen for half an hour at a time when Anne read to him--poems, short stories, things that were ended before Colin tired of them. He ate and drank hungrily and his body began to get back its strength.

At noon, when the winter sun shone, he walked, first up and down the terrace, then round and round the garden, then to the beech trees at the top of the field, and then down the hill to the Manor Farm. On mild days she drove him about the country in the dog-cart. She had tried motoring but had had to give it up because Colin was frightened at the hooting, grinding and jarring of the car.

As winter went on Anne found that Colin was no worse in cold or wet weather. He couldn't stand the noise and rush of the wind, but his strange malady took no count of rain or snow. He shivered in the clear, still frost, but it braced him all the same. Driving or strolling, she kept him half the day in the open air.

She saw that he liked best the places they had gone to when they were children--the Manor Farm fields, High Slaughter, and Hayes Mill. They were always going to the places where they had done things together. When Colin talked sanely he was back in those times. He was safe there. There, if anywhere, he could find his real self and be well.

She had the feeling that Colin's future lay somewhere through his past. If only she could get him back there, so that he could be what he had been. There must be some way of joining up that time to this, if only she could find a bridge, a link. She didn't know that she was the way, she was the link binding his past to his present, bound up with his youth, his happiness, his innocence, with the years before

Queenie and the War.

She didn't know what Queenie had done to him. She didn't know that the war had only finished what Queenie had begun. That was Colin's secret, the hidden source of his fear.

But he was safe with Anne because they were not in love with each other. She left his senses at rest, and her affection never called for any emotional response. She took him away from his fear; she kept him back in his childhood, in his boyhood, in the years before Queenie, with a continual, "Do you remember?"

"Do you remember the walk to High Slaughter?"

"Do you remember the booby-trap we set for poor Pinkney?"

That was dangerous, for poor Pinkney was at the War.

"Do you remember Benjy?"

"Yes, rather."

But Benjy was dangerous, too; for Jerrold had given him to her. She could feel Colin shying.

"He had a butterfly smut," he said. "Hadn't he? ...Do you remember how I used to come and see you at Cheltenham?"

"And Grannie and Aunt Emily, and how you used to play on their piano. And how Grannie jumped when you came down crash on those chords in the Wald-stein."

"Do you mean the *presto?*"

"Yes. The last movement."

"No wonder she jumped. I should jump now." He turned his mournful face to her. "Anne--I shall never be able to play again."

There was danger everywhere. In the end all ways led back to Colin's malady.

"Oh yes, you wall when you're quite strong."

"I shall never be stronger."

"You will. You're stronger already."

She knew he was stronger. He could sleep three hours on end now and he had left off screaming.

And still the doors were left open between their rooms at night. He was still afraid to sleep alone; he liked to know that she was there, close to him.

Instead of the dreams, instead of the sudden rushing, crashing horror, he was haunted by a nameless dread. Dread of something he didn't know, something that waited for him, something he couldn't face. Something that hung over him at night, that was there with him in the morning, that came between him and the light of the sun.

Anne kept it away. Anne came between it and him. He was unhappy and frightened when Anne was not there.

It was always, "You're *not* going, Anne?"

"Yes. But I'm coming back."

"How soon?"

And she would say, "An hour;" or, "Half an hour," or, "Ten minutes."

"Don't be longer."

"No."

And then: "I don't know how it is, Anne. But everything seems all right when you're there, and all wrong when you're not."

The Manor Farm house stands in the hamlet of Upper Speed. It has the grey church and churchyard beside it and looks across the deep road towards Sutton's farm.

The beautiful Jacobean house, the church and church-yard, Sutton's farm and the rectory, the four cottages and the Mill, the river and its bridge, lie close together in the small flat of the valley. Green pastures slope up the hill behind them to the north; pink-brown arable lands, ploughed and harrowed, are flung off to either side, east and west.

Northwards the valley is a slender slip of green bordering the slender river. Southwards, below the bridge, the water meadows widen out past Sutton's farm. From the front windows of the Manor Farm house you see them, green between the brown trunks of the elms on the road bank. From the back you look out across orchard and pasture to the black, still water and yellow osier beds above the Mill. Beyond the water a double line of beeches, bare delicate branches, rounded head after rounded head, climbs a hillock in a steep curve, to part and meet again in a thick ring at the top.

The house front stretches along a sloping grass plot, the immense porch built out like a wing with one ball-topped gable above it, a smaller gable in the roof behind. On either side two rows of wide black windows, heavy browed, with thick stone mullions.

Barker, Jerrold Fielding's agent, used to live there; but before the spring of nineteen sixteen Barker had joined up, Wyck Manor had been turned into a home for convalescent soldiers, and Anne was living with Colin at the Manor Farm.

Half of her Ilford land had been taken by the government; and she had let the rest together with the house and orchard. Instead of her own estate she had the Manor to look after now. It had been impossible in war-time to fill Barker's place, and Anne had become Jerrold's agent. She had begun with a vague promise to give a look round now and then; but when the spring came she found herself doing Barker's work, keeping the farm accounts, ordering fertilizers, calculating so many hundredweights of superphosphate of lime, or sulphate of ammonia, or muriate of potash to the acre; riding about on Barker's horse, looking after the ploughing; plodding through the furrows of the hill slopes to see how the new drillers were working; going the round of the sheep-pens to keep count of the sick ewes and lambs; carrying the motherless lambs in her arms from the fold to the warm kitchen.

She went through February rain and snow, through March wind and sleet, and through the mists of the low meadows; her feet were loaded with earth from the ploughed fields; her nostrils filled with the cold, rich smell of the wet earth; the rank, sharp smell of swedes, the dry, pungent smell of straw and hay; the thick, oily, woolly smell of the folds, the warm, half-sweet, half sour smell of the cattle sheds, of champed fodder, of milky cow's breath; the smell of hot litter and dung.

At five and twenty she had reached the last clear decision of her beauty. Dressed in riding coat and breeches, her body showed more slender and more robust than ever. Rain, sun and wind were cosmetics to her firm, smooth skin. Her eyes were bright dark, washed with the clean air.

On her Essex farm and afterwards at the War she had learned how to handle men. Sulky Curtis, who grumbled under Barker's rule, surrendered to Anne without a scowl. When Anne came riding over the Seven Acre field, lazy Ballinger pulled himself together and ploughed through the two last furrows that he would have left for next day in Barker's time. Even for Ballinger and Curtis she had smiles that atoned for her little air of imperious command.

And Colin followed her about the farmyard and up the fields till he tired and turned back. She would see him standing by the gate she had passed through, looking after her with the mournful look he used to have when he was a little boy and they left him behind.

He would stand looking till Anne's figure, black on her black horse, stood up against the skyline from the curve of the round-topped hill. It dipped; it dipped and disappeared and Colin would go slowly home.

At the first sound of her horse's hoofs in the yard he came out to meet her.

One day he said to her, "Jerrold'll be jolly pleased with what you've done when he comes home."

And then, "If he ever can be pleased with anything again."

It was the first time he had said Jerrold's name.

"That's what's been bothering me," he went on. "I can't think how Jerrold's going to get over it. You remember what he was like when Father died?"

"Yes." She remembered.

"Well--what's the War going to do to him? Look what it's done to me. He minds things so much more than I do."

"It doesn't take everybody the same way, Colin."

"I don't suppose Jerrold'll get shell-shock. But he might get something worse. Something that'll hurt him more. He must mind so awfully."

"You may be sure he won't mind anything that could happen to himself."

"Of course he won't. But the things that'll happen to other people. Seeing the other chaps knocked about and killed."

"He minds most the things that happen to the people he cares about. To you and Eliot. They're the sort of things he can't face. He'd pretend they couldn't happen. But the war's so big that he can't say it isn't happening; he's got to stand up to it. And the things you stand up to don't hurt you. I feel certain he'll come through all right."

That was the turning point in Colin's malady. She thought: "If he can talk about Jerrold he's getting well."

The next day a letter came to her from Jerrold. He wrote: "I wish to goodness I could get leave. I don't want it *all* the time. I'm quite prepared to stick this beastly job for any reasonable period; but a whole year without leave, it's a bit thick..."

"About Colin. Didn't I tell you he'd be all right? And it's all *you*, Anne. You've made him; you needn't pretend you haven't. I want most awfully to see you again. There are all sorts of things I'd like to say to you, but I can't write 'em."

She thought: "He's got over it at last, then. He won't be afraid of me any more."

Somehow, since the war she had felt that Jerrold would come back to her. It was as if always, deep down and in secret, she had known that he belonged to her and that she belonged to him as no other person could; that whatever happened and however long a time he kept away from her he would come back at some time, in some way. She couldn't distinguish between Jerrold and her sense of Jerrold; and as nothing could separate her from the sense of him, nothing could separate her from Jerrold himself. He had part in the profound and secret life of her blood and nerves and brain.

IX
JERROLD

At last, in March, nineteen-sixteen, Jerrold had got leave.

Anne was right; Jerrold had come through because he had had to stand up to the War and face it. He couldn't turn away. It was too stupendous a fact to be ignored or denied or in any way escaped from. And as he had to "take" it, he took it laughing. Once in the thick of it, Jerrold was sustained by his cheerful obstinacy, his inability to see the things he didn't want to see. He admitted that there was a war, the most appalling war, if you liked, that had ever been; but he refused, all the time, to believe that the Allies would lose it; he refused from moment to moment to believe that they could be beaten in any single action; he denied the possibility of disaster to his own men. Disaster to himself--possibly; probably, in theory; but not in practice. Not when he turned back in the rain of the enemy's fire to find his captain who had dropped wounded among the dead, when he swung him over his shoulder and staggered to the nearest stretcher. He knew he would get through. It was inconceivable to Jerrold that he should not get through. Even in his fifth engagement, when his men broke and gave back in front of the German parapet, and he advanced alone, shouting to them to come on, it was inconceivable that they should not come on. And when they saw him, running forward by himself, they gathered again and ran after him and the trench was taken in a mad rush.

Jerrold got his captaincy and two weeks' leave together. He had meant to spend three days in London with his mother, three days in Yorkshire with the Durhams, and the rest of his time at Upper Speed with Anne and Colin. He was not quite sure whether he wanted to go to the Durhams. More than anything he wanted to see Anne again.

His last unbearable memory of her was wiped out by five years of India and a year of war. He remembered the child Anne who played with him, the girl Anne who went about with him, and the girl woman he had found in her room at dawn. He tried to join on to her the image of the Anne that Eliot wrote to him about, who had gone out to the war and come back from it to look after Colin. He was in love with this image of her and ready to be in love again with the real Anne. He would go back now and find her and make her care for him.

There had been a time, after his father's death, when he had tried to make himself think that Anne had never cared for him, because he didn't want to think she cared. Now that he did want it he wasn't sure.

Not so sure as he was about little Maisie Durham. He knew Maisie cared. That was why she had gone out to India. It was also why she had been sent back again. He was afraid it might be why the Durhams had asked him to stay with them as soon as he had leave. If that was so, he wasn't sure whether he ought to stay with them, seeing that he didn't care for Maisie. But since they had asked him, well, he could only suppose that the Durhams knew what they were about. Perhaps Maisie had got over it. The little thing had lots of sense.

It hadn't been his fault in the beginning, Maisie's caring. Afterwards, perhaps, in India, when he had let himself see more of her than he would have done if he had known she cared; but that, again, was hardly his fault since he didn't know. You don't see these things unless you're on the lookout for them, and you're not on the lookout unless you're a conceited ass. Then when he did see it, when he couldn't help seeing, after other people had seen and made him see, it had been too late.

But this was five years ago, and of course Maisie had got over it. There would be somebody else now. Perhaps he would go down to Yorkshire. Perhaps he wouldn't.

At this point Jerrold realised that it depended on Anne.

But before he saw Anne he would have to see his mother. And before he saw his mother his mother had seen Anne and Colin.

And while Anne in Gloucestershire was answering Jerrold's letter, Jerrold sat in the drawing-room of the house in Montpelier Square and talked to his mother. They talked about Colin and Anne.

"What's Colin's wife doing?" he said.

"Queenie? She's driving a field ambulance car in Belgium."

"Why isn't she looking after Colin?"

"That isn't in Queenie's line. Besides--"

"Besides what?"

"Well, to tell the truth, I don't suppose she'll live with Colin after--"

"After *what*?"

"Well, after Colin's living with Anne."

Jerrold stiffened. He felt the blood rushing to his heart, betraying him. His face was God only knew what awful colour.

"You don't mean to say they--"

"I don't mean to say I blame them, poor darlings. What were they to do?"

"But" (he almost stammered it) "you don't know--you can't know--it doesn't follow."

"Well, of course, my dear, they haven't *told* me. You don't shout these things from the house-tops. But what is one to think? There they are; there they've been for the last five months, living together at the Farm, absolutely alone. Anne won't leave him. She won't have anybody there. If you tell her it's not proper she laughs in your face. And Colin swears he won't go back to Queenie. What *is* one to think?"

Jerrold covered his face with his hands. He didn't know.

His mother went on in a voice of perfect sweetness. "Don't imagine I think a bit the worse of Anne. She's been simply splendid. I never saw anything like her devotion. She's brought Colin round out of the most appalling state. We've no business to complain of a situation we're all benefitting by. Some people can do these things and you forgive them. Whatever Anne does or doesn't do she'll always be a perfect darling. As for Queenie, I don't consider her for a minute. She's been simply asking for it."

He wondered whether it were really true. It didn't follow that Anne and Colin were lovers because his mother said so; even supposing that she really thought it.

"You don't go telling everybody, I hope?" he said.

"My dear Jerrold, what do you think I'm made of? I haven't even told Anne's father. I've only told you because I thought you ought to know."

"I see; you want to put me off Anne?"

"I don't *want* to. But it would, wouldn't it?"

"Oh Lord, yes, if it was true. Perhaps it isn't."

"Jerry dear, it may be awfully immoral of me, but for Colin's sake I can't help hoping that it is. I did so want Anne to marry Colin--really he's only right when he's with her--and if Queenie divorces him I suppose she will."

"But, mother, you *are* going ahead. You may be quite wrong."

"I may. You can only suppose--"

"How on earth am I to know? I can't ask them."

"No, you can't ask them."

Of course he couldn't. He couldn't go to Colin and say, "Are you Anne's lover?" He couldn't go to Anne and say, "Are you Colin's mistress?"

"If they wanted us to know," said Adeline, "they'd have told us. There you are."

"Supposing it isn't true, do you imagine he cares for her?"

"Yes, Jerrold. I'm quite, quite sure of that. I was down there last week and saw them. He can't bear her out of his sight one minute. He couldn't not care."

"And Anne?"

"Oh, well, Anne isn't going to give herself away. But I'm certain... Would she stick down there, with everybody watching them and thinking things and talking, if she didn't care so much that nothing matters?"

"But would she--would she--"

The best of his mother was that in these matters her mind jumped to meet yours halfway. You hadn't got to put things into words.

"My dear, if you think she wouldn't, supposing she cared enough, you don't know Anne."

"I shall go down," he said, "and see her."

"If you do, for goodness' sake be careful. Even supposing there's nothing in it, you mustn't let Colin see you think there is. He'd feel then that he ought to leave her for fear of compromising her. And if he leaves her he'll be as bad as ever again. And *I* can't manage him. Nobody can manage him but Anne. That's how they've tied our hands. We can't say anything."

"I see."

"After all, Jerrold, it's very simple. If they're innocent we must leave them in their innocence. And if they're not----"

"If they're not?"

"Well, we must leave them in *that*."

Jerrold laughed. But he was not in the least amused.

He went down to Wyck the next day; he couldn't wait till the day after.

Not that he had the smallest hope of Anne now. Even if his mother's suspicion were unfounded, she had made it sufficiently clear to him that Anne was necessary to Colin; and, that being so, the chances were that Colin cared for her. In these matters his mother was not such a fool as to be utterly mistaken. On every account, therefore, he must be prepared to give Anne up. He couldn't take her away from Colin, and he wouldn't if he could. It was his own fault. What was done was done six years ago. He should have loved Anne then.

Going down in the train he thought of her, a little girl with short black hair, holding a black-and-white rabbit against her breast, a little girl with a sweet mouth ready for kisses, who hung herself round his neck with sudden, loving arms. A big girl with long black hair tied in an immense black bow, a girl too big for kisses. A girl sitting in her room between her white bed and the window with a little black cat in her arms. Her platted hair lay in a thick black rope down her back. He remembered how he had kissed her; he remembered the sliding of her sweet face against his, the pressure of her darling head against his shoulder, the salt taste of her tears. It was inconceivable that he had not loved Anne then. Why hadn't he? Why had he let his infernal cowardice stop him? Eliot had loved her.

Then he remembered Colin. Little Col-Col running after them down the field, calling to them to take him with them; Colin's hands playing; Colin's voice singing *Lord Rendal*. He tried to think of Queenie, the woman Colin had married. He had no image of her. He could see nothing but Colin and Anne.

She was there alone at the station to meet him. She came towards him along the platform. Their eyes looked for each other. Something choked his voice back. She spoke first.

"Jerrold------"

"Anne." A strange, thick voice deep down in his throat.

Their hands clasped one into the other, close and strong.

"Colin wanted to come, but I wouldn't let him. It would have been too much for him. He might have cried or something ... You mustn't mind if he cries when he sees you. He isn't quite right yet."

"No, but he's better."

"Ever so much better. He can do things on the farm now. He looks after the lambs and the chickens and the pigs. It's good for him to have something to do."

Jerrold agreed that it was good.

They had reached the Manor Farm now.

"Don't take any notice if he cries," she said.

Colin waited for him in the hall of the house. He was trying hard to control himself, but when he saw Jerrold coming up the path he broke down in a brief convulsive crying that stopped suddenly at the touch of Jerrold's hand.

Anne left them together.

"Don't go, Anne."

Colin called her back when she would have left them, again after dinner.

"Don't you want Jerrold to yourself?" she said.

"We don't want you to go, do we, Jerrold?"

"Rather not."

Jerrold found himself looking at them all the time. He had tried to persuade himself that what his mother had told him was not true. But he wasn't sure. Look as he would, he was not sure.

If only his mother hadn't told him, he might have gone on believing in what she had called their innocence. But she had shown him what to look for, and for the life of him he couldn't help seeing it at every turn: in Anne's face, in the way she looked at Colin, the way she spoke to him; in her kindness to him, her tender, quiet absorption. In the way Colin's face turned after her as she came and went; in his restlessness when she was not there; in the peace, the sudden smoothing of his vexed brows, when having gone she came back again.

Supposing it were true that they--

He couldn't bear it to be true; his mind struggled against the truth of it, but if it *were* true he didn't blame them. So far from being untrue or even improbable, it seemed to Jerrold the most likely thing in the world to have happened. It had happened to so many people since the war that he couldn't deny its likelihood. There was only one thing that could have made it impossible--if Anne had cared for him.

And what reason had he to suppose she cared? After six years? After he had told her he was trying to get away from her? He had got away; and he saw a sort of dreadful justice in the event that made it useless for him to come back. If anybody was to blame it was himself. Himself and Queenie, that horrible girl Colin had married.

When he asked himself whether it was the sort of thing that Anne would be likely to do he thought: Why not, if she loved him, if she wanted to make him happy? How could he tell what Anne would or would not do? She had said long ago that he couldn't, that she might do anything.

They spent the evening talking, by fits and starts, with long silences in between. They talked about the things that happened before the war, before Colin's marriage, the things they had done together. They talked about the farm and Anne's work, about Barker and Curtis and Ballinger, about Mrs. Sutton who watched them from her house across the road.

Mrs. Sutton had once been Colin's nurse up at the Manor: she had married old Sutton after his first wife's death; old Sutton who wouldn't die and let Anne have his farm. And now she watched them as if she were afraid of what they might do next.

"Poor old Nanna," Jerrold said.

"Goodness knows what she thinks of us," said Anne.

"It doesn't matter what she thinks," said Colin.

And they laughed; they laughed; and Jerrold was not quite sure, yet.

But before the night was over he thought he was.

They had given him the little room in the gable. It led out of Colin's room. And there on the chimneypiece he saw an old photograph of himself at the age of thirteen, holding a puppy in his arms. He had given it to Anne on the last day of the midsummer holidays, nineteen hundred. Also he found a pair of Anne's slippers under the bed, and, caught in a crack of the dressing-table, one long black hair. This room leading out of Colin's was Anne's room.

And Colin called out to him, "Do you mind leaving the door open, Jerry? I can't sleep if it's shut."

It was Jerrold's second day. He and Anne climbed the steep beech walk to the top of the hillock and sat there under the trees. Up the fields on the opposite rise they could see the grey walls and gables of the Manor, and beside it their other beech ring at the top of the last field.

They were silent for a while. He was intensely aware of her as she turned her head round, slowly, to look at him, straight and full.

And the sense of his nearness came over her, soaking in deeper, swamping her brain. Her wide open eyes darkened; her breathing came in tight, short jerks; her nerves quivered. She wondered whether he could feel their quivering, whether he could hear her jerking breath, whether he could see something queer about her eyes. But she had to look at him, not shyly, furtively, but straight and full, taking him in.

He was changed. The war had changed him. His face looked harder, the mouth closer set under the mark of the little clipped fawn-brown moustache. His eyes that used to flash their blue so gayly, to rest so lightly, were fixed now, dark and heavy with memory. They had seen too much. They would never lose that dark memory of the things they had seen. She wondered, was Colin right? Had the war done worse things to Jerrold than it had done to him? He would never tell her.

"Jerrold," she said, suddenly, "did you have a good time in India?"

"I suppose so. I dare say I thought I had."

"And you hadn't?"

"Well, I can't conceive how I could have had."

"You mean it seems so long ago."

"No, I don't mean that."

"You've forgotten."

"I don't mean that, either."

Silence.

"Look here, Anne, I want to know about Colin. Has he been very bad?"

"Yes, he has."

"How bad?"

"So bad that sometimes I was glad you weren't there to see him. You remember when he was a kid, how frightened he used to be at night. Well, he's been like that all the time. He's like that now, only he's a bit better. He doesn't scream now.... All the time he kept on worrying about you. He only told me that the other day. He seemed to think the war must have done something more frightful to you than it had done to him; he said, because you'd mind it more. I told him it wasn't the sort of thing you'd mind most."

"It isn't the sort of thing it's any good minding. I don't suppose I minded more than the other chaps. If anything had happened to you, or him, or Eliot, I'd have minded that."

"I know. That's what I told him. I knew you'd come through."

"Eliot was dead right about Colin. He knew he wouldn't. He ought never to have gone out."

"He wanted so awfully to go. But Eliot could have stopped him if it hadn't been for Queenie. She hunted and hounded him out. She told him he was funking. Fancy Colin funking!"

"What's Queenie like?"

"She's like that. She never funks herself, but she wants to make out that everybody else does."

"Do you like Queenie?"

"No. I hate her. I don't mind her hounding him out so much since she went herself; I *do* mind her leaving him. Do you know, she's never even tried to come and see him."

"Good God! what a beast the woman must be. What on earth made him marry her?"

"He was frightfully in love. An awful sort of love that wore him out and made him wretched. And now he's afraid for his life of her. I believe he's afraid of the war ending because then she'll come back."

"And if she does come back?"

"She may try and take Colin away from me. But she shan't. She can't take him if he doesn't want to go. She left him to me to look after and I mean to stick to him. I won't have him frightened and made all ill again just when I've got him well."

"I'm afraid you've had a very hard time."

"Not so hard as you think."

She smiled a mysterious, quiet smile, as if she contemplated some happy secret. He thought he knew it, Anne's secret.

"Do you think it's funny of me to be living here with Colin?"

He laughed.

"I suppose it's all right. You always had pluck enough for anything."

"It doesn't take pluck to stick to Colin."

"Moral pluck."

"No. Not even moral."

"You were always fond of him, weren't you?"

That was about as far as he dare go.

She smiled her strange smile again.

"Yes. I was always fond of him.... You see, he wants me more than anybody else ever did or ever will."

"I'm not so sure about that. But he always did get what he wanted."

"Oh, does he! How about Queenie?"

"Even Queenie. I suppose he wanted her at the time."

"He doesn't want her now. Poor Colin."

"You mustn't ask me to pity him."

"Ask you? He'd hate you to pity him. I'd hate you to pity *me*."

"I shouldn't dream of pitying you, any more than I should dream of criticising you."

"Oh, you may criticise as much as you like."

"No. Whatever you did it would make no difference. I should know it was right because you did it."

"It wouldn't be. I do heaps of wrong things, but *this* is right."

"I'm sure it is." "Here's Colin," she said.

He had come out to look for them. He couldn't bear to be alone.

Jerrold had gone to Sutton's Farm to say good-bye to their old nurse, Nanny Sutton.

Nanny talked about the war, about the young men who had gone from Wyck and would not come back, about the marvel of Sutton's living on through it all, and he so old and feeble. She talked about Colin and Anne.

"Oh, Master Jerrold," she said, "I do think it's a pity she should be livin' all alone with Mr. Colin like this 'ere."

"They're all right, Nanny. You needn't worry."

"Well--well, Miss Anne was always one to go her own way and make it seem the right way."

"You may be perfectly sure it is the right way."

"I'm not sayin' as 'tisn't. And I dunnow what Master Colin'd a done without her. But it do make people talk. There's a deal of strange things said in the place."

"Don't listen to them."

"Eh dear, I'll not 'ear a word. When anybody says anything to me I tell 'em straight they'd oughter be ashamed of themselves, back-bitin' and slanderin'."

"That's right, Nanny, you give it them in the neck."

"If it'd only end in talk, but there's been harm done to the innocent. There's Mr. and Mrs. Kimber. Kimber, 'e's my 'usband's cousing." Nanny paused.

"What about him?"

"Well, 'tis this way. They're doin' for Miss Anne, livin' in the house with her. Kimber, 'e sees to the garden and Mrs. Kimber she cooks and that. And Kimber-- that's my 'usband's cousin--'e was gardener at the vicarage. And now 'e's lost his job along of Master Colin and Miss Anne."

"What do you mean?"

"Well, sir, 'tis the vicar. 'E says they 'adn't oughter be livin' in the house with Miss Anne, because of the talk there's been. So 'e says Kimber must choose between 'em. And Kimber, 'e says 'e'd have minded what parson said if it had a bin a church matter or such like, but parson or no parson, 'e says 'e's his own master an' 'e won't have no interferin' with him and his missus. So he's lost his job."

"Poor old Kimber. What a beastly shame."

"Eh, 'tis a shame to be sure."

"Never mind; I can give him a bigger job at the Manor."

"Oh, Master Jerrold, if you would, it'd be a kindness, I'm sure. And Kimber 'e deserves it, the way they've stuck to Miss Anne."

"He does indeed. It's pretty decent of them. I'll see about that before I go."

"Thank you, sir. Sutton and me thought maybe you'd do something for him, else I shouldn't have spoken. And if there's anything I can do for Miss Anne I'll do it. I've always looked on her as one of you. But 'tis a pity, all the same."

"You mustn't say that, Nanny. I tell you it's all perfectly right."

"Well, I shall never say as 'tisn't. No, nor think it. You can trust me for that, Master Jerrold."

He thought: Poor old Nanny. She lies like a brick.

He said to himself that he would never know the truth about Anne and Colin. If he went to them and asked them he would be no nearer knowing. They would have to lie to him to save each other. In any case, his mother had made it clear to him that as long as Anne had to look after Colin he couldn't ask them. If they were innocent their innocence must be left undisturbed. If they were not innocent, well--he had lost the right to know it. Besides, he was sure, as sure as if they had told him.

He knew how it would be. Colin's wife would come home and she would divorce Colin and he would marry Anne. So far as Jerrold could see, that was his brother's only chance of happiness and sanity.

As for himself, there was nothing he could do now but clear out and leave them.

And, as he had no desire to go back to his mother and hear about Anne and Colin all over again, he went down to the Durhams' in Yorkshire for the rest of his leave.

He hadn't been there five days before he and Maisie were engaged; and before the two weeks were up he had married her.

X
ELIOT

Eliot stood in the porch of the Manor Farm house. There was nobody there to greet him. Behind him on the oak table in the hall the wire he had sent lay unopened.

It was midday in June.

All round the place the air was sweet with the smell of the mown hay, and from the Broad Pasture there came the rattle and throb of the mowing-machines.

Eliot went down the road and through the gate into the hay-field. Colin and Anne were there. Anne at the top of the field drove the mower, mounted up on the shell-shaped iron seat, white against the blue sky. Colin at the bottom, slender and tall above the big revolving wheel, drove the rake. The tedding machine, driven by a farm hand, went between. Its iron-toothed rack caught the new-mown hay, tossed it and scattered it on the field. Beside the long glistening swaths the cut edge of the hay stood up clean and solid as a wall. Above it the raised plane of the grass-tops, brushed by the wind, quivered and swayed, whitish green, greenish white, in a long shimmering undulation.

Eliot went on to meet Anne and Colin as they turned and came up the field again.

When they saw him they jumped down and came running.

"Eliot, you never told us."

"I wired at nine this morning."

"There's nobody in the house and we've not been in since breakfast at seven," Colin said.

"It's twelve now. Time you knocked off for lunch, isn't it?"

"Are you all right, Eliot?" said Anne.

"Rather."

He gave a long look at them, at their sun-burnt faces, at their clean, slender grace, Colin in his cricketing flannels, and Anne in her land-girl's white-linen coat, knickerbockers, and grey wideawake.

"Colin doesn't look as if there was much the matter with him. He might have been farming all his life."

"So I have," said Colin; "considering that I haven't lived till now."

And they went back together towards the house.

Colin's and Anne's work was done for the day. The hay in the Broad Pasture was mown and dried. Tomorrow it would be heaped into cocks and carried to the stackyard.

It was the evening of Eliot's first day. He and Anne sat out under the apple trees in the orchard.

"What on earth have you done to Colin?" he said. "I expected to find him a perfect wreck."

"He was pretty bad three months ago. But it's good for him being down here in the place he used to be happy in. He knows he's safe here. It's good for him doing jobs about the farm, too."

"I imagine it's good for him being with you."

"Oh, well, he knows he's safe with me."

"Very safe. He owes it to you that he's sane now. You must have been astonishingly wise with him."

"It didn't take much wisdom. Not more than it used to take when he was a little frightened kid. That's all he was when he came back from the war, Eliot."

"The point is that you haven't treated him like a kid. You've made a man of him again. You've given him a man's life and a man's work."

"That's what I want to do. When he's trained he can look after Jerrold's land. You know poor Barker died last month of septic pneumonia. The camp was full of it."

"I know."

"What do you think of my training Colin?"

"It's all right for him, Anne. But how about you?"

"Me? Oh, *I'm* all right. You needn't worry about me."

"I do worry about you. And your father's worrying."

"Dear old Daddy. It *is* silly of him. As if anything mattered but Colin."

"You matter. You see, your father doesn't like your being here alone with him. He's afraid of what people may think."

"I'm not. I don't care what people think. They've no business to."

"No; but they will, and they do...You know what I mean, Anne, don't you?"

"I suppose you mean they think I'm Colin's mistress. Is that it?"

"I'm afraid it is. They can't think anything else. It's beastly of them, I know, but this is a beastly world, dear, and it doesn't do to go on behaving as if it wasn't."

"I don't care. If people are beastly it's their look-out, not mine. The beastlier they are the less I care."

"I don't suppose you care if the vicar's wife won't call or if Lady Corbett and the Hawtreys cut you. But that's why."

"Is it? I never thought about it. I'm too busy to go and see them and I supposed they were too busy to come and see me. I certainly don't care."

"If it was people you cared about?"

"Nobody I care about would think things like that of me."

"Anne dear, I'm not so sure."

"Then it shows how much they care about *me*."

"But it's because they care."

"I can't help it. They may care, but they don't know. They can't know anything about me if they think that."

"And you honestly don't mind?"

"I mind what *you* think. But you don't think it, Eliot, do you?"

"I? Good Lord no! Do you mind what mother thinks?"

"Yes, I mind. But it doesn't matter very much."

"It would matter if Jerrold thought it."

"Oh Eliot--does he?"

"I don't suppose he thinks precisely that. But I'm pretty sure he thought you and Colin cared for each other."

"What makes you think so?"

"His marrying Maisie like that."

"Why shouldn't he marry her?"

"Because it's you he cares about."

Eliot's voice was quiet and heavy. She knew that what he said was true. That quiet, heavy voice was the voice of her own innermost conviction. Yet under the shock of it she sat silent, not looking at him, looking with wide, fixed eyes at the pattern the apple boughs made on the sky.

"How do you know?" she said, presently.

"Because of the way he talked to mother before he came to see you here. She says he was frightfully upset when she told him about you and Colin."

"She told him *that?*"

"Apparently."

"What did she do it for, Eliot?"

"What does mother do anything for? I imagine she wanted to put Jerrold off so that you could stick on with Colin. You've taken him off her hands and she wants him kept off."

"So she told him I was Colin's mistress."

"Mind you, she doesn't think a bit the worse of you for that. She admires you for it no end."

"Do you suppose I care what she thinks? It's her making Jerrold think it...Eliot, how could she?"

"She could, because she only sees things as they affect herself."

"Do you believe she really thinks it?"

"She's made herself think it because she wanted to."

"But why--why should she want to?"

"I've told you why. She's afraid of having to look after Colin. I've no illusions about mother. She's always been like that. She wouldn't see what she was doing to you. Before she did it she'd persuaded herself that it was Colin and not Jerrold that you cared for. And she wouldn't do it deliberately at all. I know it has all the effect of low cunning, but it isn't. It's just one of her sudden movements. She'd rush into it on a blind impulse."

Anne saw it all, she saw that Adeline had slandered her to Jerrold and to Eliot, that she had made use of her love for Colin, which was her love for Jerrold, to betray her; that she had betrayed her to safeguard her own happy life, without pity and without remorse; she had done all of these things and none of them. They were the instinctive movements of her funk. Where Adeline's ease and happiness were concerned she was one incarnate funk. You couldn't think of her as a reasonable and responsible being, to be forgiven or unforgiven.

"It doesn't matter how she did it. It's done now," she said.

"Really, Anne, it was too bad of Colin. He oughtn't to have let you."

"He couldn't help it, poor darling. He wasn't in a state. Don't put that into his head. It just had to happen... I don't care, Eliot. If it was to be done again to-morrow I'd do it. Only, if I'd known, I could have told Jerrold the truth. The others can think what they like. It'll only make me stick to Colin all the more. I promised Jerrold I'd look after him and I shall as long as he wants me. It serves them all right. They all left him to me--Daddy and Aunt Adeline and Queenie, I mean--and they can't stop me now."

"Mother doesn't want to stop you. It's your father."

"I'll write and tell Daddy. Besides, it's too late. If I left Colin to-morrow it wouldn't stop the scandal. My reputation's gone and I can't get it back, can I?"

"Dear Anne, you don't know how adorable you are without it."

"Look here, Eliot, what did your mother tell *you* for?"

"Same reason. To put me off, too."

They looked at each other and smiled. Across their memories, across the years of war, across Anne's agony they smiled. Besides its courage and its young, candid cynicism, Anne's smile expressed her utter trust in him.

"As if," Eliot said, "it would have made the smallest difference."

"Wouldn't it have?"

"No, Anne. Nothing would."

"That's what Jerrold said. And *he* thought it. I wondered what he meant."

"He meant what I mean."

The moments passed, ticked off by the beating of his heart, time and his heart beating violently together. Not one of them was his moment, not one would serve him for what he had to say, falling so close on their intolerable conversation. He meant to ask Anne to marry him; but if he did it now she would suspect him of chivalry; it would look as if he wanted to make up to her for all she had lost through Colin; as if he wanted more than anything to save her.

So Eliot, who had waited so long, waited a little longer, till the evening of his last day.

Anne had gone up with him to Wyck Manor, to see the soldiers. Ever since they had come there she had taken cream and fruit to them twice a week from the Farm. Unaware of what was thought of her, she never knew that the scandal of young Fielding and Miss Severn had penetrated the Convalescent Home with the fruit and cream. And if she had known it she would not have stayed away. People's beastliness was no reason why she shouldn't go where she wanted, where she had always gone. The Convalescent Home belonged to the Fieldings, and the Fieldings were her dearest friends who had been turned into relations by her father's marriage. So this evening, absorbed in the convalescents, she never saw the matron's queer look at her or her pointed way of talking only to Eliot.

Eliot saw it.

He thought: "It doesn't matter. She's so utterly good that nothing can touch her. All the same, if she marries me she'll be safe from this sort of thing."

They had come to the dip of the valley and the Manor Farm water.

"Let's go up the beech walk," he said.

They went up and sat in the beech ring where Anne had sat with Jerrold three months ago. Eliot never realised how repeatedly Jerrold had been before him.

"Anne," he said, "it's more than five years since I asked you to marry me."

"Is it, Eliot?"

"Do you remember I said then I'd never give you up?"

"I remember. Unless Jerrold got me, you said. Well, he hasn't got me."

"I wouldn't want you to tie yourself up with me if there was the remotest chance of Jerrold; but, as there isn't, don't you think--"

"No, Eliot, I don't."

"But you do care for me, Anne, a little. I know you do."

"I care for you a great deal; but not in that sort of way."

"I'm not asking you to care for me in the way you care for Jerrold. You may care for me any way you please if you'll only marry me. You don't know how awfully little I'd be content to take."

"I shouldn't be content to give it, though. You oughtn't to have anything but the best."

"It would be the best for me, you see."

"Oh no, Eliot, it wouldn't. You only think it would because you're an angel. It would be awful of me to give so little when I take such a lot. I know what your loving would be."

"If you know you must have thought of it. And if you've thought of it--"

"I've only thought of it to see how impossible it is. It mightn't be if I could leave off loving Jerrold. But I can't...Eliot, I've got the queerest feeling about him. I know you'll think me mad, when he's gone and married somebody else, but I feel all the time as if he hadn't, as if he belonged to me and always had; and I to him. Whoever Maisie's married it isn't Jerrold. Not the real Jerrold."

"The fact remains that she's married him."

"No. Not him. Only a bit of him. Some bit that doesn't matter."

"Anne darling, I'd try not to think that."

"I don't think it. I feel it. Down there, deep inside me. I've always felt that Jerrold would come back to me and he came back. Then there was Colin. He'll come back again."

"Then there'll be Maisie."

"No, then there won't be Maisie. There won't be anything if he really comes... Now you see how mad I am. Now you see how awful it would be to marry me."

"No, Anne. I see it's the only way to keep you safe."

"Safe from what? Safe from Jerrold? I don't want to be safe from him. Eliot, I'm telling you this because you trust me. I want you to see me as I really am, so that you won't want to marry me any more."

"Ah, that's not the way to make me. Nothing you say makes any difference. Nothing you could do would make any difference."

"Supposing it had been true what your mother said, wouldn't that?"

"No. If you'd given yourself to Colin I should only have thought it was your goodness. It would have been good because you did it."

"How queer. That's what Jerrold said. Then he *did* love me."

"I told you he loved you."

"Then I don't care. Nothing else matters."

"That's all you have to say to me?"

"Yes. Unless I lie."

"You'd lie for Jerrold."

"For him. Not to him. I should never need to."

"You've no need to lie to me, dear. I know you better than he does. You forget that I didn't think what he thought."

"That only shows that he knew."

"Knew what?"

"What I am. What I might do if I really cared."

"There are things you'd never do. You'd never do anything mean or dishonourable or cruel."

"Oh, you don't know what I'd do...Don't worry, Eliot. I shall be too busy with the land and with Colin to do very much."

"I'm not worrying."

All the same he wondered which of them knew Anne best, he or Anne herself, or Jerrold.

XI
INTERIM

Colin thought with terror of the time when Queenie would come back from the war. At any moment she might get leave and come; if she had not had it yet that only made it more likely that she would have it soon. The vague horror that waited for him every morning had turned into this definite fear of Queenie. He was afraid of her temper, of her voice and eyes, of her crude, malignant thoughts, of her hatred of Anne. More than anything he was afraid of her power over him, of her vehement, exhausting love. He was afraid of her beauty.

One morning, early in September, the wire came. Colin shook with agitation as he read it.

"What is it?" Anne said.

"Queenie. She's got leave. She'll be here today. At four o'clock."

"Don't you want to see her?"

"No, I don't."

"Then you'd better drive over to Kingden and look at those bullocks of Ledbury's."

"I don't know anything about bullocks. They ought to be straight lines from their heads to their tails. That's about all I know."

"Never mind, you'll have gone to look at bullocks. And you can tell Ledbury I'm coming over to-morrow. Do you mind driving yourself?"

Colin did mind. He was afraid to drive by himself; but he was much more afraid of Queenie.

"You can take Harry. And leave me to settle Queenie."

Colin went off with Harry to Chipping Kingden. And at four o'clock Queenie came. Her hard, fierce eyes stared past Anne, looking for Colin.

"Where's Colin?" she said.

"He had to go out, but he'll be back before dinner."

Presently Queenie asked if she might go upstairs. As they went you could see her quick, inquisitive eyes sweeping and flashing.

The door of Colin's room stood open.

"Is that Colin's room?"

"Yes."

She went in, opened the inner door and looked into the gable room.

"Who sleeps here?" she said.

"I do," said Anne.

"You?"

"Have you any objection?"

"You might as well sleep in my husband's room."

"Oh no, this is near enough. I can tell whether he's asleep or awake."

"Can you? And, please, how long has this been going on?"

"I've been sleeping in this room since November. Before that we had our old rooms at the Manor. There was a passage between, you remember. But I left the doors wide open."

"Oh no, this is near enough. I can tell whether he's asleep or awake."

"Can you? And, please, how long has this been going on?"

"I've been sleeping in this room since November. Before that we had our old rooms at the Manor. There was a passage between, you remember. But I left the doors wide open."

"I suppose," said Queenie, with furious calm, "you want me to divorce him?"

"Divorce him? Why on earth should you? Just because I looked after him at night? I *had* to. There wasn't anybody else. And he was afraid to sleep alone. He is still. But he's all right as long as he knows I'm there."

"You expect me to believe that's all there is in it?"

"No, I don't, considering what your mind's like."

"Oh yes, when people do dirty things it's always other people's dirty minds. Do you imagine I'm a fool, Anne?"

"You're an awful fool if you think Colin's my lover."

"I think it, and I say it."

"If you think it you're a fool. If you say it you're a liar. A damned liar."

"And is Colin's mother a liar, too?"

"Yes, but not a damned one. It would serve you jolly well right, Queenie, if he *was* my lover, after the way you left him to me."

"I didn't leave him to you. I left him to his mother."

"Anyhow, you left him."

"I couldn't help it. *You* were not wanted at the front and I was. I couldn't leave hundreds of wounded soldiers just for Colin."

"I had to. He was in an awful state. I've looked after him day and night; I've got him almost well now, and I think the least you can do is to keep quiet and let him alone."

"I shall do nothing of the sort. I shall divorce him as soon as the war's over."

"It isn't over yet. And I don't advise you to try. No decent barrister would touch your case, it's so rotten."

"Not half so rotten as you'll look when it's in all the papers."

"You can't frighten me that way."

"Can't I? I suppose you'll say you were looking, poor darling, if you do bring your silly old action. Only please don't do it till he's quite well, or he'll be ill again...I think that's tea going in. Will you go down?"

They went down. Tea was laid in the big bare hall. The small round oak table brought them close together. Anne waited on Queenie with every appearance of polite attention. Queenie ate and drank in long, fierce silences; for her hunger was even more imperious than her pride.

"I don't *want* to eat your food," she said at last. "I'm only doing it because I'm starving. I dined with Colin's mother last night. It was the first dinner I've eaten since I went to the war."

"You needn't feel unhappy about it," said Anne. "It's Eliot's house and Jerrold's food. How's Cutler?"

"Much the same as when you saw him." Queenie answered quietly, but her face was red.

"And that Johnnie--what was his name?--who took my place?"

Queenie's flush darkened. She was holding her mouth so tight that the thin red line of the lips faded.

"Noel Fenwick," said Anne, suddenly remembering.

"What about him?" Queenie's throat moved as if she swallowed something big and hard.

"Is he there still?"

"He was when I left."

Her angry, defiant eyes were fixed on the open doorway. You could see she was waiting for Colin, ready to fall on him and tear him as soon as he came in.

"Am I to see Colin or not?" she said as she rose.

"Have you anything to say to him?"

"Only what I've said to you."

"Then you won't see him. In fact I think you'd better not see him at all."

"You mean he funks it?"

"I funk it for him. He isn't well enough to be raged at and threatened with proceedings. It'll upset him horribly and I don't see what good it'll do you."

"No more do I. I'm not going to live with him after this. You can tell him that. Tell him I don't want to see him or speak to him again."

"I see. You just came down to make a row."

"You don't suppose I came down to stay with you two?"

Queenie was so far from coming down to stay that she had taken rooms for the night at the White Hart in Wyck. Anne drove her there.

Two and a half years passed. Anne's work on the farm filled up her days and marked them. Her times were ploughing time and the time for sowing: wheat first, and turnips after the wheat, barley after the turnips, sainfoin, grass and clover after the barley. Oats in the five-acre field this year; in the seven-acre field the next. Lambing time, calving time, cross-ploughing and harrowing, washing and shearing time, time for hoeing; hay time and harvest. Then threshing time and ploughing again.

All summer the hard fight against the charlock, year after year the same. You harrowed it out and ploughed it down and sprayed it with sulphate of copper; you sowed vetches and winter corn to crowd it out; and always it sprang up again, flaring in bright yellow stripes and fans about the hills. The air was sweet with its smooth, delicious smell.

Always the same clear-cut pattern of the fields; but the colors shifted. The slender, sharp-pointed triangle that was jade-green last June, this June was yellow-brown. The square under the dark comb of the plantation that had been yellow-brown was emerald; the wide-open fan beside it that had been emerald was pink. By August the emerald had turned to red-gold and the jade-green to white.

These changes marked the months and the years, a bright patterned, imperceptibly moving measure, rolling time off across the hills.

Nineteen-sixteen, seventeen. Nineteen-eighteen and the armistice. Nineteen-nineteen and the peace.

In the spring of that year Anne and Colin were still together at the Manor Farm. He was stronger. But, though he did more and more work every year, he was still unfit to take over the management himself. Responsibility fretted him and he tired soon. He could do nothing without Anne.

He was now definitely separated from his wife. Queenie had come back from the war a year ago. As soon as it was over she had begun to rage and consult lawyers and write letters two or three times a week, threatening to drag Anne and Colin through the Divorce Court. But Miss Mullins (once the secretary of Dr. Cutler's Field Ambulance Corps), recovering at the Farm from an excess of war work, reassured them. Queenie, she said, was only bluffing. Queenie was not in a position to bring an action against any husband, she had been too notorious herself. Miss Mullins had seen things, and she intimated that no defence could stand against the evidence she could give.

And in the end Queenie left off talking about divorce and contented herself with a judicial separation.

Colin still woke every morning to his dread of some blank, undefined disaster; but, as if Queenie and the war had made one obsession, he was no longer haunted by the imminent crash of phantom shells. It was settled that he was to live with Jerrold and Maisie when they came back to the Manor, while Anne stayed on by herself at the Farm.

Every now and then Eliot came down to see them. He had been sent home early in nineteen-seventeen with a shrapnel wound in his left leg, the bone shattered. He obtained his discharge at the price of a permanent limp, and went back to his research work.

For the last two years he had been investigating trench fever, with results that were to make him famous. But that was not for another year.

In February, nineteen-nineteen, Jerrold had come back. He and Maisie had been living in London ever since he had left the Army, filling in time till Wyck Manor would be no longer a Home for Convalescent Soldiers. He had tried to crowd into this interval all the amusement he hadn't had for four years. His way was to crush down the past with the present; to pile up engagements against the future, party on party, dances on suppers and suppers on plays; to dine every evening at some place where they hadn't dined before; to meet lots of nice amusing people with demobilised minds who wouldn't talk to him about the war; to let himself go in bursts of exquisitely imbecile laughter; never to be quiet for an hour, never to be alone with himself, never to be long alone with Maisie.

After the first week of it this sort of thing ceased to amuse him, but he went on with it because he thought it amused Maisie.

There was something he missed; something he wanted and hadn't got. At night, when he lay awake, alone with himself at last, he knew that it was Anne.

And he went on laughing and amusing Maisie; and Maisie, with a heart-breaking sweetness, laughed back at him and declared herself amused. She had never had such a jolly time in all her life, she said.

Then, very early in the spring, Maisie went down to her people in Yorkshire to recover from the jolly time she had had. The convalescent soldiers had all gone, and Wyck Manor, rather worn and shabby, was Wyck Manor again.

Jerrold came back to it alone.

XII
COLIN, JERROLD, AND ANNE

He went through the wide empty house, looking through all the rooms, trying to find some memory of the happiness he had had there long ago. The house was full of Anne. Anne's figure crossed the floors before him, her head turned over her shoulder to see if he were coming; her voice called to him from the doorways, her running feet sounded on the stairs. That was her place at the table; that was the armchair she used to curl up in; just there, on the landing, he had kissed her when he went to school.

They had given his mother's room to Maisie, and they had put his things into the room beyond, his father's room. Everything was in its place as it had been in his father's time, the great wardrobe, the white marble-topped washstand, the bed he had died on. He saw him lying there and Anne going to and fro between the washstand and the bed. The parrot curtains hung from the windows, straight and still.

Jerrold shuddered as he looked at these things.

They had thought that he would want to sleep in that room because he was married, because Maisie would have the room it led out of.

But he couldn't sleep in it. He couldn't stay in it a minute; he would never pass its door without that sickening pang of memory. He moved his things across the gallery into Anne's room.

He would sleep there; he would sleep in the white bed that Anne had slept in.

He told himself that he had to be near Colin; there was only the passage between and their doors could stand open; that was why he wanted to sleep there. But he knew that was not why. He wanted to sleep there because there was no other room where he could feel Anne so near him, where he could see her so clearly. When the dawn came she would be with him, sitting in her chair by the window.

The window looked to the west, to Upper Speed and the Manor Farm house. The house was down there behind the trees, and somewhere there, jutting out above the porch, was the window of Anne's room.

He looked at his watch. One o'clock. At two he would go and see Anne.

When Jerrold called at the Manor Farm house Anne was out. Old Ballinger came slouching up from the farmyard to tell him that Miss Anne had gone up to the Far Acres field to try the new tractor.

The Far Acres field lay at the western end of the estate. Jerrold followed her there. Five furrows, five bright brown bands on the sallow stubble, marked out the Far Acres into five plots. In the turning space at the top corner he saw Anne on her black horse and Colin standing beside her.

With a great clanking and clanging the new American, tractor struggled towards them up the hill, dragging its plough. It stopped and turned at the "headland" as Jerrold came up.

A clear, light wind blew over the hill and he felt a sudden happiness and excitement. He was beginning to take an interest in his land. He shouted:

"I say, Anne, you look like Napoleon at the battle of Waterloo."

"Oh, not Waterloo, I hope. I'm going to win *my* battle."

"Well, Marengo--Austerlitz--whatever battles he did win. Does Curtis understand that infernal thing?"

Young Curtis, sulky and stolid on his driver's seat, stared at his new master.

"Yes. He's been taught motor mechanics. He's quite good at it ... If only he'd do what you tell him. Curtis, I said you were not to use those disc coulters for this field. I've had three smashed in two weeks. They're no earthly good for stony soil."

"'Tis n' so bad 'ere as it is at the east end, miss."

"Well, we'll see. You can let her go now."

With a fearful grinding and clanking the tractor started. The revolving disc coulter cut the earth; the three great shares gripped it and turned it on one side. But the earth, instead of slanting off clear from the furrows, fell back again. Anne dismounted and ran after the tractor and stopped it.

"He hasn't got his plough set right," she said. "It's too deep in."

She stooped, and did something mysterious and efficient with a lever; the wheels dipped, raising the shares to their right level, and the tractor set off again. This time the earth parted clean from the furrows with the noise of surge, and three slanting, glistening waves ran the length of the field in the wake of the triple plough.

"Oh, Jerrold, look at those three lovely furrows. Look at the pace it goes. This field will be ploughed up in a day or two. Colin, aren't you pleased?"

The tractor was coming towards them, making a most horrible noise.

"No," he said, "I don't like the row it makes. Can't I go, now I've seen what the beastly thing can do?"

"Yes. You'd better go if you can't stand it."

Colin went with quick, desperate strides down the field away from the terrifying sound of the tractor.

They looked after him sorrowfully.

"He's not right yet. I don't think he'll ever be able to stand noises."

"You must give him time, Anne."

"Time? He's had three years. It's heart-breaking. I must just keep him out of the way of the tractors, that's all."

She mounted her horse and went riding up and down the field, abreast of the plough.

Jerrold waited for her at the gate of the field.

It was Sunday evening between five and six.

Anne was in the house, in the great Jacobean room on the first floor. Barker had judged it too large and too dilapidated to live in, and it had been left empty in his time. Eliot had had it restored and Jerrold had furnished it. Black oak bookcases from the Manor stretched along the walls, for Jerrold had given Eliot half of their father's books. This room would be too dilapidated to live in, and it had been left empty in his time. Eliot had had it restored and Jerrold had furnished it. Black oak bookcases from the Manor stretched along the walls, for Jerrold had given Eliot half of their father's books. This room would be Eliot's library when he came down. It was now Anne's sitting-room.

The leaded windows were thrown open to the grey evening and a drizzling rain; but a fire blazed on the great hearth under the arch of the carved stone chimney-piece. Anne's couch was drawn up before it. She lay stretched out on it, tired with her week's work.

She was all alone in the house. The gardener and his wife went out together every Sunday to spend the evening with their families at Medlicote or Wyck. She was not sorry when they were gone; the stillness of the house rested her. But she missed Colin. Last Sunday he had been there, sitting beside her in his chair by the hearth, reading. Today he was with Jerrold at the Manor. The soft drizzle turned to a quick patter of rain; a curtain of rain fell, covering the grey fields between the farm and the Manor, cutting her off.

She was listening to the rain when she heard the click of the gate and feet on the garden path. They stopped on the flagstones under her window. Jerrold's voice called up to her.

"Anne--Anne, are you there? Can I come up?"

"Rather."

He came rushing up the stairs. He was in the room now.

"How nice of you to come on this beastly evening."

"That's why I came. I thought it would be so rotten for you all alone down here."

"What have you done with Colin?"

"Left him up there. He was making no end of a row on the piano."

"Oh Jerrold, if he's playing again he'll be all right."

"He didn't sound as if there was much the matter with him."

"You never can tell. He can't stand those tractors."

"We must keep him away from the beastly things. I suppose we've got to have 'em?"

"I'm afraid so. They save no end of labour, and labour's short and dear."

"Is that why you've been working yourself to death?"

"I haven't. Why, do I look dead?"

"No. Eliot told me. He saw you at it."

"I only take a hand at hay time and harvest. All the rest of the year it's just riding about and seeing that other people work. And Colin does half of that now."

"All the same, I think it's about time you stopped."

"But if I stop the whole thing'll stop. The men must have somebody over them."

"There's me."

"You don't know anything about farming, Jerry dear. You don't know a teg from a wether."

"I suppose I can learn if Colin's learnt. Or I can get another Barker."

"Not so easy. Don't you like my looking after your land, then? Aren't you pleased with me? I haven't done so badly, you know. Seven hundred acres."

"You've been simply splendid. I shall never forget what you've done. And I shall never forgive myself for letting you do it. I'd no idea what it meant."

"It's only meant that Colin's better and I've been happier than I ever thought I could have been."

"Happier? Weren't you happy then?"

She didn't answer. They were on dangerous ground. If they began talking about happiness--

"If I gave it up to-morrow," she said, "I should only go and work on another farm."

"Would you?"

"Jerrold--do you want me to go?"

"Want you?"

"Yes. You did once. At least, you wanted to get away from *me*."

"I didn't know what I was doing. If I had known I shouldn't have done it. I can't talk about that, Anne. It doesn't bear thinking about."

"No. But, Jerrold--tell me the truth. Do you want me to go because of Colin?"

"Colin?"

"Yes. Because of what your mother told you?"

"How do you know what she told me?"

"She told Eliot."

"And he told *you*? Good God! what was he thinking of?"

"He thought it better for me to know it. It *was* better."

"How could it be?"

"I can't tell you...Jerrold, it isn't true."

"I know it isn't."

"But you thought it was."

"When did I think?"

"Then; when you came to see me."

"Did I?"

"Yes. And you're not going to lie about it now."

"Well, if I did I've paid for it."

(What did he mean? Paid for it? It was she who had paid.)

"When did you know it wasn't true?" she said.

"Three months after, when Eliot wrote and told me. It was too late then.... If only you'd told me at the time. Why didn't you?"

"But I didn't know you thought it. How could I know?"

"No. How could you? Who would have believed that things could have happened so damnably as that?"

"But it's all right now. Why did you say it was too late?"

"Because it *was* too late. I was married."

"What *do* you mean?"

"I mean that I lied when I told you it made no difference. It made that difference. If I hadn't thought that you and Colin were...if I hadn't thought that, I wouldn't have married Maisie. I'd have married you."

"Don't say that, Jerrold."

"Well--you asked for the truth, and there it is."

She got up and walked away from him to the window. He followed her there. She spread out her hands to the cold rain.

"It's raining still," she said.

He caught back her hands.

"Would you have married me?"

"Don't, Jerrold, don't. It's cruel of you."

He was holding her by her hands.

"Would you? Tell me. Tell me."

"Let go my hands, then."

He let them go. They turned back to the fireplace. Anne shivered. She held herself to the warmth.

"You haven't told me," he said.

"No, I haven't told you," she repeated, stupidly.

"That's because you *would*. That's because you love me. You do love me."

"I've always loved you."

She spoke as if from some far-off place; as if the eternity of her love removed her from him, put her beyond his reach.

"But--what's the good of talking about it?" she said.

"All the good in the world. We owed each other the truth. We know it now; we know where we are. We needn't humbug ourselves and each other any more. You see what comes of keeping back the truth. Look how we've had to pay for it. You and me. Would you rather go on thinking I didn't care for you?"

"No, Jerrold, no. I'm only wondering what we're to do next."

"Next?"

"Yes. *That's* why you want me to go away."

"It isn't. It's why I want you to stay. I want you to leave off working and do all the jolly things we used to do."

"You mustn't make me leave off working. It's my only chance."

They turned restlessly from the fireplace to the couch. They sat one at each end of it, still for a long time, without speaking. The fire died down. The evening darkened in the rain. The twilight came between them, poignant and disquieting, dimming their faces, making them strange and wonderful to each other. Their bodies loomed up through it, wonderful and strange. The high white stone chimney-piece glimmered like an arch into some inner place.

Outside, from the church below the farm house, the bell tinkled for service.

It ceased.

Suddenly they rose and he came towards her to take her in his arms. She beat down his hands and hung on them, keeping him off.

"Don't, Jerry, please, please don't hold me."

"Oh Anne, let me. You let me once. Don't you remember?"

"We can't now. We mustn't."

And yet she knew that it would happen in some time, in some way. But not now. Not like this.

"We mustn't."

"Don't you want me to take you in my arms?"

"No. Not that."

"What, then?" He pressed tighter.

"I want you not to hurt Maisie."

"It's too late to think of Maisie now."

"I'm not thinking of her. I'm thinking of you. You'll hurt yourself frightfully if you hurt her." She wrenched his hands apart and went from him to the door.

"What are you going to do?" he said.

"I'm going to fetch the lamp."

She left him standing there.

A few minutes later she came back carrying the lighted lamp. He took it from her and set it on the table.

"And now?"

"Now you're going back to Colin. And we're both going to be good...You do want to be good--don't you?"

"Yes. But I don't see how we're going to manage it."

"We could manage it if we didn't see each other. If I went away."

"Anne, you wouldn't. You can't mean that. I couldn't stand not seeing you. You couldn't stand it, either."

"I have stood it. I can stand it again."

"You can't. Not now. It's all different. I swear I'll be decent. I won't say another word if only you won't go."

"I don't see how I can very well. There's the land... No. Colin must look after that. I'll go when the ploughing's done. And some day you'll be glad I went."

"Go. Go. You'll find out then."

Their tenderness was over. Something hard and defiant had come in to them with the light. He was at the door now.

"And you'll come back," he said. "You'll see you'll come back."

XIII
ANNE AND JERROLD

When he was gone she turned on herself in fury. What had she done it for? Why had she let him go? She didn't want to be good. She wanted nothing in the world but Jerrold.

She hadn't done it for Maisie. Maisie was nothing to her. A woman she had never seen and didn't want to see. She knew nothing of her but her name, and that was sweet and vague like a perfume coming from some place unknown. She had no sweet image of Maisie in her mind. Maisie might never have existed for all that Anne thought about her.

What did she do it for, then? Why didn't she take him when he gave himself? When she knew that in the end it must come to that?

As far as she could see through her darkness it was because she knew that Jerrold had not meant to give himself when he came to her. She had driven him to it. She had made him betray his secret when she asked for the truth. At that moment she was the stronger; she had him at a disadvantage. She couldn't take him like that, through the sudden movement of his weakness. Before she surrendered she must know first whether Jerrold's passion for her was his weakness or his strength. Jerrold didn't know yet. She must give him time to find out.

But before all she had been afraid that if Jerrold hurt Maisie he would hurt himself. She must know which was going to hurt him more, her refusal or her surrender. If he wanted "to be good" she must go away and give him his chance.

And before the ploughing was all over she had gone.

She went down into Essex, to see how her own farm was getting on. The tenant who had the house wanted to buy it when his three years' lease was up. Anne had decided that she would let him. The lease would be up in June. Her agent advised her to sell what was left of the farm land for building, which was what Anne had meant to do. She wanted to get rid of the whole place and be free. All this had to be looked into.

She had not been gone from Jerrold a week before the torture of separation became unbearable. She had said that she could bear it because she had borne it before, but, as Jerrold had pointed out to her, it wasn't the same thing now. There was all the difference in the world between Jerrold's going away from her because he didn't want her, and her going away from Jerrold because he did. It was the difference between putting up with a dull continuous pain you had to bear, and enduring a sharp agony you could end at any minute. Before, she had only given up what she couldn't get; now, she was giving up what she could have to-morrow by simply going back to Wyck.

She loathed the flat Essex country and the streets of little white rough cast and red-tiled houses on the Ilford side where the clear fields had once lain beyond the tall elm rows. She was haunted by the steep, many-coloured pattern of the hills round Wyck, and the grey gables of the Manor. Love-sickness and home-sickness tore at her together till her heart felt as if it were stretched out to breaking point.

She had only to go back and she would end this pain. Then on the sixth day Jerrold's wire came: "Colin ill again. Please come back. Jerrold."

It was not her fault and it was not Jerrold's. The thing had been taken out of their hands. She had not meant to go and Jerrold had not meant to send for her. Colin must have made him. They had lost each other through Colin and now it was Colin who had brought them together.

Colin's terror had come again. Again he had the haunting fear of the tremendous rushing noise, the crash always about to come that never came. He slept in brief fits and woke screaming.

Eliot had been down to see him and had gone. And again, as before, nobody could do anything with him but Anne.

"I couldn't," Jerrold said, "and Eliot couldn't. Eliot made me send for you."

They had left Colin upstairs and were together in the drawing-room. He stood in the full wash of the sunlight that flooded in through the west window. It showed his face drawn and haggard, and discoloured, as though he had come through a long illness. His mouth was hard with pain. He stared away from her with heavy, wounded eyes. She looked at him and was frightened.

"Jerrold, have you been ill?"

"No. What makes you think so?"

"You look ill. You look as if you hadn't slept for ages."

"I haven't. I've been frightfully worried about Colin."

"Have you any idea what set him off again?"

"I believe it was those infernal tractors. He would go out with them after you'd left. He said he'd have to, as long as you weren't there. And he couldn't stand the row. Eliot said it would be that. And the responsibility, the feeling that everything depended on him."

"I see. I oughtn't to have left him."

"It looks like it."

"What else did Eliot say?"

"Oh, he thinks perhaps he might be better at the Farm than up here. He thinks it's bad for him sleeping in that room where he was frightened when he was a kid. He says it all hooks on to that. What's more, he says he may go on having these relapses for years. Any noise or strain or excitement'll bring them on. Do you mind his being at the Farm again?"

"Mind? Of course I don't. If I'm to look after him *and* the land it'll be very much easier there than here."

For every night at Colin's bedtime Anne came up to the Manor. She slept in the room that was to be Maisie's. When Colin screamed she went to him and sat with him till he slept again. In the morning she went back to the Farm.

She had been doing this for a week now, and Colin was better.

But he didn't want to go back. If, he said, Jerrold didn't mind having him.

Jerrold wanted to know why he didn't want to go back and Colin told him.

"Hasn't it occurred to you that I've hurt Anne enough without beginning all over again? All these damned people here think I'm her lover."

"You can't help that. You're not the only one that's hurt her. We must try and make it up to her, that's all."

"How are we going to do it?"

"My God! I don't know. I shall begin by cutting the swine who've cut her."

"That's no good. She doesn't care if they do cut her. She only cares about us. She's done everything for us, and among us all we've done nothing for her. Absolutely nothing. We can't give her anything. We haven't got anything to give her that she wants."

Jerrold was silent.

Presently he said, "She wants Sutton's farm. Sutton's dying. I shall give it to her when he's dead."

"You think that'll make up?"

"No, Colin, I don't. Supposing we don't talk about it any more."

"All right. I say, when's Maisie coming home?"

"God only knows. I don't."

He wondered how much Colin knew.

February had gone. They were in the middle of March, and still Maisie had not come back.

She wrote sweet little letters to him saying she was sorry to be so long away, but her mother wanted her to stay on another week. When Jerrold wrote asking her to come back (he did this so that he might feel that he had really played the game) she answered that they wouldn't let her go till she was rested, and she wasn't quite rested yet. Jerrold mustn't imagine she was the least bit ill, only rather tired after the winter's racketing. It would be heavenly to see him again.

Then when she was rested her mother got ill and she had to go with her to Torquay. And at Torquay Maisie stayed on and on.

And Jerrold didn't imagine she had been the least bit ill, or even very tired, or that Lady Durham was ill. He preferred to think that Maisie stayed away because she wanted to, because she cared about her people more than she cared about him. The longer she stayed the more obstinately he thought it. Here was he, trying to play the game, trying to be decent and keep straight, and there was Maisie leaving him alone with Anne and making it impossible for him.

Anne had been back at the Farm a week and he had not been to see her. But Maisie's last letter made him wonder whether, really, he need try any more. He was ill and miserable. Why should he make himself ill and miserable for a woman who didn't care whether he was ill and miserable or not? Why shouldn't he go and see

Anne? Maisie had left him to her.

And on Sunday morning, suddenly, he went.

There had been a sharp frost overnight. Every branch and twig, every blade of grass, every crinkle in the road was edged with a white fur of rime. It crackled under his feet. He drank down the cold, clean air like water. His whole body felt cold and clean. He was aware of its strength in the hard tension of his muscles as he walked. His own movement exhilarated and excited him. He was going to see Anne.

Anne was not in the house. He went through the yards looking for her. In the stockyard he met her coming up from the sheepfold, carrying a young lamb in her arms. She smiled at him as she came.

She wore her farm dress, knee breeches and a thing like an old trench coat, and looked superb. She went bareheaded. Her black hair was brushed up from her forehead and down over her ears, the length of it rolled in on itself in a curving mass at the back. Over it the frost had raised a crisp web of hair that covered its solid smoothness like a net. Anne's head was the head of a hunting Diana; it might have fitted into the sickle moon.

The lamb's queer knotted body was like a grey ligament between its hind and fore quarters. It rested on Anne's arms, the long black legs dangling. The black-faced, hammer-shaped head hung in the hollow of her elbow.

"This is Colin's job," she said.

"What are you doing with it?"

"Taking it indoors to nurse it. It's been frozen stiff, poor darling. Do you mind looking in the barn and seeing if you can find some old sacks there?"

He looked, found the sacks and carried them, following her into the kitchen. Anne fetched a piece of old blanket and wrapped the lamb up. They made a bed of the sacks before the fire and laid it on it. She warmed some milk, dipped her fingers in it and put them into the lamb's mouth to see if it would suck.

"I didn't know they'd do that," he said.

"Oh, they'll suck anything. When you've had them a little time they'll climb into your lap like puppies and suck the buttons on your coat. Its mother's dead and we shall have to bring it up by hand."

"I doubt if you will."

"Oh yes, I shall save it. It can suck all right. You might tell Colin about it. He looks after the sick lambs."

She got up and stood looking down at the lamb tucked in its blanket, while Jerrold looked at her. When she looked down Anne's face was divinely tender, as if all the love in the world was in her heart. He loved to agony that tender, downward-looking face.

She raised her eyes and saw his fixed on her, heavy and wounded, and his face strained and drawn with pain. And again she was frightened.

"Jerrold, you *are* ill. What is it?"

"Don't. They'll hear us." He glanced at the open door.

"They can't. He's in church and she's upstairs in the bedrooms."

"Can't you leave that animal and come somewhere where we can talk?"

"Come, then."

He followed her out through the hall and into the small, oak-panelled dining-room. They sat down there in chairs that faced each other on either side of the fireplace.

"What is it?" she repeated. "Have you got a pain?"

"A beastly pain."

"How long have you had it?"

"Ever since you went away. I lied when I told you it was Colin. It isn't."

"What is it, then? Tell me. Tell me."

"It's not seeing you. It's this insane life we're leading. It's making me ill. You don't know what it's been like. And I can't keep my promise. I--I love you too damnably."

"Oh, Jerrold--does it hurt as much as that?"

"You know how it hurts."

"I don't want you to be hurt----But--darling--if you care for me like that how could you marry Maisie?"

"Because I cared for you. Because I was so mad about you that nothing mattered. I thought I might as well marry her as not."

"But if you didn't care for her?"

"I did. I do, in a way. Maisie's awfully sweet. Besides, it wasn't that. You see, I was going out to France, and I thought I was bound to be killed. Nobody could go on having the luck I'd had. I wanted to be killed."

"So you were sure it would happen. You always thought things would happen if you wanted them."

"I was absolutely sure. I was never more sold in my life than when it didn't. Even then I thought it would be all right till Eliot told me. Then I knew that if I hadn't been in such a damned hurry I might have married you."

"Poor Maisie."

"Poor Maisie. But she doesn't know. And if she did I don't think she'd mind much. I married her because I thought she cared about me--and because I thought I'd be killed before I could come back to her--But she doesn't care a damn. So you needn't bother about Maisie. And you won't go away again?"

"I won't go away as long as you want me."

"That's all right then."

He looked at his watch.

"I must be off. They'll be coming out of church. I don't want them to see me here now because I'm coming back in the evening. We shall have to be awfully careful how we see each other. I say--I *may* come this evening, mayn't I?"

"Yes."

"Same time as last Sunday? You'll be alone then?"

"Yes." Her voice sounded as if it didn't belong to her. As if some other person stronger than she, were answering for her.

When he had gone she called after him.

"Don't forget to tell Colin about the lamb."

She went upstairs and slipped off her farm clothes and put on the brown-silk frock she had worn when he last came to her. She looked in the glass and was glad that she was beautiful.

She began to count the minutes and the hours till Jerrold came. Dinner time passed.

All afternoon she was restless and excited. She wandered from room to room, as if she were looking for something she couldn't find. She went to and fro between the dining-room and kitchen to see how the lamb was getting on. Wrapped in its blanket, it lay asleep after its meal of milk. Its body was warm to the touch and under its soft ribs she could feel the beating of its heart. It would live.

Two o'clock. She took up the novel she had been reading before Jerrold had come and tried to get back into it. Ten minutes passed. She had read through three pages without taking in a word. Her mind went back and back to Jerrold, to the morning of today, to the evening of last Sunday, going over and over the things they had said to each other; seeing Jerrold again, with every movement, every gesture, the sudden shining and darkening of his eyes, and his tense drawn look of pain. How she must have hurt him!

It was his looking at her like that, as if she had hurt him--Anne never could hold out against other people's unhappiness.

Half past two.

She kicked off her shoes, put on her thick boots and her coat, and walked two miles up the road towards Medlicote, for no reason but that she couldn't sit still. It was not four o'clock when she got back. She went into the kitchen and looked at the lamb again.

She thought: Supposing Colin comes down to see it when Jerrold's here? But he wouldn't come. Jerrold would take care of that. Or supposing the Kimbers stayed in? They wouldn't. They never did. And if they did, why not? Why shouldn't Jerrold come to see her?

Four o'clock struck. She had the fire lit in the big upstairs sitting-room. Tea was brought to her there. Mrs. Kimber glanced at her where she lay back on the couch, her hands hanging loose in her lap.

"You're tired after all your week's work, miss?"

"A little."

"And I dare say you miss Mr. Colin?"

"Yes, I miss him very much."

"No doubt he'll be coming down to see the lamb."

"Oh yes; he'll want to see the lamb."

"And you're sure you don't mind me and Kimber going out, miss?"

"Not a bit. I like you to go."

"It's a wonder to me," said Mrs. Kimber, "as you're not afraid to be left alone in this 'ere house. But Kimber says, Miss Anne, she isn't afraid of nothing. And I don't suppose you are, what with going out to the war and all."

"There's not much to be afraid of here."

"That there isn't. Not unless 'tis people's nasty tongues."

"They don't frighten me, Mrs. Kimber."

"No, miss. I should think not indeed. And no reason why they should."

And Mrs. Kimber left her.

A sound of pails clanking came from the yard. That was Minchin, the cow man, going from the dairy to the cow sheds. Milking time, then. It must be half past four.

Five o'clock, the slamming of the front door, the click of the gate, and the Kimbers' voices in the road below as they went towards Wyck.

Anne was alone.

Only half an hour and Jerrold would be with her. The beating of her heart was her measure of time now. What would have happened before he had gone again? She didn't know. She didn't try to know. It was enough that she knew herself, and Jerrold; that she hadn't humbugged herself or him, pretending that their passion was anything but what it was. She saw it clearly in its reality. They couldn't go on as they were. In the end something must happen. They were being drawn to each other, irresistibly, inevitably, nearer and nearer, and Anne knew that a moment would come when she would give herself to him. But that it would come today or to-morrow or at any fore-appointed time she did not know. It would come, if it came at all, when she was not looking for it. She had no purpose in her, no will to make it come. She couldn't think. It was no use trying to. The thumping of her heart beat down her thoughts. Her brain swam in a warm darkness. Every now and then names drifted to her out of the darkness: Colin--Eliot--Maisie.

Maisie. Only a name, a sound that haunted her always, like a vague, sweet perfume from an unknown place. But it forced her to think.

What about Maisie? It would have been awful to take Jerrold away from Maisie, if she cared for him. But she wasn't taking him away. She couldn't take away what Maisie had never had. And Maisie didn't care for Jerrold; and if she didn't care she had no right to keep him. She had nothing but her legal claim.

Besides, what was done was done. The sin against Maisie had been committed already in Jerrold's heart when it turned from her. Whatever happened, or didn't happen, afterwards, nothing could undo that. And Maisie wouldn't suffer.

She wouldn't know. Her thoughts went out again on the dark flood. She couldn't think any more.

Half past five.

She started up at the click of the gate. That was Jerrold.

He came to her quickly and took her in his arms. And her brain was swamped again with the warm, heavy darkness. She could feel nothing but her pulses beating, beating against his, and the quick droning of the blood in her ears. Her head was bent to his breast; he stooped and kissed the nape of her neck, lightly, brushing the smooth, sweet, roseleaf skin. They stood together, pressed close, closer, to each other. He clasped his hands at the back of her head and drew it to him. She leaned it hard against the clasping hands, tilting it so that she saw his face, before it stooped again, closing down on hers.

Their arms slackened; they came apart, drawing their hands slowly, reluctantly, down from each other's shoulders.

They sat down, she on her couch and he in Colin's chair.

"Is Colin coming?" she said.

"No, he isn't."

"Well--the lamb's better."

"I never told him about the lamb. I didn't want him to come."

"Is he all right?"

"I left him playing."

The darkness had gone from her brain and the tumult from her senses. She felt nothing but her heart straining towards him in an immense tenderness that was half pity.

"Are you thinking about Colin?" he said.

"No. I'm not thinking about anything but you... *Now* you know why I was happy looking after Colin. Why I was happy working on the land. Because he was your brother. Because it was your land. Because there wasn't anything else I could do for you."

"And I've done nothing for you. I've only hurt you horribly. I've brought you nothing but trouble and danger."

"I don't care."

"No, but think. Anne darling, this is going to be a very risky business. Are you sure you can go through with it? Are you sure you're not afraid?"

"I've never been much afraid of anything."

"I ought to be afraid for you."

"Don't. Don't be afraid. The more dangerous it is the better I shall like it."

"I don't know. It was bad enough in all conscience for you and Colin. It'll be worse for us if we're found out. Of course we shan't be found out, but there's always a risk. And it would be worse for you than for me, Anne."

"I don't care. I want it to be. Besides, it won't. It'll be far worse for you because of Maisie. That's the only thing that makes it wrong."

"Don't think about that, darling."

"I don't. If it's wrong, it's wrong. I don't care how wrong it is if it makes you happy. And if God's going to punish either of us I hope it'll be me."

"God? The God doesn't exist who could punish *you*."

"I don't care if he does punish me so long as you're let off."

She came over to him and slid to the floor and crouched beside him and laid her head against his knees. She clasped his knees tight with her arms.

"I don't want you to be hurt," she said. "I can't bear you to be hurt. But what can I do?"

"Stay like that. Close. Don't go."

She stayed, pressing her face down tighter, rubbing her cheek against his rough tweed. He put his arm round her shoulder, holding her there; his fingers stroked, stroked the back of her neck, pushed up through the fine roots of her hair, giving her the caress she loved. Her nerves thrilled with a sudden secret bliss.

"Jerrold, it's heaven when you touch me."

"I know. It's hell for me when I don't."

"I didn't know. I didn't know. If only I'd known."

"We know now."

There was a long silence. Now and again she felt him stirring uneasily. Once he sighed and her heart tightened. At last he bent over her and lifted her up and set her on his knee. She lay back gathered in his arms, with her head on his breast, satisfied, like a child.

"Jerrold, do you remember how you used to hold me to keep me from falling in the goldfish pond?"

"Yes."

"I've loved you ever since then."

"Do you remember how I kissed you when I went to school?"

"Yes."

"And the night that Nicky died?"

"Yes."

"I've been sleeping in that room, because it was yours."

"Have you? Did you love me *then*, that night?"

"Yes. But I didn't know I did. And then Father's death came and stopped it."

"I know. I know."

"Anne, what a brute I was to you. Can you ever forgive me?"

"I forgave you long ago."

"Talk of punishments--"

"Don't talk of punishments."

Presently they left off talking, and he kissed her. He kissed her again and again, with light kisses brushing her face for its sweetness, with quick, hard kisses that hurt, with slow, deep kisses that stayed where they fell; kisses remembered and unremembered, longed for, imagined and unimaginable.

The church bell began ringing for service, short notes first, tinkling and tinkling; then a hurrying and scattering of sounds, sounds falling together, running into each other, covering each other; one long throbbing and clanging sound; and then hard, slow strokes, measuring out the seconds like a clock. They waited till the bell ceased. The dusk gathered. It spread from the corners to the middle of the room. The tall white arch of the chimney-piece jutted out through the dusk.

Anne stirred slightly.

"I say, how dark it's getting."

"Yes. I like it. Don't get the lamp."

They sat clinging together, waiting for the dark.

The window panes were a black glimmer in the grey. He got up and drew the curtains, shutting out the black glimmer of the panes. He came to her and lifted her in his arms and carried her to the couch and laid her on it.

She shut her eyes and waited.

XIV
MAISIE

He didn't know what he was going to do about Maisie.

On a fine, warm day in April Maisie had come home. He had motored her up from the station, and now the door of the drawing-room had closed on them and they were alone together in there.

"Oh, Jerrold--it *is* nice--to see you--again."

She panted a little, a way she had when she was excited.

"Awfully nice," he said, and wondered what on earth he was going to do next.

He had been all right on the station platform where their greetings had been public and perfunctory, but now he would have to do something intimate and, above all, spontaneous, not to stand there like a stick.

They looked at each other and he took again the impression she had always given him of delicate beauty and sweetness. She was tall and her neck bent slightly forward as she walked; this gave her the air of bowing prettily, of offering you something with a charming grace. Her shoulders and her hips had the same long, slenderly sloping curves. Her hair was mole brown on the top and turned back in an old-fashioned way that uncovered its hidden gold. Her face was white; the thin bluish whiteness of skim milk. Her mauve blue eyes looked larger than they were because of their dark brows and lashes, and the faint mauve smears about their lids. The line of her little slender nose went low and straight in the bridge, then curved under, delicately acquiline, its nostrils were close and clean cut. Her small, close up-per lip had a flying droop; and her chin curved slightly, ever so slightly, away to her throat. When she talked Maisie's mouth and the tip of her nose kept up the same sensitive, quivering play. But Maisie's eyes were still; they had no sparkling speech; they listened, deeply attentive to the person who was there. They took up the smile her mouth began and was too small to finish.

And now, as they looked at him, he felt that he ought to take her in his arms, suddenly, at once. In another instant it would be too late, the action would have lost the grace of spontaneous impulse. He wondered how you simulated a spontaneous impulse.

But Maisie made it all right for him. As he stood waiting for his impulse she came to him and laid her hands on his shoulders and kissed him, gently, on each cheek. Her hands slid down; they pressed hard against his arms above the elbow, as if to keep back his too passionate embrace. It was easy enough to return her kiss, to pass his arms under hers and press her slight body, gently, with his cramped hands. Did she know that his heart was not in it?

No. She knew nothing.

"What have you been doing with yourself?" she said. "You do look fit."

"Do I? Oh, nothing much."

He turned away from her sweet eyes that hurt him.

At least he could bring forward a chair for her, and put cushions at her back, and pour out her tea and wait on her. He tried by a number of careful, deliberate attentions to make up for his utter lack of spontaneity. And she sat there, drinking her tea, contented; pleased to be back in her happy home; serenely unaware that anything was missing.

He took her over the house and showed her her room, the long room with the two south windows, one on each side of the square, cross-lighted bay above the porch. It was full of the clear April light.

Maisie looked round, taking it all in, the privet-white panels, the lovely faded Persian rugs, the curtains of old rose damask. An armchair and a round table with a bowl of pink tulips on it stood in the centre of the bay.

"Is this mine, this heavenly room?"

"I thought so."

He was glad that he had something beautiful to give her, to make up.

She glanced at the inner door leading to his father's room. "Is that yours in there?"

"Mine? No. That door's locked. It... I'm on the other side next to Colin."

"Show me."

He took her into the gallery and showed her.

"It's that door over there at the end."

"What a long way off," she said.

"Why? You're not afraid, are you?"

"Dear me, no. Could anybody be afraid here?"

"Poor Colin's pretty jumpy still. That's why I have to be near him."

"I see."

"You won't mind having him with us, will you?"

"I shall love having him. Always. I hope he won't mind *me*."

"He'll adore you, of course."

"Now show me the garden."

They went out on to the green terraces where the peacocks spread their great tails of yew. Maisie loved the peacocks and the clipped yew walls and the goldfish pond and the flower garden.

He walked quickly, afraid to linger, afraid of having to talk to her. He felt as if the least thing she said would be charged with some unendurable emotion and that at any minute he might be called on to respond. To be sure this was not like what he knew of Maisie; but, everything having changed for him, he felt that at any minute Maisie might begin to be unlike herself.

She was out of breath. She put her hand on his arm. "Don't go so fast, Jerry. I want to look and look."

They went up on to the west terrace and stood there, looking. Brown-crimson velvet wall-flowers grew in a thick hedge under the terrace wall; their hot sweet smell came up to them.

"It's too beautiful for words," she said.

"I'm glad you like it. It is rather a jolly old place."

"It's the most adorable place I've ever been in. It looks so good and happy. As if everybody who ever lived in it had been good and happy."

"I don't know about that. It was a hospital for four years. And it hasn't quite recovered yet. It's all a bit worn and shabby, I'm afraid."

"I don't care. I love its shabbiness. I don't want to forget what it's been.... To think that I've missed seven weeks of it."

"You haven't missed much. We've had beastly weather all March."

"I've missed *you*. Seven weeks of you."

"I think you'll get over that," he said, perversely.

"I shan't. It's left a horrid empty space. But I couldn't help it. I really couldn't, Jerry."

"All right, Maisie, I'm sure you couldn't."

"Torquay was simply horrible. And this is heaven. Oh, Jerry dear, I'm going to be so awfully happy."

He looked at her with a sudden tenderness of pity. She was visibly happy. He remembered that her charm for him had been her habit of enjoyment. And as he looked at her he saw nothing but sadness in her happiness and in her sweetness and her beauty. But the sadness was not in her, it was in his own soul. Women like Maisie were made for men to be faithful to them. And he had not been faithful to her. She was made for love and he had not loved her. She was nothing to him. Looking at her he was filled with pity for the beauty and sweetness that were nothing to him. And in that pity and that sadness he felt for the first time the uneasy stirring of his soul.

If only he could have broken the physical tie that had bound him to her until now; if only they could give it all up and fall back on some innocent, immaterial relationship that meant no unfaithfulness to Anne.

When he thought of Anne he didn't know for the life of him how he was going through with it.

Maisie had been talking to him for some seconds before he understood. At last he saw that, for reasons which she was unable to make clear to him, she was letting him off. He wouldn't have to go through with it.

As Jerrold's mind never foresaw anything he didn't want to see, so in this matter of Maisie he had had no plan. Not that he trusted to the inspiration of the moment; in its very nature the moment wouldn't have an inspiration. He had simply refused to think about it at all. It was too unpleasant. But Maisie's presence forced the problem on him with some violence. He had given himself to Anne without a scruple, but when it came to giving himself to Maisie his conscience developed a sudden sense of guiltiness. For Jerrold was essentially faithful; only his fidelity was all for Anne. His marrying Maisie had been a sin against Anne, its sinfulness disguised because he had had no pleasure in it. The thought of going back to Maisie after Anne revolted him; the thought of Anne having to share him with Maisie revolted him. Nobody, he said to himself, was ever less polygamous than he.

At the same time he was sorry for Maisie. He didn't want her to suffer, and if she was not to suffer she must not know, and if she was not to know they must go on as they had begun. He was haunted by the fear of Maisie's knowing and suffering. The pity he felt for her was poignant and accusing, as if somehow she did know and suffer. She must at least be aware that something was wanting. He would have to make up to her somehow for what she had missed; he would have to give her all the other things she wanted for that one thing. Maisie's coldness might have made it easy for him. Nothing could move Jerrold from his conviction that Maisie was cold, that she was incapable of caring for him as Anne cared. His peace of mind and the freedom of his conscience depended on this belief. But, in spite of her coldness, Maisie wanted children. He knew that.

According to Jerrold's code Maisie's children would be an injury to Anne, a perpetual insult. But Anne would forgive him; she would understand; she wouldn't want to hurt Maisie.

So he went through with it.

And now he made out that mercifully, incredibly, he was being let off. He wouldn't have to go on.

He stood by Maisie's bed looking down at her as she lay there. She had grasped his hands by the wrists, as if to hold back their possible caress. And her little breathless voice went on, catching itself up and tripping.

"You won't mind--if I don't let you--come to me?"

"I'm sorry, Maisie. I didn't know you felt like that about it."

"I don't. It isn't because I don't love you. It's just my silly nerves. I get frightened."

"I know. I know. It'll be all right. I won't bother you."

"Mother said I oughtn't to ask you. She said you wouldn't understand and it would be too hard for you. *Will* it?"

"No, of course it won't. I understand perfectly."

He tried to sound like one affectionately resigned, decently renouncing, not as though he felt this blessedness of relief, absolved from dread, mercifully and incredibly let off.

But Maisie's sweetness hated to refuse and frustrate; it couldn't bear to hurt him. She held him tighter. "Jerrold--if it *is*--if you can't stand it, you mustn't mind about me. You must forget I ever said anything. It's nothing but nerves."

"I shall be all right. Don't worry."

"You *are* a darling."

Her grasp slackened. "Please--please go. At once. Quick."

As he went she put her hand to her heart. She could feel the pain coming. It filled her with an indescribable dread. Every time it came she thought she should die of it. If only she didn't get so excited; excitement always brought it on. She held her breath tight to keep it back.

Ah, it had come. Splinters of glass, sharp splinters of glass, first pricking, then piercing, then tearing her heart. Her heart closed down on the splinters of glass, cutting itself at every beat.

She looked under the pillow for the little silver box that held her pearls of nitrate of amyl. She always had it with her, ready. She crushed a pearl in her pocket handkerchief and held it to her nostrils. The pain left her. She lay still.

And every Sunday at six in the evening, or nine (he varied the hour to escape suspicion), Jerrold came to Anne.

In the weeks before Maisie's coming and after, Anne's happiness was perfect, intense and secret like the bliss of a saint in ecstasy, of genius contemplating its finished work. In giving herself to Jerrold she had found reality. She gave herself without shame and without remorse, or any fear of the dangerous risks they ran. Their passion was too clean for fear or remorse or shame. She thought love was a finer thing going free and in danger than sheltered and safe and bound. The game of love should be played with a high, defiant courage; you were not fit to play it if you fretted and cowered. Both she and Jerrold came to it with an extreme simplicity, taking it for granted. They never vowed or protested or swore not to go back on it or on each other. It was inconceivable that they should go back on it. And as Anne saw no beginning to it, she saw no end. All her past was in her love for Jerrold; there never had been a time when she had ceased to love him. This moment when they embraced was only the meeting point between what had been and what would be.

Nothing could have disturbed Anne's conscience but the sense that Jerrold didn't belong to her, that he had no right to love her; and she had never had that sense. They had belonged to each other, always, from the time when they were children playing together. Maisie was the intruder, who had no right, who had taken what didn't belong to her. And Anne could have forgiven even that if Maisie had had the excuse of a great passion; but Maisie didn't care.

So Anne, unlike Jerrold, was not troubled by thinking about Maisie. She had never seen Jerrold's wife; she didn't want to see her. So long as she didn't see her it was as if Maisie were not there.

And yet she *was* there. Next to Jerrold she was more there for Anne than the people she saw every day. Maisie's presence made itself felt in all the risks they ran. She was the hindrance, not to perfect bliss, but to a continuous happiness. She was the reason why they could only meet at intervals for one difficult and dangerous hour. Because of Maisie, Jerrold, instead of behaving like himself with a reckless disregard of consequences, had to think out the least revolting ways by which they might evade them. He had to set up some sort of screen for his Sunday visits to the Manor Farm. Thus he made a habit of long walks after dark on week-days and of unpunctuality at meals. To avoid being seen by the cottagers he approached the house from behind, by the bridge over the mill-water and through the orchard to the back door. Luckily the estate provided him with an irreproachable and permanent pretext for seeing Anne.

For Jerrold, going about with Anne over the Manor Farm, had conceived a profound passion for his seven hundred acres. At last he had come into his inheritance; and if it was Anne Severn who showed him how to use it, so that he could never separate his love of it from his love of her, the land had an interest of its own that soon excited and absorbed him. He determined to take up farming seriously and look after his estate himself when Anne had Sutton's farm. Anne would teach him all she knew, and he could finish up with a year or two at the Agricultural College in Cirencester. He had found the work he most wanted to do, the work he believed he could do best. All the better if it brought him every day this irreproachable companionship with Anne. His conscience was appeased by Maisie's coldness, and Jerrold told himself that the life he led now was the best possible life for a sane man. His mind was clear and keen; his body was splendidly fit; his love for Anne was perfect, his companionship with her was perfect, their understanding of each other was perfect. They would never be tired of each other and never bored. He rode with her over the hills and tramped with her through the furrows in all weathers.

At times he would approach her through some sense, sharper than sight or touch, that gave him her inmost immaterial essence. She would be sitting quietly in a room or standing in a field when suddenly he would be thus aware of her. These moments had a reality and certainty more poignant even than the moment of his passion.

At last they ceased to think about their danger. They felt, ironically, that they were protected by the legend that made Anne and Colin lovers. In the eyes of the Kimbers and Nanny Sutton and the vicar's wife, and the Corbetts and Hawtreys and Markhams, Jerrold was the stern guardian of his brother's morals. They were saying now that Captain Fielding had put a stop to the whole disgraceful affair; he had forced Colin to leave the Manor Farm house; and he had taken over the estate in order to keep an eye on his brother and Anne Severn.

Anne was not concerned with what they said. She felt that Jerrold and she were safe so long as she didn't know Maisie. It never struck her that Maisie would want to know *her*, since nobody else did.

But Maisie did want to know Anne and for that reason. One day she came to Jerrold with the visiting cards.

"The Corbetts and Hawtreys have called. Shall I like them?"

"I don't know. *I* won't have anything to do with them."

"Why not?"

"Because of the beastly way they've behaved to Anne Severn."

"What have they done?"

"Done? They've been perfect swine. They've cut her for five years because she looked after Colin. They've said the filthiest things about her."

"What sort of things?"

"Why, that Colin was her lover."

"Oh Jerrold, how abominable. Just because she was a saint."

"Anne wouldn't care what anybody said about her. My mother left her all by herself here to take care of him and she wouldn't leave him. She thought of nothing but him."

"She must be a perfect angel."

"She is."

"But about these horrible people--what do you want me to do?"

"Do what you like."

"I don't want to know them. I'm thinking what would be best for Anne."

"You needn't worry about Anne. It isn't as if she was *your* friend."

"But she *is* if she's yours and Colin's. I mean I want her to be.... I think I'd better call on these Corbett and Hawtrey people and just show them how we care about her. Then cut them dead afterwards if they aren't decent to her. It'll be far more telling than if I began by being rude.... Only, Jerrold, how absurd--I don't know Anne. *She* hasn't called yet."

"She probably thinks you wouldn't want to know her."

"Do you mean because of what they've said? That's the very reason. Why, she's the only person here I do want to know. I think I fell in love with the sound of her when you first told me about her and how she took care of Colin. We must do everything we can to make up. We must have her here a lot and give her a jolly time."

He looked at her.

"Maisie, you really *are* rather a darling."

"I'm not. But I think Anne Severn must be.... Shall I go and see her or will you bring her?"

"I think--perhaps--I'd better bring her, first."

He spoke slowly, considering it.

Tomorrow was Sunday. He would bring her to tea, and in the evening he would walk back with her.

On Sunday afternoon he went down to the Manor Farm. He found Anne upstairs in the big sitting-room.

"Oh Jerrold, darling, I didn't think you'd come so soon."

"Maisie sent me."

"Maisie?"

For the first time in his knowledge of her Anne looked frightened.

"Yes. She wants to know you. I'm to bring you to tea."

"But--it's impossible. I can't know her. I don't want to. Can't you see how impossible it is?"

"No, I can't. It's perfectly natural. She's heard a lot about you."

"I've no doubt she has. Jerrold--do you think she guesses?"

"About you and me? Never. It's the last thing she'd think of. She's absolutely guileless."

"That makes it worse."

"You don't know," he said, "how she feels about you. She's furious with these brutes here because they've cut you. She says she'll cut *them* if they won't be decent to you."

"Oh, worse and worse!"

"You're afraid of her?"

"I didn't know I was. But I am. Horribly afraid."

"Really, Anne dear, there's nothing to be afraid of. She's not a bit dangerous."

"Don't you see that that makes her dangerous, her not being? You've told me a hundred times how sweet she is. Well--I don't want to see how sweet she is."

"Her sweetness doesn't matter."

"It matters to me. If I once see her, Jerrold, nothing'll ever be the same again."

"Darling, really it's the only thing you can do. Think. If you don't, can't you see how it'll give the show away? She'd wonder what on earth you meant by it. We've got to behave as if nothing had happened. This isn't behaving as if nothing had happened, is it?"

"No. You see, it has happened. Oh Jerrold, I wouldn't mind if only we could be straight about it. But it'll mean lying and lying, and I can't bear it. I'd rather go out and tell everybody and face the music."

"So would I. But we can't.... Look here, Anne. We don't care a damn what people think. You wouldn't care if we were found out to-morrow----"

"I wouldn't. It would be the best thing that could happen to us."

"To us, yes. If Maisie divorced me. Then we could marry. It would be all right for us. Not for Maisie. You do care about hurting Maisie, don't you?"

"Yes. I couldn't bear her to be hurt. If only I needn't see her."

"Darling, you must see her. You can't not. I want you to."

"Well, if you want it so awfully, I will. But I tell you it won't be the same thing, afterwards, ever."

"I shall be the same, Anne. And you."

"Me? I wonder."

He rose, smiling down at her.

"Come," he said. "Don't let's be late."

She went.

In the garden with Maisie, the long innocent conversation coming back and back; Maisie's sweetness haunting her, known now and remembered. Maisie walking in the garden among the wall flowers and tulips, between the clipped walls of yew, showing Anne her flowers. She stooped to lift their faces, to caress them with her little thin white fingers.

"I don't know why I'm showing you round," she said; "you know it all much better than I do."

"Oh, well, I used to come here a lot when I was little. I sort of lived here."

Maisie's eyes listened, utterly attentive.

"You knew Jerrold, then, when he was little, too?"

"Yes. He was eight when I was five."

"Do you remember what he was like?"

"Yes."

Maisie waited to see whether Anne were going on or not, but as Anne stopped dead she went on herself.

"I wish *I'd* known Jerry all the time like that. I wish I remembered running about and playing with him.... You were Jerrold's friend, weren't you?"

"And Elliot's and Colin's."

The lying had begun. Falsehood by implication. And to this creature of palpable truth.

"Somehow, I've always thought of you as Jerrold's most. That's what makes me feel as if you were mine, as if I'd known you quite a long time. You see, he's told me things about you."

"Has he?"

Anne's voice was as dull and flat as she could make it. If only Maisie would leave off talking about Jerrold, making her lie.

"I've wanted to know you more than anybody I've ever heard of. There are heaps of things I want to say to you." She stooped to pick the last tulip of the bunch she was gathering for Anne. "I think it was perfectly splendid of you the way you looked after Colin. And the way you've looked after Jerry's land for him."

"That was nothing. I was very glad to do it for Jerrold, but it was my job, anyway."

"Well, you've saved Colin. And you've saved the land. What's more, I believe you've saved Jerrold."

"How do you mean, 'saved' him? I didn't know he wanted saving."

"He did, rather. I mean you've made him care about the estate. He didn't care a rap about it till he came down here this last time. You've found his job for him."

"He'd have found it himself all right without me."

"I'm not so sure. We were awfully worried about him after the war. He was all at a loose end without anything to do. And dreadfully restless. We thought he'd never settle to anything again. And I was afraid he'd want to live in London."

"I don't think he'd ever do that."

"He won't now. But, you see, he used to be afraid of this place."

"I know. After his father's death."

"And he simply loves it now. I think it's because he's seen what you've done with it. I know he hadn't the smallest idea of farming it before. It's what he ought to have been doing all his life. And when you think how seedy he was when he came down here, and how fit he is now."

"I think," Anne said, "I'd better be going."

Maisie's innocence was more than she could bear.

"Jerry'll see you home. And you'll come again, won't you? Soon…. Will you take them? I gathered them for you."

"Thanks. Thanks awfully." Anne's voice came with a jerk. Her breath choked her.

Jerrold was coming down the garden walk, looking for her. She said good-bye to Maisie and turned to go with him home.

"Well," he said, "how did you and Maisie get on?"

"It was exactly what I thought it would be, only worse."

He laughed. "Worse?"

"I mean she was sweeter.... Jerrold, she makes me feel such a brute. Such an awful brute. And if she ever knows--"

"She won't know."

When he had left her Anne flung herself down on the couch and cried.

All evening Maisie's tulips stood up in the blue-and-white Chinese bowl on the table. They had childlike, innocent faces that reproached her. Nothing would ever be the same again.

XV
ANNE, JERROLD, AND MAISIE

It was a Sunday in the middle of April.

Jerrold had motored up to London on the Friday and had brought Eliot back with him for the week-end. Anne had come over as she always did on a Sunday afternoon. She and Maisie were sitting out on the terrace when Eliot came to them, walking with the tired limp that Anne found piteous and adorable. Very soon Maisie murmured some gentle, unintelligible excuse, and left them.

There was a moment of silence in which everything they had ever said to each other was present to them, making all other speech unnecessary, as if they held a long intimate conversation. Eliot sat very still, not looking at her, yet attentive as if he listened to the passing of those unuttered words. Then Anne spoke and her voice broke up his mood.

"What are you doing now? Bacteriology?"

"Yes. We've found the thing we were looking for, the germ of trench fever."

"You mean *you* have."

"Well, somebody would have spotted it if I hadn't. A lot of us were out for it."

"Oh Eliot, I am so glad. That means you'll stamp out the disease, doesn't it?"

"Probably. In time."

"I knew you'd do it. I knew you'd do something big before you'd finished."

"My dear, I've only just begun. But there's nothing big about it but the research, and we were all in that. All looking for the same thing. Happening to spot it is just heaven's own luck."

"But aren't you glad it was you?"

"It doesn't matter who it is. But I suppose I'm glad. It's the sort of thing I wanted to do and it's rather more important than most things one does."

He said no more. Years ago, when he had done nothing, he had talked excitedly and arrogantly about his work; now that he had done what he had set out to do he was reserved, impassive and very humble.

"Do Jerrold and Colin know?" she said.

"Not yet. You're the first."

"Dear Eliot, you *did* know I'd be glad."

"It's nice of you to care."

Of course she cared. She was glad to think that he had that supreme satisfaction to make up for the cruelty of her refusal to care more. Perhaps, she thought, he wouldn't have had it if he had had her. He would have been torn in two; he would have had to give himself twice over. She felt that he didn't love her more than he loved his science, and science exacted an uninterrupted and undivided service. One life hadn't room enough for two such loves, and he might not have done so much if she had been there, calling back his thoughts, drawing his passion to herself.

"What are you going to do next?" she said.

"Next I'm going off for a month's holiday. To Sicily--Taormina. I've been over-working and I'm a bit run down. How about Colin?"

"He's better. Heaps better. He soon got over that relapse he had when I was away in February."

"You mean he got over it when you came back."

"Well, yes, it was when I came back. That's just what I don't like about him, Eliot. He's getting dependent on me, and it's bad for him. I wish he could go away somewhere for a change. A long change. Away from me, away from the farm, away from Wyck, somewhere where he hasn't been before. It might cure him, mightn't it?"

"Yes," he said. "Yes. It would be worth trying."

He didn't look at her. He knew what she was going to say. She said it.

"Eliot--do you think you could take him with you? Could you stand the strain?"

"If you could stand it for four years I ought to be able to stand it for a month."

"If he gets better it won't be a strain. He isn't a bit of trouble when he's well. He's adorable. Only--perhaps--if you're run down you oughtn't to."

"I'm not so bad as all that. The only thing is, you say he ought to get away from you, and I wanted you to come too."

"Me?"

"You and Maisie and Jerrold."

"I can't. It's impossible. I can't leave the farm."

"My dear girl, you mustn't be tied to it like that. Don't you ever get away?"

"Not unless Jerrold or Colin are here. We can't all three be away at once. But it's awfully nice of you to think of it."

"I didn't. It was Maisie."

Maisie? Would she never get away from Maisie, and Maisie's sweetness and kindness, breaking her down?

"She'll be awfully disappointed if you don't go."

"Why should she be?"

"Because she wants you to."

"Maisie?"

"Yes. Surely you know she likes you?"

"I was afraid she was beginning to--"

"Why? Don't you want her to like you? Don't you like *her*?"

"Yes. And I don't want to like her. If I once begin I shall end by loving her."

"My dear, it would be the best thing you could do."

"No, Eliot, it wouldn't. You don't know.... Here she is."

Maisie came to them along the terrace. She moved with an unresisting grace, a delicate bowing of her head and swaying of her body, and breathless as if she went against a wind. Eliot gave up his chair and limped away from them.

"Has he told you about Taormina?" she said.

"Yes. It's sweet of you to ask me to go with you----"

"You're coming, aren't you?"

"I'm afraid I can't."

"Why ever not?"

"I can't leave the land for one thing. Not if Jerrold and Colin aren't here."

"Oh, bother the old land! You *must* leave it. It can get on without you for a month or two. Nothing much can happen in that time."

"Oh, can't it! Things can happen in a day if you aren't there to see that they don't."

"Well, Jerrold won't mind much if they do. But he'll mind awfully if you don't come. So shall I. Besides, it's all settled. He's to come back with Eliot in time for the hay harvest, and you and I and Colin are to go on to the Italian Lakes. My father and mother are joining us at Como in June. We shall be there a month and come home through Switzerland."

"It would be heavenly, but I can't do it. I can't, really, Maisie." She was thinking: He'll be back for the hay harvest.

"But you must. You can't go and spoil all our pleasure like that. Jerrold's and Eliot's and Colin's. **And** mine. I never dreamed of your not coming."

"Do you mean you really want me?"

"Of course I want you. So does Jerrold. It won't be the same thing at all without you. I want to see you enjoying yourself for once. You'd do it so well. I believe I want to see that more than Taormina and the Italian Lakes. Do say you'll come."

"Maisie--why are you such an angel to me?"

"I'm not. I want you to come because--oh **because** I want you. Because I like you. I'm happy when you're there. So's Jerrold. Don't go and say you care more for the land than Jerrold and me."

"I don't. I--It isn't the land altogether. It's Colin. I want him to get away from me for a time and do without me. It's frightfully important that he should get away."

"We could send Colin to another part of the island with Eliot. Only that wouldn't be very kind to Eliot."

"No. It won't do, Maisie. I'll go off somewhere when you've come back."

"But that's no good to **us**. Jerrold will be here for the haying, if you're thinking of that."

"I'm not thinking of that. I'm thinking of Colin."

As she said it she knew that she was lying. Lying to Maisie. Lying for the first time. That came of knowing Maisie; it came of Maisie's sweetness. She would have to lie and lie. She was not thinking of Colin now; she was thinking that if Jerrold came back for the hay harvest and Maisie went on with Colin to the Italian Lakes, she would have her lover to herself; they would be alone together all June. She would lie in his arms, not for their short, reckless hour of Sunday, but night after night, from long before midnight till the dawn.

For last year, when the warm weather came, Anne and Colin had slept out of doors in wooden shelters set up in the Manor fields, away from the noises of the farm. A low stone wall separated Anne's field from Colin's. This year, when Jerrold came home, Colin's shelter had been moved up from the field to the Manor garden. In the summer Anne would sleep again in her shelter. The path to her field from the Manor garden lay through three pastures and two strips of fir plantation with a green drive between.

Jerrold would come to her there. He would have his bed in Colin's shelter in the garden, and when the night was quiet he would get up and go down the Manor fields and through the fir plantation to her shelter at the bottom. They would lie there in each other's arms, utterly safe, hidden from passing feet and listening ears, and eyes that watched behind window panes.

And as she thought of his coming to her, and heard her own voice lying to Maisie, the blood mounted to her face, flooding it to the roots of her hair.

"I'm thinking of Colin."

Her voice kept on sounding loud and dreadful in her brain, while Maisie's voice floated across it, faint, as if it came from somewhere a long way off.

"You never think of yourself. You're too good for anything, Anne."

She would never be safe from Maisie and Maisie's innocence that accused, reproached and threatened her. Maisie's sweetness went through her like a thrusting sword, like a sharp poison; it had words that cut deeper than threats, reproaches, accusations. Before she had seen Maisie she had been fearless, pitiless, remorseless; now, because of Maisie, she would never be safe from remorse and pity and fear.

She recovered. She told herself that she hadn't lied; that she *had* been thinking of Colin; that she had thought of him first; that she had refused to go to Taormina before she knew that Jerrold was coming back for the hay harvest. She couldn't help it if she knew that now. It was not as if she had schemed for it or counted on it. She had never for one moment counted on anything or schemed. And still, as she thought of Jerrold, her heart tightened on the sharp sword-thrust of remorse.

Because of Maisie, nothing would ever be the same again.

In the last week of April they had gone, Jerrold and Maisie, Eliot and Colin, to Taormina. In the last week in May Jerrold and Eliot took Maisie up to Como on their way home. They found Sir Charles and Lady Durham there waiting for her.

They had left Colin by himself at Taormina.

From the first moment of landing Colin had fallen in love with Sicily and re-fused to be taken away from it. He was aware that his recovery was now in his own hands, and that he would not be free from his malady so long as he was afraid to be alone. He had got to break himself of his habit of dependence on other people. And here in Taormina he had come upon the place that he could bear to be alone in. There was freedom in his surrender to its enchantment and in the contempla-tion of its beauty there was peace. And with peace and freedom he had found his indestructible self; he had come to the end of its long injury.

One day, sitting out on the balcony of his hotel, he wrote to Anne.

"Don't imagine because I've got well here away from you that it wasn't you who made me well. In the first place, I should never have gone away if you hadn't made me go. You knew what you were about when you sent me here. I know now what Jerrold meant when he wanted to get away by himself after Father died. He said he wanted to grow a new memory. Well, that's what I've done here.

"It seemed to happen all at once. One day I'd left them all and gone out for a walk by myself. It came over me that between me and being well, perfectly well, there was nothing but myself, that I was really hanging on to my illness for some sort of protection that it gave me, just as I'd hung on to you. I'd been thinking about it all the time, filling my mind with my illness, hanging on to the very fear of it; to save myself, I suppose, from a worse fear, the fear of life itself. And suddenly, out there, I let go. And the beauty of the place got me. I can't describe the beauty, except that there was a lot of strong blue and yellow in it, a clear gold atmosphere, positively quivering, and streaming over everything like gold water. I seemed to remember it as if I'd been here before, a long, steady memory, not just a flash. It was like finding something you'd lost, or when a musical phrase you've been look-ing for suddenly comes back to you. It was the most utter, indescribable peace and satisfaction. And somehow this time joined on to the times at Wyck when we were all there and happy together; and the beastly time in between slipped through. It just dropped out, as if it had never happened, and I got a sense of having done with it forever. I can't tell you what it was like. But I think it means I'm well.

"And then, on the top of it all, I remembered you, Anne, and all your goodness and sweetness. I got right away from my beastly self and saw you as you are. And

I knew what you'd done for me. I don't believe I ever knew, really *knew*, before. I had to be alone with myself before I could see it, just as I always had to be alone with my music before I could get it right. I've never thanked you properly. I can't thank you. There aren't any words to do it in. And I only know now what it's cost you...."

Did he know? Did he know that it had once cost her Jerrold?

"... For instance, I know you gave up coming here with us because you thought it would be better for me without you."

Colin, too, turning it in her heart, the sharp blade of remorse. Would they never have done punishing her?

And then: "Maisie knows what you are. She told Eliot you were the most beautiful thing, morally, she had ever known. The one person, she said, whose motives would always be clean."

If he had tried he couldn't have hit on anything that would have hurt her so. It was more than she could bear to be punished like this through the innocence of innocent people, through their kindness and affection, their belief, their incorruptible trust in her. There was nothing in the world she dreaded more than Maisie's trust. It was as if she foresaw what it would do to her, how at any minute it would beat her, it would break her down.

But she was not beaten yet, not broken down. After every fit of remorse her passion asserted itself again in a superb recovery. Her motives might not be so spotless as they looked to Maisie, but her passion itself was clean as fire. Nothing, not even Maisie's innocence, Maisie's trust in her, could make her go back on it. Hard, wounding tears cut through her eyelids as she thought of Maisie, but she brushed them away and began counting the days till Jerrold should come back.

He came back the first week in June, in time for the hay harvest. And it happened as she had foreseen.

It would have been dangerous for Jerrold to have left the house at night to go to the Manor Farm. At any moment he might have been betrayed by his own footsteps treading the passages and stairs, by the slipping of locks and bolts, the sound of the opening and shutting of doors. The servants might be awake and hear him; they might go to his room and find that he was not there.

But Colin's shelter stood in a recess on the lawn, open to the fields and hidden from the house by tall hedges of yew. Nobody could see him slip out into the moonlight or the darkness; nobody could hear the soft padding of his feet on the grass. He had only to run down the three fields and cross the belt of firs to come to Anne's shelter at the bottom. The blank, projecting wall of the mill hid it from the cottages and the Manor Farm house; the firs hid it from the field path; a high bank, topped by a stone wall, hid it from the road and Sutton's Farm. Its three wooden walls held them safe.

Night after night, between eleven and midnight, he came to her. Night after night, she lay awake waiting till the light rustling of the meadow grass told her he was there: on moonlit nights a quick brushing sound; in the thick blackness a sound like a slow shearing as he felt his way. The moon would show him clear, as he stood in the open frame of the shelter, looking in at her; or she would see him grey, twilit and mysterious; or looming, darker than dark, on black nights without moon or stars.

They loved the clear nights when their bodies showed to each other white under the white moon; they loved the dark nights that brought them close, shutting them in, annihilating every sensation but that of his tense, hard muscles pressing down, of her body crushed and yielding, tightening and slackening in surrender; of their brains swimming in their dark ecstasy.

They loved the warmth of each other's bodies in the hot windless nights; they loved their smooth, clean coolness washed by the night wind. Nothing, not even the sweet, haunting ghost of Maisie, came between. They would fall asleep in each other's arms and lie there till dawn, till Anne woke in a sudden fright. Always she had this fear that some day they would sleep on into the morning, when the farm people would be up and about. Jerrold lay still, tired out with satisfaction, sunk under all the floors of sleep. She had to drag him up, with kisses first and light stroking, then with a strong undoing of their embrace, pushing back his heavy arms that fell again to her breast as she parted them. Then she would wrench herself loose and shake him by the shoulders till she woke him. He woke clean, with no ugly turning and yawning, but with a great stretching of his strong body and a short, sudden laugh, the laugh he had for danger. Then he would look at his wrist watch and show it her, laughing again as she saw that this time, again, they were safe. And they would lie a little while longer, looking into each other's faces for the sheer joy of looking, reckless with impunity. And he would start up suddenly with, "I say, Anne, I must clear out or we shall be caught." And they would get up.

Outside, the world looked young and unknown in the June dawn, in the still, clear, gold-crystal air, where green leaves and green grass shone with a strange, hard lustre like fresh paint, and yet unearthly, uncreated, fixed in their own space and time.

And she would go with him, her naked feet shining white on the queer, bright, cold green of the grass, up the field to the belt of firs that stood up, strange and eternal, under the risen sun.

They parted there, holding each other for a last kiss, a last clinging, as if never in this world they would meet again.

Dawn after dawn. They belonged to the dawn and the dawn light; the dawn was their day; they knew it as they knew no other time.

And Anne would go back to her shelter, and lie there, and live through their passion again in memory, till she fell asleep.

And when she woke she would find the sweet, sad ghost of Maisie haunting her, coming between her and the memory of her dark ecstasy. Maisie, utterly innocent, utterly good, trusting her, sending Jerrold back to her because she trusted her. Only to think of Maisie gave her a fearful sense of insecurity. She thought: If I'd loved her I could never have done it. If I were to love her even now that would end it. We couldn't go on. She prayed God that she might not love her.

By day the hard work of the farm stopped her thinking. And the next night and the next dawn brought back her safety.

The hay harvest was over by the last week of June, and in the first week of July Maisie had come back.

Maisie or no Maisie, the work of the farm had to go on; and Anne felt more than ever that it justified her. When the day of reckoning came, if it ever did come, let her be judged by her work. Because of her love for Jerrold here was this big estate held together, and kept going; because of his love for her here was Jerrold, growing into a perfect farmer and a perfect landlord; because of her he had found the one thing he was best fitted to do; because of him she herself was valuable.

Anne brought to her work on the land a thoroughness that aimed continually at perfection. She watched the starting of every tractor-plough and driller as it broke fresh ground, to see that machines and men were working at their highest pitch of efficiency. She demanded efficiency, and, on the whole, she got it; she gave it by a sort of contagion. She wrung out of the land the very utmost it was capable of yielding; she saw that there was no waste of straw or hay, of grain or fertilizers; and she knew how to take risks, spending big sums on implements and stock wherever she saw a good chance of a return.

Jerrold learned from her this perfection. Her work stood clear for the whole countryside to see. Nobody could say she had not done well by the land. When she first took on the Manor Farm it had stood only in the second class; in four years she had raised it to the first. It was now one of the best cultivated estates in the county and famous for its prize stock. Sir John Corbett of Underwoods, Mr. Hawtrey of Medlicote, and Major Markham of Wyck Wold owned to an admiration for Anne Severn's management. Her morals, they said, might be a trifle shady, but her farming was above reproach. More reluctantly they admitted that she had made something of that young rotter, Colin, even while they supposed that he had been sent abroad to keep him out of Anne Severn's way. They also supposed that as soon as he could do it decently Jerrold would get rid of Anne.

Then two things happened. In July Maisie Fielding came back and was seen driving about the country with Anne Severn; and in the same month old Sutton died and the Barrow Farm was let to Anne, thus establishing her permanence.

Anne had refused to take it from Jerrold as his gift. He had pressed her persistently.

"You might, Anne. It's the only thing I can give you. And what is it? A scrubby two hundred acres."

"It's a thundering lot of land, Jerrold. I can't take it."

"You must. It isn't enough, after all you've done for us. I'd like to give you everything I've got; Wyck Manor and the whole blessed estate to the last turnip, and every cow and pig. But I can't do that. And you used to say you wanted the Barrow Farm."

"I wanted to rent it, Jerry darling. I can't let you give it me."

"Why not? I think it's simply beastly of you not to."

At that point Maisie had passed through the room with her flowers and he had called to her to help him.

"What are you two quarrelling about?" she said.

"Why, I want to give her the Barrow Farm and she won't let me."

"Of course I won't let him. A whole farm. How could I?"

"I think you might, Anne. It would please him no end."

"She thinks," Jerrold said, "she can go on doing things for us, but we mustn't do anything for her. And I say it's beastly of her."

"It is really, Anne darling. It's selfish. He wants to give it you so awfully. He won't be happy if you won't take it."

"But a farm, a whole thumping farm. It's a big house and two hundred acres. How can I take a thing like that? You couldn't yourself if you were me."

Maisie's little white fingers flickered over the blue delphiniums stacked in the blue-and-white Chinese jar. Her mauve-blue eyes were smiling at Anne over the tops of the tall blue spires.

"Don't you want to make him happy?" she said.

"Not that way."

"If it's the only way--?"

She passed out of the room, still smiling, to gather more flowers. They looked at each other.

"Jerrold, I can't stand it when she says things like that."

"No more can I. But you know, she really does want you to take that farm."

"Don't you see why I can't take it--from *you*? It's because we're lovers."

"I should have thought that made it easier."

"It makes it impossible. I've *given* myself to you. I can't take anything. Besides, it would look as if I'd taken it for that."

"That's an appalling idea, Anne."

"It is. But it's what everybody'll think. They'll wonder what on earth you did it for. We don't want people wondering about us. If they once begin wondering they'll end by finding out."

"I see. Perhaps you're right. I'm sorry."

"It sticks out of us enough as it is. I can't think how Maisie doesn't see it. But she never will. She'll never believe that we--"

"Do you want her to see it?"

"No, but it hurts so, her not seeing.... Jerrold, I believe that's the punishment-- Maisie's trusting us. It's the worst thing she could have done to us."

"Then, if we're punished we're quits. Don't think of it, Anne darling. Don't let Maisie come in between us like that."

He took her in his arms and kissed her, close and quick, so that no thought could come between.

But Maisie's sweetness had not done its worst. She had yet to prove what she was and what she could do.

July passed and August; the harvest was over. And in September Jerrold went up to London to stay with Eliot for the week-end, and Anne stayed with Maisie, because Maisie didn't like being left in the big house by herself. Through all those weeks that was the way Maisie had her, through her need of her.

And on the Thursday before Anne came Maisie had called on Mrs. Hawtrey of Medlicote, and Mrs. Hawtrey had asked her to lunch with her on the following Monday. Maisie said she was afraid she couldn't lunch on Monday because Anne Severn would be with her, and Mrs. Hawtrey said she was very sorry, but she was afraid she couldn't ask Anne Severn.

And Maisie enquired in her tender voice, "Why not?"

And Mrs. Hawtrey replied, "Because, my dear, nobody here does ask Anne Severn."

Maisie said again, "Why not?"

Then Mrs. Hawtrey said she didn't want to go into it, the whole thing was so unpleasant, but nobody *did* call on Anne Severn. She was too well known.

And at that Maisie rose in her fragile dignity and said that nobody knew Anne Severn so well as she and her husband did, and that there was nobody in the world so absolutely *good* as Anne, and that she couldn't possibly know anybody who refused to know her, and so left Mrs. Hawtrey.

The evening Jerrold came home, Maisie, flushed with pleasure, entertained him with a report of the encounter.

"So you've given an ultimatum to the county."

"Yes. I told you I'd cut them all if they went on cutting Anne. And now they know it."

"That means that you won't know anybody, Maisie. Except for Anne and me you'll be absolutely alone here."

"I don't care. I don't want anybody but you and Anne. And if I do we can ask somebody down. There are lots of amusing people who'd come. And Eliot can bring his scientific crowd. It simply means that Corbetts and Hawtreys won't be asked to meet them, that's all."

She went upstairs to lie down before dinner, and presently Anne came to him in the drawing-room. She was dressed in her riding coat and breeches as she had come off the land.

"What do you think Maisie's done now?" he said.

"I don't know. Something that'll make me feel awful, I suppose."

"If you're going to take it like that I won't tell you."

"Yes. Tell me. Tell me. I'd rather know."

He told her as Maisie had told him.

"Can't you see her, standing up to the whole county? Pounding them with her little hands."

His vision of the gentle thing, rising up in that sudden sacred fury of protection, moved him to admiring, tender laughter. It made Anne burst into tears.

"Oh, Jerrold, that's the worst that's happened yet. Everybody'll cut her, because of me."

"Bless you, she won't care. She says she doesn't care about anybody but you and me."

"But that's the awful thing, her caring. That's the punishment. The punishment."

Again he took her in his arms and comforted her.

"What am I to do, Jerry? What am I to *do?*"

"Go to her," he said, "and say something nice."

"Go to her and take my punishment?"

"Well, yes, darling, I'm afraid you've got to take it. We can't have it both ways. It wouldn't *be* a punishment if you weren't so sweet, if you didn't mind so. I wish to God I'd never told you."

She held her head high.

"I made you. I'm glad you told me."

She went up to Maisie in her room. Maisie had dressed for dinner and lay on her couch, looking exquisite and fragile in a gown of thick white lace. She gave a little soft cry as Anne came to her.

"Anne, you've been crying. What is it, darling?"

"Nothing. Only Jerrold told me what you'd done."

"Done?"

"Yes, for me. Why did you do it, Maisie?"

"Why? I suppose it was because I love you. It was the least I could do."

She held out her hands to her. Anne knelt down, crouching on the floor beside her, with her face hidden against Maisie's body. Maisie put her arm round her.

"But why are you crying about it, Anne? You never cry. I can't bear it. It's like seeing Jerrold cry."

"It's because you're so good, so good, and I'm such a brute. You don't know what a brute I am."

"Oh yes, I know."

"Do you?" she said, sharply. For one moment she thought that Maisie did indeed know, know and understand so perfectly that she forgave. This was forgiveness.

"Of course I do. And so does Jerrold. *He* knows what a brute you are."

It was not forgiveness. It was Maisie's innocence again, her trust--the punishment. Anne knelt there and took the pain of it.

She lay awake, alone in her shelter. She had given the excuse of a racking headache to keep Jerrold from coming to her. For that she had had to lie. But what was her whole existence but a lie? A lie told by her silence under Maisie's trust in her, by her acceptance of Maisie's friendship, by her acquiescence in Maisie's preposterous belief. Every minute that she let Maisie go on loving and trusting and believing in her she lied. And the appalling thing was that she couldn't be alone in her lying. So long as Maisie trusted him Jerrold lied, too--Jerrold, who was truth itself. One moment she thought: That's what I've brought him to. That's how I've dragged him down. The next she saw that reproach as the very madness of her conscience. She had not dragged Jerrold down; she had raised him to his highest intensity of loving, she had brought him, out of the illusion of his life with Maisie, to reality and kept him there in an immaculate faithfulness. Not even for one insane moment did Anne admit that there was anything wrong or shameful in their passion itself. It was Maisie's innocence that made them liars, Maisie's goodness that put them in the wrong and brought shame on them, her truth that falsified them.

No woman less exquisite in goodness could have moved her to this incredible remorse. It took the whole of Maisie, in her unique perfection, to beat her and break her down. Her first instinct in refusing to know Maisie had been profoundly right. It was as if she had foreseen, even then, that knowing Maisie would mean loving her, and that, loving her, she would be beaten and broken down. The awful thing was that she did love Maisie; and she couldn't tell which was the worse to bear, her love for Maisie or Maisie's love for her. And who could have foreseen the pain of it? When she prayed that she might take the whole punishment, she had not reckoned on this refinement and precision of torture. God knew what he was about. With all his resources he couldn't have hit on anything more delicately calculated to hurt. Nothing less subtle would have touched her. Not discovery; not the grossness of exposure; but this intolerable security. What could discovery and exposure do but set her free in her reality? Anne would have rejoiced to see her lie go up in one purifying flame of revelation. But to go safe in her lie, hiding her reality, and yet defenceless under the sting of Maisie's loving, was more than she could bear. She had brought all her truth and all her fineness to this passion which Maisie's innocence made a sin, and she was punished where she had sinned, wounded by the subtle God in her fineness and her truth. If only Jerrold could have escaped, but he was vulnerable, too; there was fineness and truth in him. To suffer really he had to be wounded in his soul.

If Jerrold was hurt then they must end it.

As yet he had given no sign of feeling; but that was like him. Up to the last minute he would fight against feeling, and when it came he would refuse to own that he suffered, that there was any cause for suffering. It would be like the time when his father was dying, when he refused to see that he was dying. So he would refuse to see Maisie and then, all at once, he would see her and he would be beaten and broken down.

And suddenly he did see her.

It was on the first Sunday after Jerrold's return. Maisie had had another of her heart attacks, by herself, in her bed, the night before; and she had been lying down all day. The sun had come round on to the terrace, and she now rested there, wrapped in a fur coat and leaning back on her cushions in the garden chair.

They were sitting out there, all three, Jerrold and Anne talking together, and Maisie listening with her sweet, attentive eyes. Suddenly she shut her eyes and ceased to listen. Jerrold and Anne went on talking with hushed voices, and in a little while Maisie was asleep. Her head, rising out of the brown fur, was tilted back on the cushions, showing her innocent white throat; her white violet eyelids were shut down on her eyes, the dark lashes lying still; her mouth, utterly innocent, was half open; her breath came through it unevenly, in light jerks.

"She's asleep, Jerrold."

They sat still, making no sound.

And as she looked at Maisie sleeping, tears came again into Anne's eyes, the hard tears that cut her eyelids and spilled themselves, drop by slow drop, heavily. She tried to wipe them away secretly with her hand before Jerrold saw them; but they came again and again and he had seen. He had risen to his feet as if he would go, then checked himself and stood beside her; and together they looked on at Maisie's sleeping; they felt together the infinite anguish, the infinite pathos of her goodness and her trust. The beauty of her spirit lay bare to them in the white, tilted face, slackened and smoothed with sleep. Sleep showed them her innocence again, naked and helpless. They saw her in her poignant being, her intense reality. She was so real that in that moment nothing else mattered to them.

Anne set her teeth hard to keep her mouth still. She saw Jerrold glance at her, she heard him give a soft groan of pity or of pain; then he moved away from them and stood by the terrace wall with his back to her. She saw his clenched hands, and through his terrible, tense quietness she knew by the quivering of his shoulders that his breast heaved. Then she saw him grasp the terrace wall and grind the edge of it into the palms of his hands. That was how he had stood by his father's deathbed, gripping the foot-rail; and when presently he turned and came to her she saw the look on his face she had seen then, of young, blind agony, sharpened now with some more piercing spiritual pain.

"Come," he said, "come into the house."

They went together, side by side, as they had gone when they were children, along the terrace and down the steps into the drive. In the shelter of the hall she gave way and cried, openly and helplessly, like a child, and he put his arm round her and led her into the library, away from the place where Maisie was. They sat together on the couch, holding each other's hands, clinging together in their suffering, their memory of what Maisie had made their sin. Even so they had sat in Anne's room, on the edge of Anne's bed, when they were children, holding each other's hands, miserable and yet glad because they were brought together, because what they had done and what they had borne they had done and borne together. And now as then he comforted her.

"Don't cry, Anne darling; it isn't your fault. I made you."

"You didn't. You didn't. I wanted you and I made you come to me. And I knew what it would be like and you didn't."

"Nobody could have known. Don't go back on it."

"I'm not going back on it. If only I'd never seen Maisie--then I wouldn't have cared. We could have gone on."

"Do you mean we can't now?"

"Yes. How can we when she's such an angel to us and trusts us so?"

"It does make it pretty beastly," he said.

"It makes me feel absolutely rotten."

"So it does me, when I think about it."

"It's knowing her, Jerry. It's having to love her, and knowing that she loves me; it's knowing what she is.... Why did you make me see her?"

"You know why."

"Yes. Because it made it safer. That's the beastliness of it. I knew how it would be. I knew she'd beat us in the end--with her goodness."

"Darling, it *isn't* your fault."

"It *is*. It's all my fault. I'm not going back on it. I'd do it again to-morrow if it weren't for Maisie. Even now I don't know whether it's right or wrong. I only know it's the most real and valuable part of me that loves you, and it's the most real and valuable part of you that loves me; and I feel somehow that that makes it right. I'd go on with it if it made you happy. But you aren't happy now."

"I'm not happy because you're not. I don't mind for myself so much. Only I hate the beastly way we've got to do it. Covering it all up and pretending that we're not lovers. Deceiving her. That's what makes it all wrong. Hiding it."

"I know. And I made you do that."

"You didn't. We did it for Maisie. Anyhow, we must stop it. We can't go on like this any more. We must simply tell her."

"Tell her?"

"Yes; tell her, and get her to divorce me, so that I can marry you. It's the only straight thing."

"How can we? It would hurt her so awfully."

"Not so much as you think. Remember, she doesn't care for me. She's not like you, Anne. She's frightfully cold."

As he said it there came to her a sudden awful intimation of reality, a sense that behind all their words, all the piled-up protection of their outward thinking, there hid an unknown certainty, a certainty that would wreck them if they knew it. It was safer not to know, to go on hiding behind those piled-up barriers of thought. But an inward, ultimate honesty drove her to her questioning.

"Are you sure she's cold?"

"Absolutely sure. You go on thinking all the time that she's like you, that she takes things as hard as you do; but she doesn't. She doesn't feel as you do. It won't hurt her as it would hurt you if I left you for somebody else."

"But--it'll hurt her."

"It's better to hurt her a little now than to go on humbugging and shamming till she finds out. That would hurt her damnably. She'd hate our not being straight with her. But if we tell her the truth she'll understand. I'm certain she'll understand and she'll forgive *you*. She can't be hard on you for caring for me."

"Even if she doesn't care?"

"She cares for *you*," he said.

She couldn't push it from her, that importunate sense of a certainty that was not his certainty. If Maisie did care for him Jerrold wouldn't see it. He never saw what he didn't want to see.

"Supposing she *does* care all the time? How do you know she doesn't?"

"I don't think I can tell you."

"But I *must* know, Jerrold. It makes all the difference."

"It makes none to me, Anne. I'd want you whether Maisie cared for me or not. But she doesn't."

"If I thought she didn't--then--then I shouldn't mind her knowing. Why are you so certain? You might tell me."

Then he told her.

After all, that sense of hidden certainty was an illusion.

"When was that, Jerrold?"

"Oh, a night or two after she came down here in April. She didn't know, poor darling, how she let me off."

"April--September. And she's stuck to it?"

"Oh--stuck to it. Rather."

"And before that?"

"Before that we were all right."

"And she'd been away, too."

"Yes. Ages. That made it all the funnier."

"I wish you'd told me before."

"I wish I had, if it makes you happier."

"It does. Still, we can't go on, Jerrold, till she knows."

"Of course we can't. It's too awful. I'll tell her. And we'll go away somewhere while she's divorcing me, and stay away till I can marry you.... It'll be all different when we've got away."

"When you've told her. We ought to have told her long ago, before it happened."

"Yes. But now--what the devil *am* I to tell her?"

He saw, as if for the first time, what telling her would mean.

"Tell her the truth. The whole truth."

"How can I--when it's *you*?"

"It's because it *is* me that you've got to tell her. If you don't, Jerrold, I'll tell her myself."

"All right. I'll tell her at once and get it over. I'll tell her tonight."

"No. Not tonight, while she's so tired. Wait till she's rested."

And Jerrold waited.

XVI
ANNE, MAISIE, AND JERROLD

Jerrold waited, and Maisie got her truth in first.

It was on the Wednesday, a fine bright day in September, and Jerrold was to have driven Maisie and Anne over to Oxford in the car. And, ten minutes before starting, Maisie had declared herself too tired to go. Anne wouldn't go without her, and Jerrold, rather sulky, had set off by himself. He couldn't understand Maisie's sudden fits of fatigue when there was nothing the matter with her. He thought her capricious and hysterical. She was acquiring his mother's perverse habit of upsetting your engagements at the last moment; and lately she had been particularly tiresome about motoring. Either they were going too fast or too far, or the wind was too strong; and he would have to turn back, or hold himself in and go slowly. And the next time she would refuse to go at all for fear of spoiling their pleasure. She liked it better when Anne drove her.

And today Jerrold was annoyed with Maisie because of Anne. If it hadn't been for Maisie, Anne would have been with him, enjoying a day's holiday for once. Really, Maisie might have thought of Anne and Anne's pleasure. It wasn't like her not to think of other people. Yet he owned that she hadn't wanted Anne to stay with her. He could hear her pathetic voice imploring Anne to go "because Jerry won't like it if you don't." Also he knew that if Anne was determined not to do a thing nothing you could say would make her do it.

He had had time to think about it as he sat in the lounge of the hotel at Oxford waiting for the friends who were to lunch with him. And suddenly his annoyance had turned to pity.

It was no wonder if Maisie was hysterical. His life with her was all wrong, all horribly unnatural. She ought to have had children. Or he ought never to have married her. It had been all wrong from the beginning. Perhaps she had been aware that there was something missing. Perhaps not. Maisie had seemed always singularly unaware. That was because she didn't care for him. Perhaps, if he had loved her passionately she would have cared more. Perhaps not. Maisie was incurably cold. She shrank from the slightest gesture of approach; she was afraid of any emotion. She was one of those unhappy women who are born with an aversion from warm contacts, who cannot give themselves. What puzzled him was the union of such a temperament with Maisie's sweetness and her charm He had noticed that other men adored her. He knew that if it had not been for Anne he might have adored her, too. And again he wondered whether it would have made any difference to Maisie if he had.

He thought not. She was happy, as it was, in her gentle, unexcited way. Happy and at peace. Giving happiness and peace, if peace were what you wanted. It was that happiness and peace of Maisie's that had drawn him to her when he gave Anne up three years ago.

And again he couldn't understand this combination of hysteria and perfect peace. He couldn't understand Maisie.

Perhaps, after all, she had got what she had wanted. She wouldn't have been happy and at peace if she had been married to some brute who would have had no pity, who would have insisted on his rights. Some faithful brute; or some brute no more faithful to her than he, who had been faithful only to Anne.

As he thought of Anne darkness came down over his brain. His mind struggled through it, looking for the light.

The entrance of his friends cut short his struggling.

Maisie lay on the couch in the library, and Anne sat with her. Maisie's eyes had been closed, but now they had opened, and Anne saw them looking at her and smiling.

"You are a darling, Anne; but I wish you'd gone with Jerrold."

"I don't. I wouldn't have liked it a bit."

"He would, though."

"Not when he thought of you left here all by yourself."

Maisie smiled again.

"Jerry doesn't think, thank Goodness."

"Why 'thank Goodness'?"

"Because I don't want him to. I don't want him to see."

"To see what?"

"Why, that I can't do things like other people."

"Maisie--why can't you? You used to. Jerrold's told me how you used to rush about, dancing and golfing and playing tennis."

"Why? Did he say anything?"

"Only that you took a lot of exercise, and he thinks it's awfully bad for you knocking it all off now."

"Dear old Jerry. Of course he must think it frightfully stupid. But I can't help it, Anne. I can't do things now like I used to. I've got to be careful."

"But--why?"

"Because there's something wrong with my heart. Jerry doesn't know it. I don't want him to know."

"You don't mean seriously wrong?"

"Not very serious. But it hurts."

"Hurts?"

"Yes. And the pain frightens me. Every time it comes I think I'm going to die. But I don't die."

"Oh--Maisie--what sort of pain?"

"A disgusting pain, Anne. As if it was full of splintered glass, mixed up with bubbling blood, cutting and tearing. It grabs at you and you choke; you feel as if your face would burst. You're afraid to breathe for fear it should come again."

"But, Maisie, that's angina."

"It isn't real angina; but it's awful, all the same. Oh, Anne, what must the real thing be like?"

"Have you seen a doctor?"

"Yes, two. A man in London and a man in Torquay."

"Do they say it isn't the real thing?"

"Yes. It's all nerves. But it's every bit as bad as if it was real, except that I can't die of it."

"Poor little Maisie--I didn't know."

"I didn't mean you to know. But I *had* to tell somebody. It's so awful being by yourself with it and being frightened. And then I'm afraid all the time of Jerrold finding out. I'm afraid of his *seeing* me when it comes on."

"But, Maisie darling, he ought to know. You ought to tell him."

"No. I haven't told my father and mother because they'd tell him. Luckily it's only come on in the night, so that he hasn't seen. But it might come on anywhere, any minute. If I'm excited or anything … That's the awful thing, Anne; I'm afraid of getting excited. I'm afraid to feel. I'm afraid of everything that makes me feel. I'm afraid of Jerrold's touching me, even of his saying something nice to me. The least thing makes my silly heart tumble about, and if it tumbles too much the pain comes. I daren't let Jerrold sleep with me."

"Yet you haven't told him."

"No; I daren't."

"You *must* tell him, Maisie."

"I won't. He'd mind horribly. He'd be frightened and miserable, and I can't bear him to be frightened and miserable. He's had enough. He's been through the war. I don't mean that that frightened him; but this would."

"Do you mean to say he doesn't see it?"

"Bless you, no. He just thinks I'm tiresome and hysterical. I'd rather he thought that than see him unhappy. Nothing in the world matters but Jerrold. You see I care for him so frightfully…. You don't know how awful it is, caring like that, and yet having to beat him back all the time, never to give him anything. I daren't let him come near me because of that ghastly fright. I know you oughtn't to be afraid of pain, but it's a pain that makes you afraid. Being afraid's all part of it. So I can't help it."

"Of course you can't help it."

"I wouldn't mind if it wasn't for Jerry. I ought never to have married him."

"But, Maisie, I can't understand it. You're always so happy and calm. How can you be calm and happy with *that* hanging over you?"

"I've got to be calm for fear of it. And I'm happy because Jerrold's there. Simply knowing that he's there…. I can't think what I'd do, Anne, if he wasn't such an angel. Some men wouldn't be. They wouldn't stand it. And that makes me care all the more. He'll never know how I care."

"You must tell him."

"There it is. I daren't even try to tell him. I just live in perpetual funk."

"And you're the bravest thing that ever lived."

"Oh, I've got to cover it up. It wouldn't do to show it. But I'm glad I've told you."

She leaned back, panting.

"I mustn't talk--any more now."

"No. Rest."

"You won't mind?... But--get a book--and read. You'll be--so bored."

She shut her eyes.

Anne got a book and tried to read it; but the words ran together, grey lines tangled on a white page. Nothing was clear to her but the fact that Maisie had told the truth about herself.

It was the worst thing that had happened yet. It was the supreme reproach, the ultimate disaster and defeat. Yet Maisie had not told her anything that surprised her. This was the certainty that hid behind the defences of their thought, the certainty she had foreseen when Jerrold told her about Maisie's coldness. It meant that Jerrold couldn't escape, and that his punishment would be even worse than hers. Nothing that Maisie could have done would have been more terrible to Jerrold than her illness and the way she had hidden it from him; the poor darling going in terror of it, lying in bed alone, night after night, shut in with her terror. Jerrold was utterly vulnerable; his belief in Maisie's indifference had been his only protection against remorse. How was he going to bear Maisie's wounding love? How would he take the knowledge of it? Anne saw what must come of his knowing. It would be the end of their happiness. After this they would have to give each other up; he would never take her in his arms again; he would never come to her again in the fields between midnight and dawn. They couldn't go on unless they told Maisie the truth; and they couldn't tell Maisie the truth now, because the truth would bring the pain back to her poor little heart. They could never be straight with her; they would have to hide what they had done for ever. Maisie had silenced them for ever when she got her truth in first. To Anne it was not thinkable, either that they should go on being lovers, knowing about Maisie, or that she should keep her knowledge to herself. She would tell Jerrold and end it.

She stayed on with Maisie till the evening.

Jerrold had come back and was walking home with her through the Manor fields when she made up her mind that she would tell him now; at the next gate-- the next--when they came to the belt of firs she would tell him.

She stopped him there by the fence of the plantation. The darkness hid them from each other, only their faces and Anne's white coat glimmered through.

"Wait a minute, Jerrold. I want to tell you something. About Maisie."

He drew himself up abruptly, and she felt the sudden start and check of his hurt mind.

"You haven't told her?" he said.

"No. It's something she told me. She doesn't want you to know. But you've got to know it. You think she doesn't care for you, and she does; she cares awfully. But--she's ill."

"Ill? She isn't, Anne. She only thinks she is. I know Maisie."

"You don't know that she gets heart attacks. Frightful pain, Jerrold, pain that terrifies her."

"My God--you don't mean she's got *angina*?"

"Not the real kind. If it was that she'd be dead. But pain so bad that she thinks she's dying every time. It's what they call false angina. That's why she doesn't want you to sleep with her, for fear it'll come on and you'll see her."

Through the darkness she could feel the vibration of his shock; it came to her in his stillness.

"You said she didn't feel. She's afraid to feel because feeling brings it on."

He spoke at last. "Why on earth couldn't she tell me that?"

"Because she loves you so awfully. The poor darling didn't want you to be un-happy about her."

"As if that mattered."

"It matters more than anything to her."

"Do you really mean that she's got that hellish thing? Who told her what it was?"

"Some London doctor and a man at Torquay."

"I shall take her up to-morrow and make her see a specialist."

"If you do you mustn't let her know I told you, or she'll never tell me anything again."

"What am I to say?"

"Say you've been worried about her."

"God knows I ought to have been."

"You're worried about her, and you think there's something wrong. If she says there isn't, you'll say that's what you want to be sure of."

"Look here; how do those fellows know it isn't the real thing?"

"Oh, they can tell that by the state of her heart. I don't suppose for a moment it's the real thing. She wouldn't be alive if it was. And you don't die of false angina. It's all nerves, though it hurts like sin."

He was silent for a second.

"Anne--she's beaten us. We can't tell her now."

"No. And we can't go on. If we can't be straight about it we've got to give each other up."

"I know. We can't go on. There's nothing more to be said."

His voice dropped on her aching heart with the toneless weight of finality.

"We've got to end it now, this minute," she said. "Don't come any farther."

"Let me go to the bottom of the field."

"No. I'm not going that way."

He had come close to her now, close, as though he would have taken her in his arms for the last night, the last time. He wanted to touch her, to hold her back from the swallowing darkness. But she moved out of his reach and he did not follow her. His passion was ready to flame up if he touched her, and he was afraid. They must end it clean, without a word or a touch.

The grass drive between the firs led to a gate on the hill road that skirted the Manor fields. He knew that she would go from him that way, because she didn't want to pass by their shelter at the bottom. She couldn't sleep in it tonight.

He stood still and watched her go, her white coat glimmering in the darkness between the black rows of firs. The white gate glimmered at the end of the drive. She stood there a moment. He saw her slip like a white ghost between the gate and the gate post; he heard the light thud of the wooden latch falling back behind her, and she was gone.

XVII
JERROLD, MAISIE, ANNE, ELIOT

Maisie lay in bed, helpless and abandoned to her illness. It was no good trying to cover it up and hide it any more. Jerrold knew.

The night when he left Anne he had gone up to Maisie in her room. He couldn't rest unless he knew that she was all right. He had stooped over her to kiss her and she had sat up, holding her face to him, her hands clasped round his neck, drawing him close to her, when suddenly the pain gripped her and she lay back in his arms, choking, struggling for breath.

Jerrold thought she was dying. He waited till the pain passed and she was quieted, then he ran downstairs and telephoned for Ransome. He looked on in agony while Ransome's stethoscope wandered over Maisie's thin breast and back. It seemed to him that Ransome was taking an unusually long time about it, that he must be on the track of some terrible discovery. And when Ransome took the tubes from his ears and said, curtly, "Heart quite sound; nothing wrong there," he was convinced that Ransome was an old fool who didn't know his business. Or else he was lying for Maisie's sake.

Downstairs in the library he turned on him.

"Look here; there's no good lying to me. I want truth."

"My dear Fielding, I shouldn't dream of lying to you. There's nothing wrong with your wife's heart. Nothing organically wrong."

"With that pain? She was in agony, Ransome, agony. Why can't you tell me at once that it's angina?"

"Because it isn't. Not the real thing. False angina's a neurosis, not a heart disease. Get the nervous condition cured and she'll be all right. Has she had any worry? Any shock?"

"Not that I know."

"Any cause for worry?"

He hesitated. Poor Maisie had had cause enough if she had known. But she didn't know. It seemed to him that Ransome was looking at him queerly.

"No," he said. "None."

"You're quite certain? Has she ever had any?"

"Well, I suppose she was pretty jumpy all the time I was at the front."

"Before that? Years ago?"

"That I don't know. I should say not."

"You won't swear?"

"No. I won't swear. It would be years before we were married."

"Try and find out," said Ransome. "And keep her quiet and happy. She'd better stay in bed for a week or two."

So Maisie stayed in bed, and Jerrold and Anne sat with her, together or in turn. He had a bed made up in her room and slept there when he slept at all. But half the night he lay awake, listening for the sound of her panting and the little gasping cry that would come when the pain got her. He kept on getting up to look at her and make sure that she was sleeping.

He was changed from his old happy, careless self, the self that used to turn from any trouble, that refused to believe that the people it loved could be ill and die. He was convinced that Maisie's state was dangerous. He sent for Dr. Harper of Cheltenham and for a nerve specialist and a heart specialist from London and they all told him the same thing. And he wouldn't believe them. Because Maisie's death was the most unbearable thing that his remorse could imagine, he felt that nothing short of Maisie's death would appease the powers that punished him. He was the more certain that Maisie would die because he had denied that she was ill. For Jerrold's mind remembered everything and anticipated nothing. Like most men who refuse to see or foresee trouble, he was crushed by it when it came.

The remorse he felt might have been less intolerable if he had been alone in it; but, day after day, his pain was intensified by the sight of Anne's pain. She was exquisitely vulnerable, and for every pang that stabbed her he felt himself responsible. What they had done they had done together, and they suffered for it together, but in the beginning she had done it for him, and he had made her do it. Nobody, not even Maisie, could have been more innocent than Anne. He had no doubt that, left to herself, she would have hidden her passion from him to the end of time. He, therefore, was the cause of her suffering.

It was as if Anne's consciousness were transferred to him, day after day, when they sat together in Maisie's room, one on each side of her bed, while Maisie lay between them, sleeping her helpless and reproachful sleep, and he saw Anne's piteous face, white with pain. His pity for Maisie and his pity for Anne, their pity for each other were mixed together and held them, close as passion, in an unbearable communion.

They looked at each other, and their wounded eyes said, day after day, the same thing: "Yes, it hurts. But I could bear it if it were not for you." Their pity took the place of passion. It was as if a part of each other passed into them with their suffering as it had passed into them with their joy.

And through it all their passion itself still lived its inextinguishable and tortured life. Pity, so far from destroying it, only made it stronger, pouring in its own emotion, wave after wave, swelling the flood that carried them towards the warm darkness where will and thought would cease.

And as Jerrold's soul had once stirred in the warm darkness under the first stinging of remorse, so now it pushed and struggled to be born; all his will fought against the darkness to deliver his soul. His soul knew that Anne saved it. If her will had been weaker his would not have been so strong. At this moment an unscrupulous Anne might have damned him to the sensual hell by clinging to his pity. He would have sinned because he was sorry for her.

But Anne's will refused his pity. When he showed it she was angry. Yet it was there, waiting for her always, against her will.

One day in October (Maisie's illness lasting on into the autumn) they had gone out into the garden to breathe the cold, clean air while Maisie slept.

"Jerrold," she said, suddenly, "do you think she knows?"

"No. I'm certain she doesn't."

"I'm not. I've an awful feeling that she knows and that's why she doesn't get better."

"I don't think so. If she knew she'd have said something or done something."

"She mightn't. She mightn't do anything. Perhaps she's just being angelically good to us."

"She *is* angelically good. But she doesn't know. You forget her illness began before there *was* anything to know. It isn't the sort of thing she'd think of. If somebody told her she wouldn't believe it. She trusts us absolutely.... That's bad enough, Anne, without her knowing."

"Yes. It's bad enough. It's worse, really."

"I know it is.... Anne--I'm awfully sorry to have let you in for all this misery."

"You mustn't be sorry. You haven't let me in for it. Nobody could have known it would have happened. It wouldn't, if Maisie had been different. We wouldn't have bothered then. Nothing would have mattered. Think how gloriously happy we were. All my life all my happiness has come through you or because of you. We'd be happy still if it wasn't for Maisie."

"I don't see how we're to go on like this. I can't stand it when you're not happy. And nothing makes any difference, really. I want you so awfully all the time."

"That's one of the things we mustn't say to each other."

"I know we mustn't. Only I didn't want you to think I didn't."

"I don't think it. I know you'll care for me as long as you live. Only you mustn't say so. You mustn't be sorry for me. It makes me feel all weak and soft when I want to be strong and hard."

"You *are* strong, Anne."

"So are you. I shouldn't love you if you weren't. But we mustn't make it too hard for each other. You know what'll happen if we do?"

"What? You mean we'd crumple up and give in?"

"No. But we couldn't ever see each other alone again. Never see each other again at all, perhaps. I'd have to go away."

"You shan't have to. I swear I won't say another word."

"Sometimes I think it would be easier for you if I went."

"It wouldn't. It would be simply damnable. You can't go, Anne. That *would* make Maisie think."

After weeks of rest Maisie passed into a period of painless tranquillity. She had no longer any fear of her illness because she had no longer any fear of Jerrold's knowing about it. He did know, and yet her world stood firm round her, firmer than when he had not known. For she had now in Jerrold's ceaseless devotion what seemed to her the absolute proof that he cared for her, if she had ever doubted it. And if he had doubted her, hadn't he the absolute proof that she cared, desperately? Would she have so hidden the truth from him, would she have borne her pain and the fear of it, in that awful lonely secrecy, if she had not cared for him more than for anything on earth? She had been more afraid to sleep alone than poor Colin who had waked them with his screaming. Jerrold knew that she was not a brave woman like Anne or Colin's wife, Queenie; it was out of her love for him that she had drawn the courage that made her face, night after night, the horror of her torment alone. If he had wanted proof, what better proof could he have than that?

So Maisie remained tranquil, secure in her love for Jerrold, and in his love for her, while Anne and Jerrold were tortured by their love for each other. They were no longer sustained in their renunciation by the sight of Maisie's illness and the fear of it which more than anything had held back their passion. Without that warning fear they were exposed at every turn. It might be there, waiting for them in the background, but, with Maisie going about as if nothing had happened, even remorse had lost its protective poignancy. They suffered the strain of perpetual frustration. They were never alone together now. They had passed from each other, beyond all contact of spirit with spirit and flesh with flesh, beyond all words and looks of longing; they had nothing of each other but sight, sight that had all the violence of touch without its satisfaction, that served only to excite them, to torture them with desire. They might be held at arm's length, at a room's length, at a field's length apart, but their eyes drew them together, set their hearts beating; in one moment of seeing they were joined and put asunder.

And, day after day, their minds desired each other with a subtle, incessant, intensely conscious longing, and were utterly cut off from all communion. They met now at longer and longer intervals, for their work separated them. Colin had come home in October, perfectly recovered, and he and Jerrold managed the Manor estate together while Anne looked after her own farm. Jerrold never saw her, he never tried to see her unless Colin or Maisie or some of the farm people were present; he was afraid and Anne knew that he was afraid. Her sense of his danger made her feel herself fragile and unstable. She, too, avoided every occasion of seeing him alone.

And this separation, so far from saving them, defeated its own end. Every day it brought them nearer to the breaking point. It was against all nature and all nature was against it. They had always before them that vision of the point at which they would give in. Always there was one thought that drew them to the edge of surrender: "I can bear it for myself, but I can't bear it for him," "I can bear it for myself, but I can't bear it for her."

And to both of them had come another fear, greater than their dread of Maisie's pain, the fear of each other's illness. Their splendid physical health was beginning to break down. They worked harder than ever on the land; but hard work exhausted them at the end of the day. They went on from a sense of duty, dull and implacable, but they had no more pleasure in it. Anne became every night more restless, every day more tired and anaemic. Jerrold ate less and slept less. They grew thin, and their faces took on the same look of fatigue and anxiety and wonder, as if, more than anything, they were amazed at a world whose being connived at and tolerated their pain.

Maisie saw it and felt the first vague disturbance of her peace. Her illness had worried everybody while it lasted, but she couldn't think why, when she was well again, Anne and Jerrold should go on looking like that. Maisie thought it was physical; the poor dears worked too hard.

The change had been so gradual that she saw it without consternation, but when Eliot came down in November he couldn't hide his distress. To Eliot the significant thing was not Anne's illness or Jerrold's illness but the likeness in their illnesses, the likeness in their faces. It was clear that they suffered together, with the same suffering, from the same cause. And when on his last evening Jerrold took him into the library to consult him about Maisie's case, Eliot had a hard, straight talk with him about his own.

"My dear Jerrold," he said, "there's nothing seriously wrong with Maisie. I've examined her heart. It isn't a particularly strong heart, but there's no disease in it. If you took her to all the specialists in Europe they'd tell you the same thing."

"I know, but I keep on worrying."

"That, my dear chap, is because you're ill yourself. I don't like it. I'm not bothered about Maisie, but I am bothered about you and Anne."

"Anne? Do you think *Anne's* ill?"

"I think she will be, and so will you if... What have you been doing?"

"We've been doing nothing."

"That's it. You've got to do something and do it pretty quick if it's to be any good."

Jerrold started and looked up. He wondered whether Eliot knew. He had a way of getting at things, you couldn't tell how.

"What d'you mean? What are you talking about?" His words came with a sudden sharp rapidity.

"You know what I mean."

"I don't know how *you* know anything. And, as a matter of fact, you don't."

"I don't know much. But I know enough to see that you two can't go on like this."

"Maisie and me?"

"No. You and Anne. It's Anne I'm talking about. I suppose you can make a mess of your own life if you like. You've no business to make a mess of hers."

"My God! as if I didn't know it. What the devil am I to do?"

"Leave her alone, Jerrold, if you can't have her."

"Leave her alone? I *am* leaving her alone. I've got to leave her alone, if we both die of it."

"She ought to go away," Eliot said.

"She shan't go away unless I go with her. And I can't.'"

"Well, then, it's an impossible situation."

"It's a damnable situation, but it's the only decent one. You forget there's Maisie."

"No, I don't. Maisie doesn't know?"

"Oh Lord, no. And she never will."

"You ought to tell her."

Jerrold was silent.

"My dear Jerrold, it's the only sensible thing. Tell her straight and get her to divorce you."

"I was going to. Then she got ill and I couldn't."

"She isn't ill now."

"She will be if I tell her. It'll simply kill her."

"It won't. It may--even--cure her."

"It'll make her frightfully unhappy. And it'll bring back that infernal pain. If you'd seen her, Eliot, you'd know how impossible it is. We simply can't be swine. And if I could, Anne couldn't.... No. We've got to stick it somehow, Anne and I."

"It's all wrong, Jerrold."

"I know it's all wrong. But it's the best we can do. You don't suppose Anne would be happy if we did Maisie down."

"No. No. She wouldn't. You're right there. But it's a damnable business."

"Oh, damnable, yes."

Jerrold laughed in his agony. Yet he saw, as if he had never seen it before, Eliot's goodness and the sadness and beauty of his love for Anne. He had borne for years what Jerrold was bearing now, and Anne had not loved him. He had never known for one moment the bliss of love or any joy. He had had nothing. And Jerrold remembered with a pang of contrition that he had never cared enough for Eliot. It had always been Colin, the young, breakable Colin, who had clung to him and followed him. Eliot had always gone his own queer way, keeping himself apart.

And now Eliot was nearer to him than anything in the world, except Anne.

"I'm sorry, Jerrold."

"You're pretty decent, Eliot, to be sorry--I believe you honestly want me to have Anne."

"I wouldn't go so far as that, old man. But I believe I honestly want Anne to have you.... I say, she hasn't gone yet, has she?"

"No. Maisie's keeping her for dinner in your honour. You'll probably find her in the drawing-room now."

"Where's Maisie?"

"She won't worry you. She's gone to lie down."

Eliot went into the drawing-room and found Anne there.

She looked at him. "You've been talking to Jerrold," she said.

"Yes, Anne. I'm worried about him."

"So am I."

"And I'm worried about you."

"And he's worried about Maisie."

"Yes. I suppose he began by not seeing she was ill, and now he does see it he thinks she's going to die. I've been trying to explain to him that she isn't."

"Can you explain why she's got into this state? It's not as if she wasn't happy. She *is* happy."

"She wasn't always happy. Jerrold must have made her suffer damnably."

"When?"

"Oh, long before he married her."

"But *how* did he make her suffer?"

"Oh, by just not marrying her. She found out he didn't care for her. Her people took her out to India, I believe, with the idea that he would marry her. And when they saw that Jerry wasn't on in that act they sent her back again. Poor Maisie got it well rammed into her then that he didn't care for her, and the idea's stuck. It's left a sort of wound in her memory."

"But she must have thought he cared for her when he did marry her. She thinks he cares now."

"Of course she thinks it. I don't suppose he's ever let her see."

"I know he hasn't."

"But the wound's there, all the same. She's never got over it, though she isn't conscious of it now. The fact remains that Maisie's marriage is incomplete because Jerry doesn't care for her. Part of Maisie, the adorable part we know, isn't aware of any incompleteness; it lives in a perpetual illusion. But the part we don't know, the hidden, secret part of her, is aware of nothing else.... Well, her illness is simply camouflage for that. Maisie's mind couldn't bear the reality, so it escaped into a neurosis. Maisie's behaving as though she wasn't married, so that her mind can say to itself that her marriage is incomplete because she's ill, not because Jerry doesn't care for her. It's substituted a bearable situation for an unbearable one."

"Then, you don't think she *knows*?"

"That Jerrold doesn't care for her? No. Only in that unconscious way. Her mind remembers and *she* doesn't."

"I mean, she doesn't know about Jerrold and me?"

"I'm sure she doesn't. If she did she'd do something."

"That's what Jerrold said. What would she do?"

"Oh something beautiful, or it wouldn't be Maisie. She'd let Jerrold go."

"Yes. She'd let him go. And she'd die of it."

"Oh no, she wouldn't. I told Jerrold just now it might cure her."

"How *could* it cure her?"

"By making her face reality. By making her see that her illness simply means that she hasn't faced it. All our neuroses come because we daren't live with the truth."

"It's no good making Maisie well if we make her unhappy. Besides, I don't be-lieve it. If Maisie's unhappy she'll be worse, not better."

"There *is* just that risk," he said. "But it's you I'm thinking about, not Maisie. You see, I don't know what's happened."

"Jerrold didn't tell you?"

"He only told me what I know already."

"After all, what *do* you know?"

"I know you were all right, you and he, when I saw you together here in the spring. So I suppose you were happy then. Jerrold looked wretchedly ill all the time he was at Taormina. So I suppose he was unhappy then because he was away from you. He looks wretchedly ill now. So do you. So I suppose you're both unhappy."

"Yes, we're both unhappy."

"Do you want to tell me about it, Anne?"

"No. I don't want to tell you about it. Only, if I thought you still wanted to marry me----"

"I do want to marry you. I shall always want to marry you. I told you long ago nothing would ever make any difference.

"Even if----?"

"Even if--Whatever you did or didn't do I'd still want you. But I told you--don't you remember?--that you could never do anything dishonourable or cruel."

"And I told you I wasn't sure."

"And I am sure. That's enough for me. I don't want to know anything more. I don't want to know anything you'd rather I didn't know."

"Oh, Eliot, you *are* so good. You're good like Maisie. Don't worry about Jerry and me. We'll see it through somehow."

"And if you can't stand the strain of it?"

"But I can."

"And if *he* can't? If you want to be safe----"

"I told you I should never want to be safe."

"If you want *him* to be safe, then, would you marry me?"

"That's different. I don't know, Eliot, but I don't think so."

He went away with a faint hope. She had said it would be different; what she would never do for him she might do for Jerrold.

She might, after all, marry him to keep Jerrold safe.

Nothing made any difference. Whatever Anne did she would still be Anne. And it was Anne he loved. And, after all, what did he know about her and Jerrold? Only that if they had been lovers that would account for their strange happiness seven months ago; if they had given each other up this would account for their unhappiness now. He thought: How they must have struggled.

Perhaps, some day, when the whole story was told and Anne was tired of struggling, she would come to him and he would marry her.

Even if----

XVIII
JERROLD AND ANNE

The Barrow Farm house, long, low and grey, stood back behind the tall elms and turned its blank north gable end to the road and the Manor Farm. Its nine mullioned windows looked down the field to the river. And the great barns were piled behind it, long roof-trees, steep, mouse-coloured slopes and peaks above grey walls.

Anne didn't move into the Barrow Farm house all at once. She had to wait while Jerrold had the place made beautiful for her.

This was the only thing that roused him to any interest. Through all his misery he could still find pleasure in the work of throwing small rooms into one to make more space for Anne, and putting windows into the south gable to give her the sun.

Anne's garden absorbed him more than his own seven hundred acres. Maisie and he planned it together, walking round the rank flower-beds, and bald wastes scratched up by the hens.

There was to be a flagged court on one side and a grass plot on the other, with a flower garden between. Here, Maisie said, there should be great clumps of larkspurs and there a lavender hedge. They said how nice it would be for Anne to watch the garden grow.

"He's going to make it so beautiful that you'll want to stay in it forever," she said.

And Anne went with them and listened to them, and told them they were angels, and pretended to be excited about her house and garden, while all the time her heart ached and she was too tired to care.

The house was finished by the end of November and Jerrold and Maisie helped her to furnish it. Maisie sent to London for patterns and brought them to Anne to choose. Maisie thought perhaps the chintz with the cream and pink roses, or the one with the green leaves and red tulips and blue and purple clematis was the prettiest. Anne tried to behave as if all her happiness depended on a pattern, and ended by choosing the one that Maisie liked best. And the furniture went where Maisie thought it should go, because Anne was too tired to care. Besides, she was busy on her farm. Old Sutton in his decadence had let most of his arable land run to waste, and Anne's job was to make good soil again out of bad.

Maisie was pleased like a child and excited with her planning. Her idea was that Anne should come in from her work on the land and find the house all ready for her, everything in its place, chairs and sofas dressed in their gay suits of chintz, the books on their shelves, the blue-and-white china in rows on the oak dresser.

Tea was set out on the gate-legged table before the wide hearth-place. The lamps were lit. A big fire burned. Colin and Jerrold and Maisie were there waiting for her. And Anne came in out of the fields, tired and white and thin, her black hair drooping. Her rough land dress hung slack on her slender body.

Jerrold looked at her. Anne's tired face, trying to smile, wrung his heart. So did the happiness in Maisie's eyes. And Anne's voice trying to sound as if she were happy.

"You darlings! How nice you've made it."

"Do you like it?"

Maisie was breathless with joy.

"I love it. I adore it! But--aren't there lots of things that weren't here before? Where did that table come from?"

"From the Manor Farm. Don't you remember it? That's Eliot."

"And the bureau, and the dresser, and those heavenly rugs?"

"That's Jerrold."

And the china was Colin, and the chintz was Maisie. The long couch for Anne to lie down on was Maisie. Everything that was not Anne's they had given her.

"You shouldn't have done it," she said.

"We did it for ourselves. To keep you with us," said Maisie.

"Did you think it would take all that?"

She wondered whether they saw how hard she was trying to look happy, not to be too tired to care.

Then Maisie took her upstairs to show her her bedroom and the white bathroom. Colin carried the lamp. He left them together in Anne's room. Maisie turned to her there.

"Darling, how tired you look. Are you too tired to be happy?"

"I'd be a brute if I weren't happy," Anne said.

But she wasn't happy. The minute they were gone her sadness came upon her, crushing her down. She could hear Colin and Maisie, the two innocent ones, laughing out into the darkness. She saw again Jerrold's hard, unhappy face trying to smile; his mouth jerking in the tight, difficult smile that was like an agony. And it used to be Jerrold who was always happy, who went laughing.

She turned up and down the beautiful lighted room; she looked again and again at the things they had given her, Colin and Jerrold and Maisie.

Maisie. She would have to live with the cruelty of Maisie's gifts, with Maisie's wounding kindness and her innocence. Maisie's curtains, Maisie's couch, covered with flowers that smiled at her, gay on the white ground. She thought of the other house, of the curtains that had shut out the light from her and Jerrold, of the couch where she had lain in his arms. Each object had a dumb but poignant life that reminded and reproached her.

This was the scene where her life was to be cast. Henceforth these things would know her in her desolation. Jerrold would never come to her here as he had come to the Manor Farm house; they would never sit together talking by this fireside; those curtains would never be drawn on their passion; he would never go up to that lamp and put it out; she would never lie here waiting, thrilling, as he came to her through the darkness.

She had wanted the Barrow Farm and she had got what she had wanted, and she had got it too late. She loved it. Yet how was it possible to love the place that she was to be so unhappy in? She ought to hate it with its enclosing walls, its bright-eyed, watching furniture, its air of quiet complicity in her pain.

She drew back the curtains. The lamp and its yellow flame hung out there on the darkness of the fields. The fields dropped away through the darkness to the river, and there were the black masses of the trees.

There the earth waited for her. Out there was the only life left for her to live.

The life of struggling with the earth, forcing the earth to yield to her more than it had yielded to the men who had tilled it before her, making the bad land good. Ploughing time would come and seed time, and hay harvest and corn harvest. Feeding time and milking time would come. She would go on seeing the same things done at the same hour, at the same season, day after day and year after year. There would have been joy in that if it had been Jerrold's land, if she could have gone on working for Jerrold and with Jerrold. And if she had not been so tired.

She was only twenty-nine and Jerrold was only thirty-two. She wondered how many more ploughing times they would have to go through, how many seed times and harvests. And how would they go through them? Would they go on getting more and more tired, or would something happen?

No. Nothing would happen. Nothing that they could bear to think of. They would just go on.

In the stillness of the house she could feel her heart beating, measuring out time, measuring out her pain.

That winter Adeline and John Severn came down to Wyck Manor for Christmas and the New Year.

Adeline was sitting in the drawing-room with Maisie in the heavy hour before tea time. All afternoon she had been trying to talk to Maisie, and she was now bored. Jerrold's wife had always bored her. She couldn't imagine why Jerrold had married her when it was so clear that he was not in love with her.

"It's funny," she said at last, "staying in your own house when it isn't your own any more."

Maisie hoped that Adeline would treat the house as if it were her own.

"I probably shall. Don't be surprised if you hear me giving orders to the servants. I really cannot consider that Wilkins belongs to anybody but me."

Maisie hoped that Adeline wouldn't consider that he didn't.

And there was a pause. Adeline looked at the clock and saw that there was still another half-hour till tea time. How could they possibly fill it in? Then, suddenly, from a thought of Jerrold so incredibly married to Maisie, Adeline's mind wandered to Anne.

"Is Anne dining here tonight?" she said.

And Maisie said yes, she thought Adeline and Mr. Severn would like to see as much as possible of Anne. And Adeline said that was very kind of Maisie, and was bored again.

She saw nothing before her but more and more boredom; and the subject of Anne alone held out the prospect of relief. She flew to it as she would have fled from any danger.

"By the way, Maisie, if I were you I wouldn't let Anne see too much of Jerrold."

"Why not?"

"Because, my dear, it isn't good for her."

"I should have thought," Maisie said, "it was very good for both of them, as they like each other. I should never dream of interfering with their friendship. That's the way people get themselves thoroughly disliked. I don't want Jerry to dislike me, or Anne, either. I like them to feel that if he *is* married they can go on being friends just the same."

"Oh, of course, if you like it----"

"I do like it," said Maisie, firmly.

Firm opposition was a thing that Adeline's wilfulness could never stand. It always made her either change the subject or revert to her original statement. This time she reverted.

"My point was that it isn't fair to Anne."

"Why isn't it?"

"Because she's in love with him."

"That," said Maisie, with increasing decision, "I do *not* believe. I've never seen any signs of it."

"You're the only person who hasn't then. It sticks out of her. If it was a secret I shouldn't have told you."

"It is a secret to me," said Maisie, "so I think you might let it alone."

"You ought to know it if nobody else does. We've all of us known about Anne for ages. She was always quite mad about Jerrold. It was funny when she was a little thing; but it's rather more serious now she's thirty."

"She isn't thirty," said Maisie, contradictiously.

"Almost thirty. It's a dangerous age, Maisie. And Anne's a dangerous person.

She's absolutely reckless. She always was."

"I thought you thought she was in love with Colin."

"I never thought it."

Maisie hated people who lied to her.

"Why did you tell Jerrold they were lovers, then?" she said.

"Did I tell Jerrold they were lovers?"

"He thinks you did."

"He must have misunderstood what I said. Colin gave me his word of honour that there was nothing between them."

But Maisie had no mercy.

"Why should he do that if you didn't think there was? If you were mistaken then you may be mistaken now."

"I'm not mistaken now. Ask Colin, ask Eliot, ask Anne's father."

"I shouldn't dream of asking them. You forget, if Jerrold's my husband, Anne's my friend."

"Then for goodness sake keep her out of mischief. Keep her out of Jerrold's way. Anne's a darling and I'm devoted to her, but she always did love playing with fire. If she's bent on burning her pretty wings it isn't kind to bring her where the lamp is."

"I'd trust Anne's wings to keep her out of danger."

"How about Jerrold's danger? You might think of him."

"I do think of him. And I trust him. Absolutely."

"I don't. I don't trust anybody absolutely."

"One thing's clear," said Maisie, "that it's time we had tea."

She got up, with an annihilating dignity, and rang the bell. Adeline's smile intimated that she was unbeaten and unconvinced.

That evening John Severn came into his wife's room as she was dressing for dinner.

"I wish to goodness Anne hadn't this craze for farming," he said. "She's simply working herself to death. I never saw her look so seedy. I'm sorry Jerrold let her have that farm."

"So am I," said Adeline. "I never saw Jerry look so seedy, either. Maisie's been behaving like a perfect idiot. If she wanted them to go off together she couldn't have done better."

"You don't imagine," John said, "that's what they're after?"

"How do I know what they're after? You never can tell with people like Jerrold and Anne. They're both utterly reckless. They don't care who suffers so long as they get what they want. If Anne had the morals of a--of a mouse, she'd clear out."

"I think," John said, "you're mistaken. Anne isn't like that.... I hope you haven't said anything to Maisie?"

Adeline made a face at him, as much as to say, "What do you take me for?" She lifted up her charming, wilful face and powdered it carefully.

The earth smelt of the coming rain. All night the trees had whispered of rain coming to-morrow. Now they waited.

At noon the wind dropped. Thick clouds, the colour of dirty sheep's wool, packed tight by their own movement, roofed the sky and walled it round, hanging close to the horizon. A slight heaving and swelling in the grey mass packed it tighter. It was pregnant with rain. Here and there a steaming vapour broke from it as if puffed out by some immense interior commotion. Thin tissues detached themselves and hung like a frayed hem, lengthening, streaming to the hilltops in the west.

Anne was going up the fields towards the Manor and Jerrold was coming down towards the Manor Farm. They met at the plantation as the first big drops fell.

He called out to her, "I say, you oughtn't to be out a day like this."

Anne had been ill all January with a slight touch of pleurisy after a cold that she had taken no care of.

"I'm going to see Maisie."

"You're *not*," he said. "It's going to rain like fury."

"Maisie knows I don't mind rain," Anne said, and laughed.

"Maisie'd have a fit if she knew you were out in it. Look, how it's coming down over there."

Westwards and northwards the round roof and walls of cloud were shaken and the black rain hung sheeted between sky and earth. Overhead the dark tissues thinned out and lengthened. The fir trees quivered; they gave out slight creaking, crackling noises as the rain came down. It poured off each of the sloping fir branches like a jet from a tap.

"We must make a dash for it," Jerrold said. And they ran together, laughing, down the field to Anne's shelter at the bottom. He pushed back the sliding door.

The rain drummed on the roof and went hissing along the soaked ground; it sprayed out as the grass bent and parted under it; every hollow tuft was a water spout. The fields were dim behind the shining, glassy bead curtain of the rain.

The wind rose again and shook the rain curtain and blew it into the shelter. Rain scudded across the floor, wetting them where they stood. Jerrold slid the door to. They were safe now from the downpour.

Anne's bed stood in the corner tucked up in its grey blankets. They sat down on it side by side.

For a moment they were silent, held by their memory. They were shut in there with their past. It came up to them, close and living, out of the bright, alien mystery of the rain.

He put his hand on the shoulder of Anne's coat to feel if it was wet. At his touch she trembled.

"It hasn't gone through, has it?"

"No," she said and coughed again.

"Anne, I hate that cough of yours. You never had a cough before."

"I've never had pleurisy before."

"You wouldn't have had it if you hadn't been frightfully run down."

"It's all over now," she said.

"It isn't. You may get it again. I don't feel as if you were safe for one minute. Are you warm?"

"Quite."

"Are your feet wet?"

"No. No. No. Don't worry, Jerry dear; I'm all right."

"I wouldn't worry if I was with you all the time. It's not seeing you. Not knowing."

"Don't," she said. "I can't bear it."

And they were silent again.

Their silence was more real to them than the sounding storm. There was danger in it. It drew them back and back. It was poignant and reminiscent. It came to them like the long stillness before their passion. They had waited here before, like this, through moments tense and increasing, for the supreme, toppling instant of their joy.

Their minds went round and round, looking for words to break the silence and finding none. They were held there by their danger.

At last Anne spoke.

"Do you think it's over?"

"No. It's only just begun."

The rain hurled itself against the window, as if it would pluck them out into the storm. It brimmed over from the roof like water poured out from a bucket.

"We'll have to sit tight till it stops," he said.

Silence again, long, inveterate, dangerous. Every now and then Anne coughed, the short, hard cough that hurt and frightened him. He knew he ought to leave her; every minute increased their danger. But he couldn't go. He felt that, after all they might have done and hadn't done, heaven had some scheme of compensation in which it owed them this moment.

She turned from him coughing, and that sign of her weakness, the sight of her thin shoulders shaking filled him with pity that was passion itself. He thought of the injustice life had heaped on Anne's innocence; of the cruelty that had tracked her and hunted her down; of his own complicity with her suffering. He thought of his pity for Maisie as treachery to Anne, of his honour as cowardice. Instead of piling up wall after wall, he ought never to have let anything come between him and Anne. Not even Maisie. Not even his honour. His honour belonged to Anne far more than to Maisie. The rest had been his own blundering folly, and he had no right to let Anne be punished for it.

An hour ago the walls had stood solid between them. Now a furious impulse seized him to tear them down and get through to her. This time he would hold her and never let her go.

His thoughts went the way his passion went. Then suddenly she turned and they looked at each other and he thought no more. All his thoughts went down in the hot rushing darkness of his blood.

"Anne," he said, "Anne"--His voice sounded like a cry.

They stood up suddenly and were swept together; he held her tight, shut in his arms, his body straining to her. They clung to each other as if only by clinging they could stand against the hot darkness that drowned them; and the more they clung the more it came over them, wave after wave.

Then in the darkness he heard her crying to him to let her go.

"Don't make me, Jerrold, don't make me."

"Yes. Yes."

"No. Oh, why did we ever come here?"

He pressed her closer and she tried to push him off with weak hands that had once been strong. He felt her breakable in his arms, and utterly defenceless.

"I can't," she cried. "I should feel as if Maisie were there and looking at us.... Don't make me."

Suddenly he let her go.

He was beaten by the sheer weakness of her struggle. He couldn't fight for his flesh, like a brute, against that helplessness.

"If I go, you'll stay here till the rain stops?"

"Yes. I'm sorry, Jerry. You'll get so wet."

That made him laugh. And, laughing, he left her. Then tears came, cutting through his eyelids like blood from a dry wound. They mixed with the rain and blinded him.

And Anne sat on the little grey bed in her shelter and stared out at the rain and cried.

XIX
ANNE AND ELIOT

She knew what she would do now.

She would go away and never see Jerrold again, never while their youth lasted, while they could still feel. She would go out of England, so far away that they couldn't meet. She would go to Canada and farm.

All night she lay awake with her mind fixed on the one thought of going away. There was nothing else to be done, no room for worry or hesitation. They couldn't hold out any longer, she and Jerrold, strained to the breaking-point, tortured with the sight of each other.

As she lay awake there came to her the peace that comes with all immense and clear decisions. Her mind would never be torn and divided any more. And towards morning she fell asleep.

She woke dulled and bewildered. Her mind struggled with a sense of appalling yet undefined disaster. Something had happened overnight, she couldn't remember what. Something had happened. No. Something was going to happen. She tried to fall back into sleep, fighting against the return of consciousness; it came on, wave after wave, beating her down.

Now she remembered. She was going away. She would never see Jerrold again. She was going to Canada.

The sharp, clear name made the whole thing real and irrevocable. It was something that would actually happen soon. To her. She was going. And when she had gone she would not come back.

She got up and looked out of the window. She saw the green field sloping down to the river and the road, and beyond the road, to the right, the rise of the Manor fields and the belt of firs. And in her mind, more real than they, the Manor house, the garden, and the many-coloured hills beyond, rolling, curve after curve, to the straight, dark-blue horizon. The scene that held her childhood, all her youth, all her happiness; that had drawn her back, again and again, in memory and in dreams, making her heart ache. How could she leave it? How could she live with that pain?

If she was going to be a coward, if she was going to be afraid of pain--How was she to escape it, how was Jerrold to escape? If she stayed on they would break down together and give in; they would be lovers again, and again Maisie's sweet, wounding face would come between them; they could never get away from it; and in the end their remorse would be as unbearable as their separation. She couldn't drag Jerrold through that agony again.

No. Life wasn't worth living if you were a coward and afraid. And under all her misery Anne had still the sense that life was somehow worth living even if it made you miserable. Life was either your friend or your enemy. If it was your friend you served it; if it was your enemy you stood up to it and refused to let it beat you, and your enemy became your servant. Whatever happened, your work remained. Still there would be ploughing and sowing, and reaping and ploughing again. Still the earth waited. She thought of the unknown Canadian earth that waited for her tilling.

Jerrold was not a coward. He was not afraid--well, only afraid of the people he loved getting ill and dying; and she was not going to get ill and die.

She would have to tell him. She would go to him in the fields and tell him.

But before she did that she must make the thing irrevocable. So Anne wrote to the steamship company, booking her passage in two weeks' time; she wrote to Eliot, asking him to call at the company's office and see if he could get her a decent cabin. She went to Wyck and posted her letters, and then to the Far Acres field where Jerrold was watching the ploughing.

They met at the "headland." They would be safe there on the ploughed land, in the open air.

"What is it, Anne?" he said.

"Nothing. I want to talk to you."

"All right."

Her set face, her hard voice gave him a premonition of disaster.

"It's simply this," she said. "What happened yesterday mustn't happen again."

"It shan't. I swear it shan't. I was a beast. I lost my head."

"Yes, but it may happen again. We can't go on like this, Jerry. The strain's too awful."

"You mean you can't trust me."

"I can't trust myself. And it isn't fair to you."

"Oh, me. That doesn't matter."

"Well, then, say *I* matter. It's the same for me. I'm never going to let that happen again. I'm going away."

"Going away--"

"Yes. And I'm not coming back this time."

His voice struggled in his throat. Something choked him. He couldn't speak.

"I'm going to Canada in a fortnight."

"Good God! You can't go to Canada."

"I can. I've booked my passage."

His face was suddenly sallow white, ghastly. His heart heaved and he felt sick.

"Nothing on earth will stop me."

"Won't Maisie stop you? If you do this she'll know. Can't you see how it gives us away?"

"No. It'll only give *me* away. If Maisie asks me why I'm going I shall tell her I'm in love with you, and that I can't stand it; that I'm too unhappy. I'd rather she thought I cared for you than that she should think you cared for me."

"She'll think it all the same."

"Then I shall have to lie. I must risk it.... Oh Jerry, don't look so awful! I've got to go. We've settled it that we can't go on deceiving her, and we aren't going to make her unhappy. There's nothing else to be done."

"Except to bear it."

"And how long do you suppose that'll last? We *can't* bear it. Look at it straight. It's all so horribly simple. If we were beasts and only thought of ourselves and didn't think of Maisie it wouldn't matter to us what we did. But we can't be beasts. We can't lie to Maisie, and we can't tell her the truth. We can't go on seeing each other without wanting each other--unbearably--and we can't go on wanting each other without--some day--giving in. It comes back the first minute we're alone. And we don't mean to give in. So we mustn't see each other, that's all. Can you tell me one other thing I can do?"

"But why should it be *you*? Why should you get the worst of it?"

"Because one of us has got to clear out. It can't be you, so it's got to be me. And going away isn't the worst of it. It'll be worse for you sticking on here where everything reminds you--At least I shall have new things to keep my mind off it."

"Nothing will keep your mind off it. You'll fret yourself to death."

"No, I shan't. I shall have too much to do. You're *not* to be sorry for me, Jerrold."

"But you're giving up everything. The Barrow Farm. The place you wanted. You won't have a thing."

"I don't want 'things.' It's easier to chuck them than to hang on to them when they'll remind me.... Really, if I could see any other way I'd take it."

"But you can't go. You're not fit to go. You're ill."

"I shall be all right when I get there."

"But what do you think you're going to *do* in Canada? It's not as if you'd got anything to go for."

"I shall find something. I shall work on somebody's ranch first and learn Canadian farming. Then I shall look out for land and buy it. I've got stacks of money. All Grandpapa Everitt's, and the money for the farm. Stacks. I shall get on all right."

"When did you think of all this?"

"Last night."

"I see. I made you."

"No. I made myself. After all, it's the easiest way."

"For you, or me?"

"For both of us. Honestly, it's the only straight thing. I ought to have done it long ago."

"It means never seeing each other again. You'll never come back."

"Never while we're young. When we're both old, too old to feel any more, then I'll come back some day, and we'll be friends."

And still his will beat against hers in vain, till at last he stopped; sick and exhausted.

They went together down the ploughed land into the pastures, and through the pastures to the mill water. In the opposite field they could see the brown roof and walls of the shelter.

"What are you going to plant in the Seven Acres field?"

"Barley," he said.

"You can't. It was barley last year."

"Was it?"

They were silent then. Jerrold struggled with his feeling of deadly sickness. Anne couldn't trust herself to speak. At the Barrow Farm gate they parted.

Maisie's eyes looked at him across the table, wondering. Her little drooping mouth was half open with anxiety, as if any minute she was going to say something. The looking-glass had shown him his haggard and discoloured face, a face to frighten her. He tried to eat, but the sight and smell of hot roast mutton sickened him.

"Oh, Jerrold, can't you eat it?"

"No, I can't. I'm sorry."

"There's some cold chicken. Will you have that?"

"No, thanks."

"Try and eat something."

"I can't. I feel sick."

"Don't sit up, then. Go and lie down."

"I will if you don't mind."

He went to his room and was sick. He lay down on his bed and tried to sleep. His head ached violently and every movement made him heave; he couldn't sleep; he couldn't lie still; and presently he got up and went out again, up to the Far Acres field to the ploughing. He couldn't overcome the physical sickness of his misery, but he could force himself to move, to tramp up and down the stiff furrows, watching the tractor; he kept himself going by the sheer strength of his will. The rattle and clank of the tractor ground into his head, making it ache again. He was stunned with great blows of noise and pain, so that he couldn't think. He didn't want to think; he was glad of the abominable sensations that stopped him. He went from field to field, avoiding the boundaries of the Barrow Farm lest he should see Anne.

When the sun set and the land darkened he went home.

At dinner he tried to eat, sickened again, and leaned back in his chair; he forced himself to sit through the meal, talking to Maisie. When it was over he went to bed and lay awake till the morning.

The next day passed in the same way, and the next night; and always he was aware of Maisie's sweet face watching him with frightened eyes and an unuttered question. He was afraid to tell her that Anne was going lest she should put down his illness to its true cause.

And on the third day, when he heard her say she was going to see Anne, he told her.

"Oh, Jerrold, she can't really mean it."

"She does mean it. I said everything I could to stop her, but it wasn't any good. She's taken her passage."

"But why--why should she want to go?"

"I can't tell you why. You'd better ask her."

"Has anything happened to upset her?"

"What on earth should happen?"

"Oh, I don't know. When did she tell you this?"

He hesitated. It was dangerous to lie when Maisie might get the truth from Anne.

"The day before yesterday."

Maisie's eyes were fixed on him, considering it. He knew she was saying to herself, "That was the day you came home so sick and queer."

"Jerry--did you say anything to upset her?"

"No."

"I can't think how she could want to go."

"Nor I. But she's going."

"I shall go down and see if I can't make her stay."

"Do. But you won't if I can't," he said.

Maisie went down early in the afternoon to see Anne.

She couldn't think how Anne could want to leave the Barrow Farm house when she had just got into it, when they had all made it so nice for her; she couldn't think how she could leave them when she cared for them, when she knew how they cared for her.

"You *do* care for us, Anne?"

"Oh yes, I care."

"And you *wanted* the farm. I can't understand your going just when you've got it, when you've settled, in and when Jerrold took all that trouble to make it nice for you. It isn't like you, Anne."

"I know. It must seem awful of me; but I can't help it, Maisie darling. I've *got* to go. You mustn't try and stop me. It only makes it harder."

"Then it *is* hard? You don't really want to go?"

"Of course I don't. But I must."

Maisie meditated, trying to make it out.

"Is it--is it because you're unhappy?"

Anne didn't answer.

"You *are* unhappy. You've been unhappy ever so long. Can't we do anything?"

"No. Nobody can do anything."

"It isn't," said Maisie at last, "anything to do with Jerrold?"

"You wouldn't ask me that, Maisie, if you didn't know it was."

"Perhaps I do know. Do you care for him very much, Anne?"

"Yes, I care for him, very much. And I can't stand it."

"It's so bad that you've got to go away?"

"It's so bad that I've got to go away."

"That's very brave of you."

"Or very cowardly."

"No. You couldn't be a coward.... Oh, Anne darling, I'm so sorry."

"Don't be sorry. It's my own fault. I'd no business to get into this state. Don't let's talk about it, Maisie."

"All right, I won't. But I'm sorry.... Only one thing. It--it hasn't made you hate me, has it?"

"You know it hasn't."

"Oh, Anne, you *are* beautiful."

"I'm anything but, if you only knew."

She had got beyond the pain of Maisie's goodness, Maisie's trust. No possible blow from Maisie's mind could hurt her now. Nothing mattered. Maisie's trust and goodness didn't matter, since she had done all she knew; since she was going away; since she would never see Jerrold again, never till their youth was gone and they had ceased to feel.

That afternoon Eliot arrived at Wyck Manor. His coming was his answer to Anne's letter.

He went over to the Barrow Farm about five o'clock when Anne's work would be done. Anne was still out, and he waited till she should come back.

As he waited he looked round her room. This, he thought, was the place that Anne had set her heart on having for her own; it was the home they had made for her. Something terrible must have happened before she could bring herself to leave it. She must have been driven to the breaking-point. She was broken. Jerrold must have driven and broken her.

He heard her feet on the flagged path, on the threshold of the house; she stood in the doorway of the room, looking at him, startled.

"Eliot, what are you doing there?"

"Waiting for you. You must have known I'd come."

"To say good-bye? That was nice of you."

"No, not to say good-bye. I should come to see you off if you were going."

"But I am going. You've seen about my berth, haven't you?"

"No, I haven't. We've got to talk about it first."

He looked dead tired. She remembered that she was his hostess.

"Have you had tea?"

"No. You're going to give me some. Then we'll talk about it."

"Talking won't be a bit of good."

"I think it may be," he said.

She rang the bell and they waited. She gave him his tea, and while they ate and drank he talked to her about the weather and the land, and about his work and the book he had just finished on Amoebic Dysentery, and about Colin and how well he was now. Neither of them spoke of Jerrold or of Maisie.

When the tea things were cleared away he leaned back and looked at her with his kind, deep-set, attentive eyes. She loved Eliot's eyes, and his queer, clever face that was so like and so unlike his father's, so utterly unlike Jerrold's.

"You needn't tell me why you're going," he said at last. "I've seen Jerrold."

"Did he tell you?"

"No. You've only got to look at him to see."

"Do you think Maisie sees?"

"I can't tell you. She isn't stupid. She must wonder why you're going like this."

"I told her. I told her I was in love with Jerrold."

"What did she say?"

"Nothing. Only that she was sorry. I told her so that she mightn't think he cared for me. She needn't know that."

"She isn't stupid," he said again.

"No. But she's good. She trusts him so. She trusted me.... Eliot, that was the worst of it, the way she trusted us. That broke us down."

"Of course she trusted you."

"Did you?"

"You know I did."

"And yet," she said, "I believe you knew. You knew all the time."

"If I didn't, I know now."

"Everything?"

"Everything."

"How? Because of my going away? Is that it?"

"Not altogether. I've seen you happy and I've seen you unhappy. I've seen you with Jerrold. I've seen you with Maisie. Nobody else would have seen it, but I did, because I knew you so well. And because I was afraid of it. Besides, you almost told me."

"Yes, and you said it wouldn't make any difference. Does it?"

"No. None. I know, whatever you did, you wouldn't do it only for yourself. You did this for Jerrold. And you were unhappy because of it."

"No. No. I was happy. We were only unhappy afterwards because of Maisie. It was so awful going on deceiving her, hiding it and lying. I feel as if everything I said and did then was a lie. That was how I was punished. Not being able to tell the truth. And I could have borne even that if it wasn't for Jerrold. But he hated it, too. It made him wretched."

"I know it did. If you hadn't been so fine it wouldn't have punished you."

"The horrible thing was knowing what I'd done to Jerrold, making him hide and lie."

"Oh, what you've done to Jerrold--You've done him nothing but good. You've made him finer than he could possibly have been without you."

"I've made him frightfully unhappy."

"Not unhappier than he's made you. And it's what he had to be. I told you long ago Jerrold wouldn't be any good till he'd suffered damnably. Well--he has suffered damnably. And he's got a soul because of it. He hadn't much of one before he loved you."

"How do you mean?"

"I mean he used to think of nothing but his own happiness. Now he's thinking of nothing but Maisie's and yours. He loves you better than himself. He even loves Maisie better--I mean he thinks more of her--than he did before he loved you. There are two people that he cares for more than himself. He cares more for his own honour than he did. And for yours. And that's your doing. Just think how you'd have wrecked him if you'd been a different sort of woman."

"No. Because then he wouldn't have cared for me."

"No, I believe he wouldn't. He chose well."

"You were always much too good to me."

"No, Anne. I want you to see this thing straight, and to see yourself as you really are. Not to go back on yourself."

"I don't go back on myself. That would be going back on Jerrold. I'm sorry because of Maisie, that's all. If I'd had an ounce of sense I'd never have known her. I'd have gone off to some place not too far away where Jerrold could have come to me and where I should never have seen Maisie. That's what I should have done. We should both have been happy then."

"Yes, Jerrold would have been happy. And he wouldn't have saved his soul. And he'd have been deceiving Maisie all the time. You don't really wish you'd done that, Anne."

"No. Not now. And I'm not unhappy about Maisie now. I'm going away. I'm giving Jerrold up. I can't do more than that."

"You wouldn't have to go away, Anne, if you'd do what I want and marry me.

You said perhaps you might if you had to save Jerrold."

"Did I? I don't think I did."

"You've forgotten and I haven't. You don't know what an appalling thing you're doing. You're leaving everything and everybody you ever cared for. You'll die of sheer unhappiness."

"Nonsense, Eliot. You know perfectly well that people don't die of unhappiness. They die of accidents and diseases and old age. I shall die of old age. And I'll be back in twenty years' time if I've seen it through."

"Twenty years. The best years of your life. You'll be desperately lonely. You don't know what it'll be like."

"Oh yes, I do. I've been lonely before now. And I've saved myself by working."

"Yes, in England, where you could see some of us sometimes. But out there, with people you never saw before--people who may be brutes--"

"They needn't be."

He went on relentlessly. "People you don't care for and never will care for. You've never really cared for anybody but us."

"I haven't. I'm going because I care. I can't let Jerry go on like that. I've got to end it."

"You're going simply to save Jerrold. So that you can never go back to him. Don't you see that if you married me you'd both be safe? You couldn't go back. If you were married to me Jerrold wouldn't take you from me. If you were married to me you wouldn't break faith with me. If you had children you wouldn't break faith with them. Nothing could keep you safer."

"I can't, Eliot. Nothing's changed. I belong to Jerrold. I always have belonged to him. It isn't anything physical. Even if I'm separated from him, thousands of miles, I shall belong to him still. My mind, or soul, or whatever the thing is, can't get away from him.... You say if I belonged to you I couldn't give myself to Jerrold. If I belong to Jerrold, how can I give myself to you?"

"I see. It's like that, is it?"

"It's like that."

Eliot said no more. He knew when he was beaten.

Maisie sat alone in her own room, thinking it over. She didn't know yet that Eliot had come. He had arrived while she was with Anne and she had missed him on the way to Barrow Farm, driving up by the hill road while he walked down through the fields.

She didn't think of Jerrold all at once. Her mind was taken up with Anne and Anne's unhappiness. She could see nothing else. She remembered how Adeline had told her that Anne was in love with Jerrold. She had said, "It was funny when she was a little thing." Anne had loved him all her life, then. All her life she had had to do without him.

Maisie thought: Perhaps he would have loved her and married her if it hadn't been for me. And yet Anne had loved her.

That was Anne's beauty.

She wondered next: If Anne had been in love with Jerrold all that time, and if they had all seen it, all the Fieldings and John Severn, how was it that she had never seen it? She had seen nothing but a perfect friendship, and she had tried to keep it for them in all its perfection, so that neither of them should miss anything because Jerrold had married her. She remembered how happy Anne had been when she first knew her, and she thought: If she was happy then, why is she unhappy now? If she loved Jerrold all her life, if she had done without him all her life, why go away now?

Unless something had happened.

It was then that Maisie thought of Jerrold, and his sad, drawn face and his sudden sickness the other day. That was the day he had been with Anne, when she had told him that she was going away. He had never been the same since. He had neither slept nor eaten.

Maisie had all the pieces of the puzzle loose before her, and at first sight not one of them looked as if it would fit. But this piece under her hand fitted. Jerrold's illness joined on to Anne's going. With a terrible dread in her heart Maisie put the two things together and saw the third thing. Jerrold was ill because Anne was going away. He wouldn't be ill unless he cared for her. And another thing. Anne was going away, not because she cared, but because Jerrold cared. Therefore she knew that he cared for her. Therefore he had told her. That was what had happened.

When she had put all the pieces into their places she would have the whole story.

But Maisie didn't want to know any more. She had enough to make her heart break. She still clung to her belief in their goodness. They were unhappy because they had given each other up. And under all her thinking, like a quick-running pain, there went her premonition of its end. She remembered that they had been happy once when she first knew them. If they were unhappy now because they had given each other up, had they been happy then because they hadn't? For a moment she asked herself, "Were they--?" and was afraid to finish and answer her own question. It was enough that they were all unhappy now and that none of them would ever be happy again. Not Anne. Not Jerrold. *Their* unhappiness didn't bear thinking of, and in thinking of it Maisie forgot her own.

Her heart shook her breast with its beating, and for a moment she wondered whether her pain were beginning again. Then the thought of Anne and Jerrold and herself and of their threefold undivided misery came upon her, annihilating every other thought. As if all that was physical in Maisie were subdued by the intensity of her suffering, with the coming of the supreme emotion her body had no pain.

XX
MAISIE, JERROLD, AND ANNE

She got up and dressed for dinner as if nothing had happened, or, rather, as if everything were about to happen and she were going through with it magnificently, with no sign that she was beaten. She didn't know yet what she would do; she didn't see clearly what there was to be done. She might not have to do anything; and yet again, vaguely, half-fascinated, half-frightened, she foresaw that she might be called on to do something, something that was hard and terrible and at the same time beautiful and supreme.

And downstairs in the hall, she found Eliot.

He told her that he had come down to see Anne and that he had done his best to keep her from going away and that it was all no good.

"We can't stop her. She's got an unbreakable will."

"Unbreakable," she said. "And yet she's broken."

"I know," he said.

In her nervous exaltation she felt that Eliot had been sent, that Eliot knew. Eliot was wise. He would help her.

"Eliot----" she said. "Will you see me in the library after dinner? I want to ask you something."

"If it's about Anne, I don't know that there's anything I can say."

"It's about Jerrold," she said.

After dinner he came to her in the library.

"Where's Jerrold?"

"In the drawing-room with Colin. He won't come in."

"Eliot, there's something awfully wrong with him. He can't sleep. He can't eat. He's sick if he tries."

"He looks pretty ghastly."

"Do you know what's the matter with him?"

"How can I know? He doesn't tell me anything."

"It's ever since he heard that Anne's going." "He's worried about her. So am I. So are you."

"He isn't worrying. He's fretting…. Eliot--do you think he cares for her?"

Eliot didn't answer her. He looked at her gravely, searchingly, as if he were measuring her strength before he answered.

"Don't be afraid to tell me. I'm not a coward."

"I haven't anything to tell you. It isn't altogether this affair of Anne's. Jerrold hasn't been fit for a long time."

"It's been going on for a long time."

"What makes you think so?"

"Oh," said Maisie, "everything."

"Then why don't you ask him?"

"But--if it is so--would he tell me?"

"I don't know. Perhaps he wants to tell you, only he's afraid. Anyhow, if it isn't so he'll tell you and you'll be happy."

"Somehow I don't think I'm going to be happy."

"Then," he said, "you're going to be brave."

She thought: He knows. He's known all the time, only he won't give them away.

"Yes," she said, "I'll ask him."

"Maisie--if it is so what will you do?"

"Do? There's only one thing I *can* do."

She turned to him, and her milk-white face was grey-white, ashen; the skin had a slack, pitted look, suddenly old. The soft flesh trembled. But her mouth and eyes were still. In this moment of her agony no base emotion defaced their sweetness, so that she seemed to him utterly composed. She had seen what she could do. Something hard and terrible.

"I can set him free."

That was the end she had seen before her, vaguely, as something not only hard and terrible, but beautiful and supreme. To leave off clinging to the illusion of her happiness. To let go. And with that letting go she was aware that an obscure horror had been hanging over her for three days and three nights and was now gone. She stood free of herself, in a great light and peace, so that presently when Jerrold came to her she met him with an incomparable tranquillity.

"Jerrold--"

The slight throbbing of her voice startled him coming out of her stillness.

They stood up, facing each other, in attitudes that had no permanence, as if what must pass between them now would be sudden and soon over.

"Do you care for Anne?"

The words dropped clear through her stillness, vibrating. His eyes went from her, evading the issue. Her voice came with a sharper stress.

"I **must** know. **Do** you care for her?"

"Yes."

"And that's why she's going?"

"Yes. That's why she's going. Did Eliot say anything?"

"No. He only told me to ask you. He said you'd tell me the truth."

"I have told you the truth. I'm sorry, Maisie."

"I know you're sorry. So am I."

"But, you see, it isn't as if I'd begun after I married you. I've cared for her all my life."

"Then why didn't you marry her?"

"Because, first of all, I didn't know I cared. And afterwards I thought she cared for Colin."

"You never asked her?"

"No. I thought--I thought they were lovers."

"You thought that of her?"

"Well, yes. I thought it would be just like her to give everything. I knew if she cared enough she'd stick at nothing. She wouldn't do it for herself."

"That was--when?"

"The time I came home on leave three years ago."

"The time you married me. Why did you marry me, if you didn't care for me?"

"I would have cared for you if I hadn't cared for her."

"But, when you cared for her----?"

"I thought we should find something in it. I wanted you to be happy. More than anything I wanted you to be happy. I thought I'd be killed in my next action and that nothing would matter."

"That you wouldn't have to keep it up?"

"Oh, I'd have kept it up all right if Anne hadn't been there. I cared enough for you to want you to be happy. I wanted you to have a child. You'd have liked that. That would have made you happy."

"Poor Jerrold----"

"I'd have been all right if I hadn't seen Anne again."

"When did you see her again?"

"Last spring."

"Only last spring?"

"Yes, only."

"When I was away."

She remembered. She remembered how she had first come to Wyck and found Jerrold happy and superbly well.

"But," she said, "you were happy then."

He sighed, a long, tearing sigh that hurt her.

"Yes. We were happy then."

And in a flash of terrific clarity she remembered her home-coming and the night that followed it and Jerrold's acquiescence in their separation.

"Then," she said, "if you were happy----"

"Do you want to know how far it went?"

"I want to know everything. I want the truth. I think you owe me the truth."

"It went just as far as it could go."

"Do you mean----"

He stood silent and she found his words for him.

"You were Anne's lover?"

"Yes."

Her face changed before him, as it had changed an hour ago before Eliot, ashen-white and slack, quivering, suddenly old.

Tears came into his eyes, tears of remorse and pity. She saw them and her heart ached for him.

"It didn't last long," he said.

"How long?"

"From March till--till September."

"I remember."

"Maisie--I can't ask you to forgive me. But you must forgive Anne. It wasn't her fault. I made her do it. And she's been awfully unhappy about it, because of you."

"Ah--that was why----"

"Won't you forgive her?"

"I forgive you both. I don't know how I should have felt if you'd been happy. I can't see anything but your unhappiness."

"We gave it up because of you. That was Anne. She couldn't bear going on after she knew you, when you were such an angel. It was your goodness and sweetness broke us down."

"But if I'd been the most disagreeable person it would have been just as *wrong*."

"It wouldn't, for in that case we shouldn't have deceived you. I should have told you straight and left you."

"Why didn't you tell me, Jerrold? Why didn't you tell me in the beginning?"

"We were afraid. We didn't want to hurt you."

"As if that mattered."

"It did matter. We were going to tell you. Then you were ill and we couldn't. We thought you'd die of it, with your poor little heart in that state."

"Oh, my dear, did you suppose I'd hurt you that way?"

"That was what we couldn't bear. Not being straight about it. That was why we gave each other up. It never happened again. Anne's going away so that it mayn't happen.... Maisie--you *do* believe me?"

"Yes, I believe you. I believe you did all you knew."

"We did. But it's my fault that Anne's going. I lost my head, and she was afraid."

"If only you'd told me. I shouldn't have been hard on you, Jerry. You knew that, didn't you?"

"Yes. I knew."

"And you went through all that agony rather than hurt me."

"Yes."

"The least I can do, then, is to let you go."

"Would you, Maisie?"

"Of course. I married you to make you happy. I must make you happy this way, that's all. But if I do you mustn't think I don't care for you. I care for you so much that nothing matters but your happiness."

"Maisie, I'm not fit to live in the same world with you."

"You mustn't say that. You're fit to live in the same world with Anne. I suppose I could have made this all ugly and shameful for you. But I want to keep it beautiful. I want to give you all beautiful to Anne, so that you'll never go back on it, and never feel ashamed."

"You made me ashamed every time we thought of you."

"Don't think of me. Think of each other."

"Oh--you're adorable."

"No, I'm doing this because I love you both. But if I didn't love you I should do it for myself. I should hate myself if I didn't. I can't think of anything more disgusting and dishonourable than to keep a man tied to you when he cares for somebody else. I should feel as if I were living in sin."

"Maisie--will you be awfully unhappy?"

"Yes, Jerrold. But not so unhappy as if I'd kept you."

"We'll go away somewhere where you won't have to see us."

"No. It's I who'll go away."

"But I want you to have the Manor and--and everything. Colin'll look after the estate for me."

"Do you think I could stay here after you'd gone?... No, Jerry, I can't do that for you. You can't make it up that way."

"I wasn't dreaming of making it up. I simply owe you everything, everlastingly, and there's nothing I can do. I only remembered that you liked the garden."

"I couldn't bear it. I should hate the garden. I should hate the whole place."

"I've done that to you?"

"Yes, you've done that to me. It can't be helped."

"But, what will you *do*, Maisie?"

"I shall go back to my own people. They happen to care for me."

That was her one reproach.

"Do you think *I* don't?"

"Oh no. I've done the only thing that would make you care. Perhaps that's what I did it for."

He took the hand she gave him and bowed his head over it and kissed it.

Maisie had a long talk with Eliot after Jerrold had left her.

She was still tranquil and composed, but Jerrold was worried. He was afraid lest the emotion roused by his confession should bring on her pain. That night Eliot slept in his father's room, so that he could go to her if the attack came.

But it did not come.

Late in the afternoon Jerrold went down to the Barrow Farm and saw Anne. He came back with a message from her. Anne wanted to see Maisie, if Maisie would let her.

"But she thinks you won't," he said.

"Why should I?"

"She's desperately unhappy."

She turned from him as if she would have left him, and then stayed.

"You want me to see her?"

"If you wouldn't hate it too much."

"I shall hate it. But I'll see her. Go and bring her."

She dreaded more than anything the sight of Anne. Her new knowledge of her made Anne strange and terrible. She felt that she would be somehow different. She would see something in her that she had never seen before, that she couldn't bear to see. Anne's face would show her that Jerrold was her lover.

Yet, if she had never seen that look, if she had never seen anything in Anne's face that was not beautiful, what did that mean but that Anne's love for him was beautiful? Before it had touched her body it had lived a long time in her soul. Either Anne's soul was beautiful because of it, or it was beautiful because of Anne's soul; and Maisie knew that if she too was to be beautiful she must keep safe the beauty of their passion as she had kept safe the beauty of their friendship. It was clear and hard, unbreakable as crystal. *She* had been the one flaw in it, the thing that had damaged its perfection. Now that she had let Jerrold go it would be perfect.

Anne stood in the doorway of the library, looking at her and not speaking. She was the same that she had been yesterday, and before that, and before that; dressed in the farm clothes that were the queer rough setting of her charm. The same, except that she was still more broken, still more beaten, and still more beautiful in her defeat.

"Anne--"

Maisie got up and waited, as Anne shut the door and stood there with her back to it.

"Maisie--I don't know why I've come. There were things I wanted to say to you, but I can't say them."

"You want to say you're sorry you took Jerrold from me."

"I'm bitterly sorry."

She came forward with a slender, awkward grace. Her eyes were fixed on Maisie, thrown open, expecting pain; but she didn't shrink or cower.

Maisie's voice came with its old sweetness.

"You didn't take him from me. You couldn't take what I haven't got."

"I gave him up, Maisie. I couldn't bear it."

"And I've given him up. *I* couldn't bear it, either. But," she said, "it was harder for you. You had him. I'm only giving up what I've never really had. Don't be too unhappy about it."

"I shall always be unhappy when I think of you. You've been such an angel to me. If we could only have told you."

"Yes. If only you'd told me. That was where you went wrong, Anne."

"I couldn't tell you. You were so ill. I thought it would kill you."

"Well, what if it had? You shouldn't have thought of me, you should have thought of Jerrold."

"I did think of him. I didn't want him to have agonies of remorse. It's been bad enough as it is."

"I know what it's been, Anne."

"That's what I really came for now. To see if you'd had that pain again."

"You needn't be afraid. I shall never have that pain again. Eliot told me all about it last night."

"What did he say?"

"He showed me how it all happened. I was ill because I couldn't face the truth. The truth was that Jerrold didn't care for me. It seems my mind knew it all the time when I didn't. I did know it once, and part of me went on feeling the shock of it, while the other part was living like a fool in an illusion, thinking he cared. And now I've been dragged out of it into reality. I'm facing it. *This* is real. And whatever I may be I shan't be ill again, not with that illness. I couldn't help it, but in a way it was as false as if I'd made it up on purpose to hide the truth. And the truth's cured me."

"Eliot told me it might. And I wouldn't believe him."

"You can believe him now. He said you and Jerrold were all right because you'd faced the truth about yourselves and each other. You held on to reality."

"Eliot said that?"

"Yes. He said it was the test of everybody, how they took reality, and that Jerrold had had to learn how, but that you had always known. You were so true that your worst punishment was not being able to tell me the truth. I was to think of you like that."

"How can you bear to think of me at all?"

"How can I bear to live? But I shall live."

Maisie's voice dropped, note by note, like clear, rounded tears, pressed out and shaped by pain.

Anne's voice came thick and quivering out of her dark secret anguish, like a voice from behind shut doors.

"Jerrold said you'd forgiven me. Have you?"

"It would be easier for you if I didn't. But I can't help forgiving you when you're so unhappy. I wouldn't have forgiven you if you hadn't told me the truth, if I'd had to find it out that time when you were happy. Then I'd have hated you."

"You don't now?"

"No. I don't want to see you again, or Jerrold, either, for a long time. But that's because I love you."

"Me?"

"Yes, you too, Anne."

"How *can* you love me?"

"Because I'm like you, Anne; I'm faithful."

"I wasn't faithful to you, Maisie."

"You were to Jerrold."

Anne still stood there, silent, taking in silence the pain of Maisie's goodness, Maisie's love.

Then Maisie ended it.

"He's waiting for you," she said, "to take you home."

Anne went to him where he stood by the terrace steps, illuminated by the light from the windows. In there she could hear Colin playing, a loud, tempestuous music. Jerrold waited.

She went past him down the steps without a word, and he followed her through the garden.

"Anne--" he said.

Under the blackness of the yew hedge she turned to him, and their hands met.

"Don't be afraid," he said. "Next week I'll take you away somewhere till it's over."

"Where?"

"Oh, somewhere a long way off, where you'll be happy."

Somewhere a long way off, beyond this pain, beyond this day and this night, their joy waited.

"And Maisie?" she said.

"Maisie wants you to be happy."

He held her by the hand as he used to hold her when they were children, to keep her safe. And hand in hand, like children, they went down through the twilight of the fields, together.

The Codes Of Hammurabi And Moses
W. W. Davies

QTY

The discovery of the Hammurabi Code is one of the greatest achievements of archaeology, and is of paramount interest, not only to the student of the Bible, but also to all those interested in ancient history...

Religion   ISBN: *1-59462-338-4*   **Pages:132**

MSRP $12.95

The Theory of Moral Sentiments
Adam Smith

QTY

This work from 1749. contains original theories of conscience amd moral judgment and it is the foundation for systemof morals.

Philosophy ISBN: *1-59462-777-0*   **Pages:536**

MSRP $19.95

Jessica's First Prayer
Hesba Stretton

QTY

In a screened and secluded corner of one of the many railway-bridges which span the streets of London there could be seen a few years ago, from five o'clock every morning until half past eight, a tidily set-out coffee-stall, consisting of a trestle and board, upon which stood two large tin cans, with a small fire of charcoal burning under each so as to keep the coffee boiling during the early hours of the morning when the work-people were thronging into the city on their way to their daily toil...

Pages:84

Childrens   ISBN: *1-59462-373-2*   *MSRP $9.95*

My Life and Work
Henry Ford

QTY

Henry Ford revolutionized the world with his implementation of mass production for the Model T automobile. Gain valuable business insight into his life and work with his own auto-biography... "We have only started on our development of our country we have not as yet, with all our talk of wonderful progress, done more than scratch the surface. The progress has been wonderful enough but..."

Pages:300

Biographies/   ISBN: *1-59462-198-5*   *MSRP $21.95*

www.bookjungle.com *email: sales@bookjungle.com fax: 630-214-0564 mail: Book Jungle PO Box 2226 Champaign, IL 61825*

The Art of Cross-Examination
Francis Wellman

QTY

I presume it is the experience of every author, after his first book is published upon an important subject, to be almost overwhelmed with a wealth of ideas and illustrations which could readily have been included in his book, and which to his own mind, at least, seem to make a second edition inevitable. Such certainly was the case with me; and when the first edition had reached its sixth impression in five months, I rejoiced to learn that it seemed to my publishers that the book had met with a sufficiently favorable reception to justify a second and considerably enlarged edition. ..

Pages:412

Reference   ISBN: *1-59462-647-2*   *MSRP $19.95*

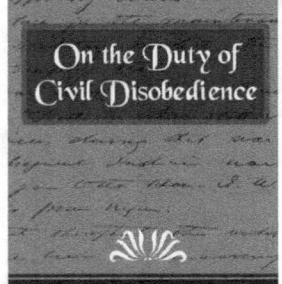

On the Duty of Civil Disobedience
Henry David Thoreau

QTY

Thoreau wrote his famous essay, On the Duty of Civil Disobedience, as a protest against an unjust but popular war and the immoral but popular institution of slave-owning. He did more than write—he declined to pay his taxes, and was hauled off to gaol in consequence. Who can say how much this refusal of his hastened the end of the war and of slavery ?

Law   ISBN: *1-59462-747-9*   **Pages:48**
                                             MSRP $7.45

Dream Psychology
Psychoanalysis for Beginners

Sigmund Freud

Dream Psychology Psychoanalysis for Beginners
Sigmund Freud

QTY

Sigmund Freud, born Sigismund Schlomo Freud (May 6, 1856 - September 23, 1939), was a Jewish-Austrian neurologist and psychiatrist who co-founded the psychoanalytic school of psychology. Freud is best known for his theories of the unconscious mind, especially involving the mechanism of repression; his redefinition of sexual desire as mobile and directed towards a wide variety of objects; and his therapeutic techniques, especially his understanding of transference in the therapeutic relationship and the presumed value of dreams as sources of insight into unconscious desires.

Pages:196

Psychology   ISBN: *1-59462-905-6*   *MSRP $15.45*

The Miracle of Right Thought
Orison Swett Marden

QTY

Believe with all of your heart that you will do what you were made to do. When the mind has once formed the habit of holding cheerful, happy, prosperous pictures, it will not be easy to form the opposite habit. It does not matter how improbable or how far away this realization may see, or how dark the prospects may be, if we visualize them as best we can, as vividly as possible, hold tenaciously to them and vigorously struggle to attain them, they will gradually become actualized, realized in the life. But a desire, a longing without endeavor, a yearning abandoned or held indifferently will vanish without realization.

Pages:360

Self Help   ISBN: *1-59462-644-8*   *MSRP $25.45*

The Rosicrucian Cosmo-Conception Mystic Christianity *by Max Heindel*   ISBN: *1-59462-188-8*   **$38.95**
The Rosicrucian Cosmo-conception is not dogmatic, neither does it appeal to any other authority than the reason of the student. It is: not controversial, but is: sent forth in the, hope that it may help to clear...   New Age/Religion Pages 646

Abandonment To Divine Providence *by Jean-Pierre de Caussade*   ISBN: *1-59462-228-0*   **$25.95**
"The Rev. Jean Pierre de Caussade was one of the most remarkable spiritual writers of the Society of Jesus in France in the 18th Century. His death took place at Toulouse in 1751. His works have gone through many editions and have been republished...   Inspirational/Religion Pages 400

Mental Chemistry *by Charles Haanel*   ISBN: *1-59462-192-6*   **$23.95**
Mental Chemistry allows the change of material conditions by combining and appropriately utilizing the power of the mind. Much like applied chemistry creates something new and unique out of careful combinations of chemicals the mastery of mental chemistry...   New Age Pages 354

The Letters of Robert Browning and Elizabeth Barret Barrett 1845-1846 vol II   ISBN: *1-59462-193-4*   **$35.95**
by Robert Browning and Elizabeth Barrett   Biographies Pages 596

Gleanings In Genesis (volume I) *by Arthur W. Pink*   ISBN: *1-59462-130-6*   **$27.45**
Appropriately has Genesis been termed "the seed plot of the Bible" for in it we have, in germ form, almost all of the great doctrines which are afterwards fully developed in the books of Scripture which follow...   Religion/Inspirational Pages 420

The Master Key *by L. W. de Laurence*   ISBN: *1-59462-001-6*   **$30.95**
In no branch of human knowledge has there been a more lively increase of the spirit of research during the past few years than in the study of Psychology, Concentration and Mental Discipline. The requests for authentic lessons in Thought Control, Mental Discipline and...   New Age/Business Pages 422

The Lesser Key Of Solomon Goetia *by L. W. de Laurence*   ISBN: *1-59462-092-X*   **$9.95**
This translation of the first book of the "Lernegton" which is now for the first time made accessible to students of Talismanic Magic was done, after careful collation and edition, from numerous Ancient Manuscripts in Hebrew, Latin, and French...   New Age/Occult Pages 92

Rubaiyat Of Omar Khayyam *by Edward Fitzgerald*   ISBN:*1-59462-332-5*   **$13.95**
Edward Fitzgerald, whom the world has already learned, in spite of his own efforts to remain within the shadow of anonymity, to look upon as one of the rarest poets of the century, was born at Bredfield, in Suffolk, on the 31st of March, 1809. He was the third son of John Purcell...   Music Pages 172

Ancient Law *by Henry Maine*   ISBN: *1-59462-128-4*   **$29.95**
The chief object of the following pages is to indicate some of the earliest ideas of mankind, as they are reflected in Ancient Law, and to point out the relation of those ideas to modern thought.   Religion/History Pages 452

Far-Away Stories *by William J. Locke*   ISBN: *1-59462-129-2*   **$19.45**
"Good wine needs no bush, but a collection of mixed vintages does. And this book is just such a collection. Some of the stories I do not want to remain buried for ever in the museum files of dead magazine-numbers an author's not unpardonable vanity..."   Fiction Pages 272

Life of David Crockett *by David Crockett*   ISBN: *1-59462-250-7*   **$27.45**
"Colonel David Crockett was one of the most remarkable men of the times in which he lived. Born in humble life, but gifted with a strong will, an indomitable courage, and unremitting perseverance...   Biographies/New Age Pages 424

Lip-Reading *by Edward Nitchie*   ISBN: *1-59462-206-X*   **$25.95**
Edward B. Nitchie, founder of the New York School for the Hard of Hearing, now the Nitchie School of Lip-Reading, Inc, wrote "LIP-READING Principles and Practice". The development and perfecting of this meritorious work on lip-reading was an undertaking...   How-to Pages 400

A Handbook of Suggestive Therapeutics, Applied Hypnotism, Psychic Science   ISBN: *1-59462-214-0*   **$24.95**
by Henry Munro   Health/New Age/Health/Self-help Pages 376

A Doll's House: and Two Other Plays *by Henrik Ibsen*   ISBN: *1-59462-112-8*   **$19.95**
Henrik Ibsen created this classic when in revolutionary 1848 Rome. Introducing some striking concepts in playwriting for the realist genre, this play has been studied the world over.   Fiction/Classics/Plays 308

The Light of Asia *by sir Edwin Arnold*   ISBN: *1-59462-204-3*   **$13.95**
In this poetic masterpiece, Edwin Arnold describes the life and teachings of Buddha. The man who was to become known as Buddha to the world was born as Prince Gautama of India but he rejected the worldly riches and abandoned the reigns of power when...   Religion/History/Biographies Pages 170

The Complete Works of Guy de Maupassant *by Guy de Maupassant*   ISBN: *1-59462-157-8*   **$16.95**
"For days and days, nights and nights, I had dreamed of that first kiss which was to consecrate our engagement, and I knew not on what spot I should put my lips..."   Fiction/Classics Pages 240

The Art of Cross-Examination *by Francis L. Wellman*   ISBN: *1-59462-309-0*   **$26.95**
Written by a renowned trial lawyer, Wellman imparts his experience and uses case studies to explain how to use psychology to extract desired information through questioning.   How-to/Science/Reference Pages 408

Answered or Unanswered? *by Louisa Vaughan*   ISBN: *1-59462-248-5*   **$10.95**
Miracles of Faith in China   Religion Pages 112

The Edinburgh Lectures on Mental Science (1909) *by Thomas*   ISBN: *1-59462-008-3*   **$11.95**
This book contains the substance of a course of lectures recently given by the writer in the Queen Street Hall, Edinburgh. Its purpose is to indicate the Natural Principles governing the relation between Mental Action and Material Conditions...   New Age/Psychology Pages 148

Ayesha *by H. Rider Haggard*   ISBN: *1-59462-301-5*   **$24.95**
Verily and indeed it is the unexpected that happens! Probably if there was one person upon the earth from whom the Editor of this, and of a certain previous history, did not expect to hear again...   Classics Pages 380

Ayala's Angel *by Anthony Trollope*   ISBN: *1-59462-352-X*   **$29.95**
The two girls were both pretty, but Lucy who was twenty-one who supposed to be simple and comparatively unattractive, whereas Ayala was credited, as her Bombwhat romantic name might show, with poetic charm and a taste for romance. Ayala when her father died was nineteen...   Fiction Pages 484

The American Commonwealth *by James Bryce*   ISBN: *1-59462-286-8*   **$34.45**
An interpretation of American democratic political theory. It examines political mechanics and society from the perspective of Scotsman James Bryce   Politics Pages 572

Stories of the Pilgrims *by Margaret P. Pumphrey*   ISBN: *1-59462-116-0*   **$17.95**
This book explores pilgrims religious oppression in England as well as their escape to Holland and eventual crossing to America on the Mayflower, and their early days in New England...   History Pages 268

QTY

The Fasting Cure *by Sinclair Upton*   ISBN: *1-59462-222-1*   **$13.95** ☐
In the Cosmopolitan Magazine for May, 1910, and in the Contemporary Review (London) for April, 1910, I published an article dealing with my experiences in fasting. I have written a great many magazine articles, but never one which attracted so much attention... New Age/Self Help/Health Pages 164

Hebrew Astrology *by Sepharial*   ISBN: *1-59462-308-2*   **$13.45** ☐
In these days of advanced thinking it is a matter of common observation that we have left many of the old landmarks behind and that we are now pressing forward to greater heights and to a wider horizon than that which represented the mind-content of our progenitors... Astrology Pages 144

Thought Vibration or The Law of Attraction in the Thought World   ISBN: *1-59462-127-6*   **$12.95** ☐
by William Walker Atkinson   *Psychology/Religion Pages 144*

Optimism *by Helen Keller*   ISBN: *1-59462-108-X*   **$15.95** ☐
Helen Keller was blind, deaf, and mute since 19 months old, yet famously learned how to overcome these handicaps, communicate with the world, and spread her lectures promoting optimism. An inspiring read for everyone... Biographies/Inspirational Pages 84

Sara Crewe *by Frances Burnett*   ISBN: *1-59462-360-0*   **$9.45** ☐
In the first place, Miss Minchin lived in London. Her home was a large, dull, tall one, in a large, dull square, where all the houses were alike, and all the sparrows were alike, and where all the door-knockers made the same heavy sound... Childrens/Classic Pages 88

The Autobiography of Benjamin Franklin *by Benjamin Franklin*   ISBN: *1-59462-135-7*   **$24.95** ☐
The Autobiography of Benjamin Franklin has probably been more extensively read than any other American historical work, and no other book of its kind has had such ups and downs of fortune. Franklin lived for many years in England, where he was agent... Biographies/History Pages 332

Name	
Email	
Telephone	
Address	
City, State ZIP	

☐ **Credit Card**   ☐ **Check / Money Order**

Credit Card Number	
Expiration Date	
Signature	

Please Mail to: Book Jungle
PO Box 2226
Champaign, IL 61825
or Fax to: 630-214-0564

ORDERING INFORMATION

web: *www.bookjungle.com*
email: *sales@bookjungle.com*
fax: *630-214-0564*
mail: *Book Jungle PO Box 2226 Champaign, IL 61825*
or PayPal *to sales@bookjungle.com*

Please contact us for bulk discounts

DIRECT-ORDER TERMS

**20% Discount if You Order
Two or More Books**
Free Domestic Shipping!
Accepted: Master Card, Visa,
Discover, American Express